Songs of a Befuddled Muse

Thirteen tales of divergent inspiration

By William Cohen-Kiraly

Copyright © 2022 William Cohen-Kiraly

All rights reserved.

ISBN: 979-8-9855769-1-7

Dedication

To my wife Lisa,

and my daughters Jamie and Jessica,

who all helped make this book happen.

Acknowledgements:

Though an author is solely responsible for what goes in the book, no book is solely the work of a single person. A lot of people helped me create this book and my thanks go to all who supported and encouraged me with a few special callouts.

First, thanks to my wife and daughters for just putting up with me in this long project, critically reading my work, giving me useful ideas, and surreptitiously being inspiration to some of the more interesting characters.

Extra special thanks has to go to my daughter Jamie Cohen-Kiraly. Without her, this book would never have happened. She challenged me to start writing again with collaborations and friendly competitions. Jamie is an exceptionally talented visual artist and besides her help fueling my inspiration, she also provided the cover "tattoos" and images for each of the story headers. To see more of her work, buy custom-painted shoes, or hire here to paint murals and theater sets, visit www.jayckarts.com.

Special thanks also go to several friends with clown-related ideas for *The Big Gumshoes*, and especially my wife, Lisa Cohen-Kiraly, who first said "I don't know why you are asking me, I'm not creative in this way" and then proceeded to give me wonderful, creative ideas. Also thanks to Kali Fencl, a friend and a wonderful comedienne who also sparked some great clown memes.

My brother Don Kiraly (a recently "retired" professor of Translation at the University of Mainz) and his good friend Paul Foster provided invaluable input for the two Lady Jane stories, particularly on parts touching linguistics and Tudor swear words. My neighbor, Jonathan Kish, is a professional chef, and he helped create the English-Spanish fusion menu for the dinner in the White Tower.

I am also thankful to Daniel Whiteson, a CERN physicist, and one of the hosts of the great podcast *Daniel and Jorge Explain the Universe* (https://sites.uci.edu/danielandjorge) for reading and critiquing the flow and the "science" of time travel in the Lady Jane stories. I highly recommend both the podcast and the podcast team's several books (https://sites.uci.edu/danieland-jorge) about what we do and don't know about this crazy universe.

The lyrics from the song *Bury My Lovely*, by Emil Adler and Julie Flanders are used by their kind permission. Watch this beautiful, haunting song (https://www.youtube.com/watch?v=puGEpGzk2hk) as performed by October Project, featuring the stunning voice of Mary Fahl.

If you want to be a writer, one of the most educational and humbling things you can do is have other writers read and critique your work. I belong the the Westside Writers Group (Cleveland) and many writers from this group have read, commented on, and — even occasionally —encouraged, my writing. Two accomplished authors in particular, Malcolm B Wood (http://malcolm-wood.com/Welcome.html), author of seven novels and a book about writing, and M.T Bass (https://mtbassauthor.wordpress.com), author of at least thirteen books including the intriguing *Murder by Munchausen* (https://www.amazon.com/dp/B079C6GNLL) series, have provided invaluable suggestions and encouragement.

My editor, Brett Kinsey (https://www.thefreelanceeditors.com), is responsible for a lot of corrections in both story flow, grammar and spelling. Any mistakes that are still here are my own, Brett is *very* thorough.

Table of Contents

Curved Space	1
The Daemon Muse	11
Times of Life and Death	23
Heart's Desire	47
A Sticky End	61
The Singer of Starfish	67
The Offering	79
The Big Gumshoes	89
A Day in the Life of the Great Space Explorer	115
Something That Will Not Let Go	125
Pea Soup	151
The Severed World	161
A Thread Across The Veil	229
About the Author	253

Curved Space

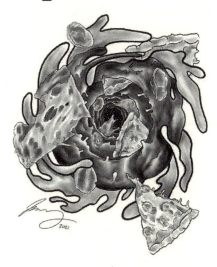

    I sat in my tiny office and pulled the mylar blanket closer around my body. My breath came out as steam in the cold air as I made my best calculations at where Earth might be. I pointed the antenna and opened the microphone.
    "Earth Ship Neil Armstrong, Captain's Log: September 9, 2637: If the chronometers can be believed, it is now 2637 Earth time, 2524 in our ship time. That means we've been asleep for over 120 years our time while something like 250 years have passed on Earth. We're lucky to be alive, if that word can be applied to us in our current predicament. The ship was designed for no more than 80 years of suspended animation life support which should have been more than enough to get us through the wormhole and into the Tau Ceti system.
    "The ship began waking us up about 24 hours ago when the SA systems started a cascading failure. Eighteen of us have survived, we've lost five of our friends and shipmates already. The dead are Master Chief Thomas Clay, Ensign Lara Hillary, Spaceman First Class Angus MacLarther, Spaceman First Class Barrow Liamyeska, and my first officer, Lieutenant Commander Agatha Leandro. These were good people, and I am proud to

have served with them. They will be missed greatly—if we ever have the leisure to do so.

"Our situation is stable for the moment but desperate in the near term. Our air and water supplies are good for now. Heat is too low—we are all cold—but it is survivable for the moment. Unfortunately, most of our food supplies have become infested with bacteria and much of it has rotted and turned poisonous. Even if we can disinfect what hasn't rotted, I doubt we'll be able to eat much of what is left.

"Since the SA chambers have failed, we can't put ourselves back under to try to get home and given our limited food supplies and poor condition, I'm not sure how we'll survive more than three or four weeks. Maybe our five dead are the lucky ones…

"We're trying to figure out what went wrong. Our best guess is that the boneheaded physicists miscalculated the far end of the wormhole. We're not sure exactly where we are, but our best guess is we're still somewhere in the vicinity of Tau Ceti, maybe within a quarter parsec. As we narrow down our calculations, I'll send out further updates.

"But at this point, I'm afraid the Armstrong's mission to take humans to another star system is going to fail. We'll keep broadcasting for as long as we're able.

"For now, I've got to stop and see if the galley crew has found us anything more to eat. I'm torturing myself, I know, but all I can think about right now is Momma Carina's pizza, where we went almost every Friday while training for this mission. Well Earth, if you get this message sometime before we starve to death—or become the first Donner party in space—please send us a bunch of Momma's Pepperoni Thick Crust specials… Captain Accardi out."

A couple days later, I was in the galley with Doc, trying to find some way to rig the crippled recyclers to turn our ship's rotted food into something edible. We were, all of us, already starting to feel lightheaded and sick from hunger. That, combined with the wooziness that normally accompanies you for a week after waking up from SA, I guess I was already starting to fade a bit when Doc nudged me and pointed at the intercom. It took me a second to register Maneesh's voice saying, "Captain to the bridge, please. Captain to the bridge, can you hear me Captain?"

I clicked the responder button. "Captain here, Lieutenant. What's up?"

"Captain, you have to come see this!" There was an edge of panic in his voice. I looked at Doc. I turned off the mike and still covered it with my hand by habit. "Can he be hallucinating already?" I asked.

She shrugged back at me. "Maybe. Everyone reacts differently." We both floated to the galley hatch and moved fore to the bridge.

We came through the bridge hatch and at first couldn't see much because Lieutenant Loke, Ensign Frischman and Spaceman Seth were all there blocking our view of the starboard viewports. Five people on the bridge of the Armstrong gets a bit crowded.

I pushed and pulled my way into the bridge enough so I could see—then stopped dead, holding on to a handhold near the viewport with a death-grip.

There was a creature in what looked like a spacesuit hanging on to our hull and holding a cardboard sign against the window. That was shocking enough until I read the sign. Then I nearly cried.

The sign read "Did somebody here order pizza?"

"Holy mother of God," I muttered to myself. "Jamie, hand me that clipboard and pen floating over there." I gestured. The Ensign snatched them and floated them to me.

"Who are you?" I wrote and held up my sign to the viewport.

The creature looked like it was trying to peer through its helmet for a moment then shook its head, threw away the cardboard sign and wrote another. As the old sign drifted away, I realized it was a pizza box. My mind was completely befuddled but my poor, abused, hungry stomach rumbled loudly in anticipation.

The new sign said, "I can't read through the porthole and my helmet. Can you let me in?"

All the old vids ran through my mind at this point, *2001, Contact, Krasper's Escape*. In my mind, I saw the weird effects as the aliens ran the travelers through sequences of pretentious, psychedelic images and I thought our meeting with a space-pizza delivery guy was just about right. Real life never lives up to the movies.

I waved my hand, pointing to where the airlock was on the ship, hoping like hell it, too, wasn't failing with age. The creature gave a thumbs up and started pulling itself along the hull towards the airlock. We all pressed our heads against the glass of the several portholes in the bridge, and by God, the creature was trailing a big rectangular box on a lead.

Doc grabbed my arm. "Al, what about the protocols on first contact?"

I stared at her, dumbfounded. "Drea, we're all about to die of starvation and you want to turn down the pizza now?"

Maneesh Loke shook his head and grinned. "I don't know how we're going to get EASA to pay the delivery charges, though."

Ten minutes later, the entire crew, those of us who could still stand, were in the airlock portal room or in the two storage rooms which connected to it. We heard the hiss of re-pressurization and opened the hatch and out of the airlock stepped something that looked human holding a sealed box tethered to its spacesuit. It put the box in a wall clamp and released the seals and pulled off its helmet to reveal a very definitely human young man, maybe in his early thirties. He had a mop of unruly red hair, a face full of freckles and a mischievous grin he kept trying to suppress.

He finally gave up and grinned broadly at us and said "It's about time you guys showed up."

We stared at him; I don't think anyone knew what to say at that moment. He laughed a bit at our staring faces and said "I'm Mikey, I do pizza runs for Thomas' (he said it 'Tō-Măz') Pizza and Subs." He pointed to the name clearly written on the tethered box, "I hear you guys are hungry." At this point, he flipped open the latches on his box and the smell of garlic and pepperoni filled the portal room. I think I could hear all of our stomachs rumbling and I could see my crew surging at the hatches from the other rooms.

"Okay," Mikey said, "I know you guys are probably really, really hungry but I only brought these three pizzas over for now. There are a bunch more on my ship and I'll bring those later. But I've heard that when you're really hungry, you're not supposed to gorge yourself, at least that's what I've seen on the vids, so I want everyone to take only one piece first and I can get you the rest later."

Doc snorted at his speech but didn't say anything. I tried to think of anything I was supposed to do to make sure this was all real and he wasn't going to poison my crew. That's when I started thinking maybe this was all a hallucination. But damn, the pizza smelled so real.

The Armstrong's crew obediently followed his instructions and took one piece each. Some shoved it into their mouths but some of us ate it daintily, trying to savor the return of the touch of food on our tongues. I don't think I was the only one crying at that moment, which is always an annoying mess in zero grav.

"Okay Mikey," I said after we had all had our slice, "Thank you for this. You've given us all a little bit of heaven now and I don't know how we can ever repay you…"

"It's on the house, guys," he said grinning. "Don't even expect a tip!"

I shook my head. "Okay, can you explain what you are doing delivering pizza to a spaceship some five or so light-years from Earth?"

"Ah, well, you see, I live on Garland, which is a planet in what you'd call the Tau Zeta system. It was probably about 50 years after you left Sol that someone developed the Star Bridges which are ways of creating temporary artificial super-curved and super-stable wormholes between star systems.

"What this means is that when the Yuri Gargarin finally reached Alpha Centauri in 2476, humans had already been settled there for 35 years.

"When the Ibn Battuta reached Barnard's Star, humans had already been there though nobody wants to live in that hellhole of a star system. But humans were able to meet the crew there and take them back to Earth.

"But nobody could figure out what the heck happened to the Armstrong. We've been watching Tau Ceti hoping to find you for more than a century. This end of the wormhole you went into had shifted erratically a number of times so we didn't know where or when you might come out and I think we'd all given up hope for you.

"So I nearly fell out of my skin when I picked up your broadcast log entry a few days ago. I'm a pilot on the Garland-Haven run. I was on my way to Haven and just happened to be in the right spot to pick up your transmission. Good thing too, your transmission was several degrees off from the right vector to hit Earth so no one would have ever heard it if I hadn't been in the right location…"

Of all the things he was telling me, I don't know why I picked up on the least relevant point, maybe because I've been a pilot and astronaut all my life and this seemed so weird at that moment. More likely, I guess, I was probably in shock and not thinking. "So you use a spaceship to deliver pizza?"

Mikey threw his head back and laughed at that question. "Naw," he said when he could talk again, "not exactly. I run a freighter between Garland and Haven for the biggest pizza franchise on Garland. Thomas is very, very picky about the produce he uses for his pies and no one grows produce like the Amish. When I go to pick up new produce though, I always bring a ton of pizzas with me. They may wear black and only drive cars that don't hover, but the Amish sure like our pizza. Everybody does, it's the best pizza in the known universe.

"When I heard your transmission, I figured the produce could wait. I could fulfill your pizza fantasy and my ship has the room to take you all back to Garland—or Haven if you are more Amish-ly inclined. It won't be luxurious — it's a freighter after all — but we have all the half-baked pies you could ever want. And the boys at home will be jealous as hell of me. You don't know this, but you guys are larger than life heroes."

"What?" Doc asked.

Mikey was grinning that lop-sided grin again. "You had one of the longest-running vid series ever. The great and sexy Capt. Accardi…" here he gave me a wink, "and his noble crew sent by a wormhole to the farthest reaches of the galaxy, trying to find their way home. I think the series went on for like thirty years in the last century and there were three different guys playing Capt. Accardi and this actress Lena Dunar Wai played his beautiful lover, Doc Cho.

"Us pilots of course, have watched every vid and can recite lines from our favorite episodes. We are all fans of the great space explorers, just like Armstrong and Gagarin. But Capt. Accardi in his beautiful form-fitting suit is the favorite with all the boys on Garland." Nodding at Doc, he continued. "You must be the real Doc. A lot of guys loved you too, even guys on Garland, but your character got killed off early saving the ship from the evil Draaks, a race whose homeworld was destroyed and who now live in spaceships, and survive by looting other worlds. Capt. Accardi always has your picture hanging in his cabin." Doc didn't seem to have anything to say about all this and just stared at him with an open mouth.

I think she was as nonplussed as me with all the things Mikey was telling us, as she, too, picked what seemed like the most irrelevant detail. "Haven is an Amish Planet?" she asked.

"Ah yes," Mikey replied, "I guess that's something else you guys probably don't know. Ever since space travel became cost-effective, a lot of humans have moved off-planet. We've found a lot of planets that can support human life but no Draaks or other intelligent life, at least not that we can tell—certainly no technological life.

"There are ruins on Tau Ceti Six that show someone once lived there, but it's pretty inhospitable now. Anyway, some of the new colonies are just extensions of general Earth society, but several of them are separatist colonies who feel like we can live a more authentic life away from human society in general.

"Some failed, like New Atlantis, which was supposed to be a progressive communal society where everyone lived like Marx prescribed, um Karl, not Groucho. They kind of starved to death. Then there was the New Aryan Paradise which went to hell in a hand basket pretty damn fast.

But most of us separatists have survived and thrived. Haven was the destination of the Amish. Of course, they couldn't navigate the Star Bridges themselves but they paid others and Haven continues to be one of the most peaceful, prosperous, pastoral planets in the human realm."

"And Garland," I asked.

"Ah," he said, "we're the queer planet. A lot of us decided we could make our own lives better without feeling so out of place among the straights. Not all gays came, but pretty much anyone who comes to live on Garland is gay or bi. But we get a lot of straight tourists all the time — something Haven prohibits, of course — because we have the best food, the best entertainment, and the best shopping anywhere in the human sphere."

One of my crew, I couldn't identify the voice, said "Too bad about Barrow, then. He would have loved your place."

Spaceman Seth asked. "So if we go with you to your planet, does that mean we have to become gay?"

Mikey laughed again. "Nooooo, like I say, we have a lot of straight visitors. And just like everyone else, we have a lot of kids of our own who don't grow up gay and many of them choose to move off planet when they grow up.

"We'll fix you up and get you ready to live in the twenty-seventh century. And you better believe we'll throw you the biggest welcome-home bash you can imagine. But after that, you'll be free to stay with us or go wherever you choose."

Then he looked at me, his mischievous grin back. "Now, you, however, are just as sexy as all guys who played you in the vids, at least you will be once you put some weight back on." He reached into his box and found one last slice of pizza and handed it to me.

"You can stay with me however long you want. Just remember, on Garland, space is really curved, there are no straight lines here." He laughed at my expression. but I have no idea what that expression was.

The Daemon Muse

1978

Danny stacked up his roommates' dirty dishes onto the old wooden wire spool that served as their coffee table, pushed the old newspapers onto the floor and laid down on the couch. He was so tired he could barely concentrate enough to build his nest. Finals week had been more brutal than usual. His work at the school paper hadn't let up even for finals with a huge student council cheating scandal. And the classes he had ignored all semester to work on the newspaper required a catch-up effort that was nearly impossible, but he had done it. He didn't have his grades yet but, in his heart of hearts, he knew that he had done okay.

He was never going to be a straight-A student, but Danny was pretty sure he was passing everything except maybe creative writing. For his final project, he had submitted a story about the dragon—a story born of an early finals week nightmare—which was the biggest piece of crap he had ever written. This pissed him off to no end, considering what he thought he was going to do for a living.

He was finally fading off when the door slammed open, and Jim and Angel walked in.

"Get your ass up, sleepyhead." Angel called out. "We're gonna go celebrate the end of finals."

"Oh fuck," said Danny. "Man, I gotta sleep. I'm so tired, I can't even think straight."

"Yeah, but Sue and Lorelei are joining us at Thalia's. You like Sue, right?"

Danny threw his arm across his face in defense against the lights they turned on and muttered another curse word. "Okay, give me a minute to get ready."

Changed into a semi-clean shirt and having splashed water on his face and underarms, Danny was soon walking with his friends to the bar. Being outside in the bracing spring air brought at least a little life back into his dead insides.

Thalia's was hopping when they walked in. A college band was playing very badly and very loudly. College kids finally released from the hell of finals week were trying to let loose and dance and yell and drink.

As promised, Sue and Lori were there. Sue came over and gave Danny a peck on his cheek. He tried to respond with a little more, but she played coy and pushed him away. But she winked at him as she grabbed her drink and went back to the pool table.

Danny knew he should follow. They weren't exactly boyfriend and girlfriend, but there was something there and he should keep it going for another night. She was smart, self-assured, pretty in her own way, and smelled like heaven. He should have followed.

Instead, he sat down and pulled out the reporter's notebook he always kept in his back pocket so inspiration could never find him unprepared. He started writing furiously.

Jim looked at him, waved his hand in front of Danny's face and said "What the fuck? That girl wants you. She's not my type but damn, I think she's yours…"

Danny vaguely waved him away.

"What are you doing, asshole?" Jim asked. "This is after finals. It's time to play. You don't have another writing assignment, do you Mr. Famous Writer who writes shit?"

"I got an idea, I gotta write it down or I'm going to lose it," Danny said.

"Come on, man. It's summer. You don't have to write anything for four months."

But Danny kept writing. And he kept writing. And he kept jotting down more notes as he looked around the bar. Every face, everybody, had a story idea for him. The man in the silly, bright red t-shirt who looked like Humphrey Bogart, he could be a PI, maybe a clown PI. The tall handsome guy who looked like an officer from *Star Trek*, he could be a spaceship captain who saves his starving crew. What about that fat girl, maybe she lived a really hard life and had an evil father she wanted to get back at.

Angel came back once or twice to check on Danny, but his friends eventually just gave up and played pool and danced and drank.

Danny kept writing, occasionally sipping his beer absentmindedly. He wrote as fiercely as he could, but it still felt like he was losing ideas faster than he could get them down.

He wrote down an idea about a sailor who had a hallucination of being saved by something called the Sea Mistress.

"Buy me a drink, sailor" asked a slightly husky female voice just as he was writing more details of that odd plot. He looked up and sitting in the other chair at his little table was a stunningly beautiful woman. She had chin length straight black hair, full lips with crimson lipstick and long fingernails in matching red. She had a powerfully built, but still very feminine body. She was older than Danny, somewhere in her mid-20s and she exuded confidence, even sensuality, without being obvious about it.

For a moment, Danny was completely speechless. Yeah, he really liked Sue and while he knew he wasn't unattractive, women like *this* never came on to him. Things like *this* didn't happen to regular, everyday guys like him.

"Um," he started out lamely, "I can only get you 3-2 beer, I'm not old enough to buy the hard stuff."

She laughed, it was a throaty laugh and the laugh rose into her eyes too. "That'll do fine," she said.

Danny wasn't sure if the tiredness was creeping back into him, but he felt just a little light-headed as he went to get her a beer and himself a refill.

He could see Sue watching him with hooded eyes but he sure as hell didn't care right at that moment. It was a relief that —at least for a moment—the torrent of story ideas had thinned to a trickle. But the old bartender looked like a guy who could forget his whole life story every night and invent a new life every day. Weird idea.

"I'm Danny," he said, handing her the beer. "Danny, uh, Dan Jackman."

"Nice to meet you," she answered. "Just call me Calli."

"Like in Colleen," Danny said, thinking about a friend from high school.

"No, actually, like Calliope," she answered, smiling at him. "Why would you think you'd meet a Colleen in a place called 'Thalia's?"

"You a student here?" he asked.

"You could say that. What were you writing so intensely in that little notebook?" she asked.

"Ideas. Maybe it's sleep deprivation from finals week but as soon as I got here, I started getting all of these story ideas. It was like they were pouring out of my brain and I had to write them down before I forgot them."

"You're a writer?" she said, brightening with interest.

"I am, or at least that's what I want to be. I haven't published anything yet but it's the only thing I can imagine doing with my life."

"Tell me about your stories," she said, sipping her own beer then putting it down in such a way her hand touched his. She didn't move it.

Danny jolted at the touch, it was like the fire hose of ideas came roaring back as he stared into her deep brown eyes. It took all his strength to fight the urge to grab his notebook again.

"I don't know, I love telling stories. When I was a kid, I used to tell my sister stories to calm her down when my dad was on one of his drunks or my mom was in one of her tirades. It's the only way I could get her to go to sleep. Later on, I wrote a bunch of stories in junior high and high school. I guess I am published 'cuz two of them were published in our school arts magazine. A lot of them were like *Star Trek* ripoffs but really, they were pretty good. It was the only way I knew how to get through those years until I got to leave home."

"How about now, you're what, a sophomore?"

"Junior. I don't know. Maybe since I'm not so miserable anymore, I can't seem to write any stories I like all that much. I write for the *Spectator*, I did the series on the two student council members who were caught cheating and the school tried to cover it up."

"Ohh, yeah, I saw that one. Hell of good story."

"Yeah, but it's like my ability to write fiction has left me for the time being. The best one I did was about a kid who went to jail rather than register for the draft, but it felt really artificial to me. I don't know anything about being in jail.

I wrote another about a girl on campus fighting for her rights after being raped by another student and I just turned in a really, really awful one about a dragon with a hole in its head that represents the worst parts of capitalism. Someday when I'm famous, I know that one will pop up somewhere and absolutely destroy my reputation."

Calli threw her head back and laughed. "Well, Mr. Dan, let's see if we can get you back on track. Why do you write such political stuff?"

"I used to just write stories that I thought were fun or interesting to me, but with the world in the shape it's in now, well you can't write just for entertainment. We have to change the world."

"And how much politics do you do outside of your writing."

"Well, I write for the newspaper, that's political, that's investigative."

"When was the last time you worked for a politician or went to a protest or even went to a candlelight vigil?" she asked, tilting her head to the side a little.

Danny looked down. "Well never, really."

"If it doesn't interest you in real life, why do you think you could write about it? A good story comes from here," she said, poking his chest, "not here" she said, playfully slapping his forehead. A wise man once said "If you write to impress it will always be bad, but if you write to express it will be good."

"Well my, my, aren't we Miss Erudite. Who said that?" Danny asked.

"Thornton Wilder. A man with impeccable writing credentials."

Danny sighed, but he was impressed. "I don't think I could ever be that good" he said.

Calli took his hands in her own and looked straight into his eyes. "I think maybe yes you can."

When she touched him, he gasped. The flood of images started fire-hosing through his head again. She smiled very sensuously at him and the flood trickled back to one image of him and her together in wild abandon and it was all he could do to not start shaking.

"Would you like to dance?" she asked him and he just nodded, it was the only movement he felt he could trust himself to make.

They danced for a long time. Angel and Jim kept playing pool, Sue and Lorelei walked out with Sue trying—and failing—to give him an unpleasant look. Dan didn't notice anything but Calli.

Later on, the rubber band safely on the doorknob to warn his apartment mates to not disturb, Dan stood in his room, savoring slowly undressing his new friend. The curves promised by her clothes were more exquisite than he had dared to hope. It was like opening a present as he took her clothes off one by one. The red blouse, the lace bra underneath, the skirt, the panties. By the time he got to the stockings, he could feel his heart beating hard against his ribcage.

They made love and it was a new experience for Dan. Though his body felt more drained than any time he had ever made love before, his mind, his soul, felt fuller but more diffuse. He closed his eyes and felt waves of passion as she caressed him and he felt her similarly moved. Their sweat made them slippery, the warmth of her skin seemed to burn him.

In the aftermath, she lay gently and perfectly in the crook of his shoulder. He could feel her left breast lying softly against his chest and he trembled just a little bit in continued ecstasy. She played with the one tiny little tuft of chest hair he had, humming to herself something he didn't recognize.

"Oh my God!" he said, trying to pull himself up on one elbow. "We didn't use any protection."

Calli pushed him down, kissing his neck and then his ear. "Don't worry Dan, you can't get me pregnant."

"Why?" he asked automatically, then apologized. "I shouldn't have asked that."

"It's okay," she said, smiling at him. "You and I can conceive our own children, over and over again, but it's not me who will give birth."

"What?" he asked, but his mind was fuzzy. "I don't think I'll ever be able to sleep with any other woman ever again." He said, again quickly regretting his words.

"You better," she said. "You can't give our children life unless you go out into the world and live a little yourself. And don't worry, I am not a jealous lover. I'll stay with you always and share your life with you."

Dan found himself falling asleep quickly and when he woke in the morning, the smell of her lingered on his body and his pillow and his sheets, but Calli was gone.

He never saw Sue again and that made him sad.

1982

Dan was sitting on his bed, bawling his eyes out. Calli sat across from him, too mad to even look at him.

"What the hell are you doing?" she demanded. "Are you fucking crazy? You have a woman who loves you, a woman with a huge heart and a huge spirit, a woman with a huge creative soul and you're leaving her for some bimbo?"

"I'm not leaving Sherry for a bimbo or for Jenny or whatever. I can't control how I feel. I can't bring myself to really be totally in love with her. I want an epic love story in my life. I know Sherry is great, it's just that I love her but I'm not *in* love with her."

"Isn't that just fucking bullshit. Dan, you are a first-class asshole. If you want an epic love then you better start living an epic life. It doesn't come to you, you have to go out and get it."

Dan whimpered. "I'm trying but I'm too scared and too young. I gotta grow up some more before I can settle down."

Calli just shook her head in sorrow. "Yeah, sorry, Jenny's not a bimbo, but she's not what you need. You haven't written anything but city council meetings and stupid interviews with high school football players since college. You need someone like Sherry to pull you out of yourself."

"She can't. I'm stuck in there myself and I have to get me out first before I can be what she needs."

Calli stood squarely in front of him, grabbed Dan's chin hard and forced his eyes level with hers. "I am not a jealous lover, but I am an impatient one. Do what you have to do to bring our children into the world. Grow up, learn to live. But don't waste your time. We are not guaranteed enough time to finish our work and I don't want us to die before we create something worthy."

"Us to die?" he said, trying to pull his chin out of her hand and failing.

"What, you think your creativity outlives you. You die, I die. You give up and I am barren and I will not be childless. Grow up!" she said and slapped him hard across the face.

2003

For years, Dan had not seen Calli. Sometimes she was there just beyond his perception, but he always looked away. She tried to talk to him and he hummed things to himself and drowned her out.

Today, on the verge of falling asleep after a long day at the office, he let his guard down and looked where he shouldn't have looked. What he saw shocked him.

The beautiful, sensuous woman he had made love to so long ago was changed. It was not just that she was older, he was older too, but that her hair was a frazzled graying mess, her cheeks were hollowed, her skin sallow, her eyes were bloodshot, and her teeth were yellow and crooked.

"So you make me like this and now you won't look at me or even acknowledge I exist. I am still trying to bring you back to what you should be doing and you ignore every idea I try to give you. Why are you so cruel?" Her voice wavered with pain.

"My God Calli, I'm a grown man. I have work I have to do, I have a family I have to take care of. I have a son and a daughter who need me. I don't have time to waste chasing a pipedream…" There was pain in Dan's voice too though he tried to hide it.

"Besides, I've written several stories over the last few years…"

"Three" she spat out at him, "three lousy stories in twenty five years. That's your epic life for you?"

"I have to put Justin and Ellie through college. He wants to be a game designer; she wants to be a painter. You know how unlikely it is I can make any money writing books, like maybe one out of a hundred writers ever makes any money at all. And I can't leave everything up to Emily."

"Oh Emily, you mean the woman who won't even read the piddling few stories you have written. The one who says she'll read them only when you become famous and make lots of money?"

"She's a good woman and a good mother." Said Dan with a flash of anger.

"And a good inspiration to you?" Calli shot back.

"What the fuck is the use of me locking myself away from my family if all I'm doing is writing books that no one will ever read? I don't have time for foolish dreams. I'm too fucking old now to start a writing career."

"My God, is that what you think? You have to have someone read your work to make it worthwhile? Sure, it's nice, but you write for you and for me, not for anyone else. If you write, you can still have that epic life you thought you would have, maybe even have that epic love affair you gave Sherry up for.

But if you don't write, this is what you'll see in the mirror." Once again she gripped his chin firmly in her hand and pulled his face to look at hers eye to eye. Calli's breath was foul and boozy and she held his gaze until he couldn't look any more and forced his eyes shut.

2014

Dan and Calli saw each other much more now. Sometimes, when Emily was away, they made love like the old days.

Ellie, Dan's crazy daughter, had a great idea several months ago to do 'creative prompts.' They would agree on a prompt and she would paint a picture and Dan would write a story and by God, even if no one but Ellie ever read his words, he discovered he loved doing it again.

With both the kids out of the house and on their own, he could find the time to write and deep in his imagination, he found himself plotting the book he knew he had in him. No, the first of many books he had in him.

It was while starting to plot this book that Calli had returned to him, no longer sallow and rheumy. She was still as old as he was but her smile had returned and her eyes crinkled with crows feet that looked more like joy than age.

Ellie didn't see her but sometimes when they were working together with Ellie at her easel and Dan pounding on his laptop, he would see Calli walk up behind his daughter to ostensibly look closer at her painting. Calli would brush up against Ellie and Dan could see inspiration light up his daughter's eyes with delight.

Calli would let out one of her glorious laughs and look back at Dan as if to say "What? I didn't do anything."

She had been right all those years ago, write for the pure pleasure of imagination and everything will fall into place.

Like Calli, he felt and looked better than he had in years. He had dropped twenty five pounds and rediscovered the spring in his own step as well. Even Emily seemed to have taken some notice. Sure, he was in his late 50s now but he still had time to create a body of work. He still had time to get published if he put his mind to it. With the bright new world of self-publishing, maybe he could find a few hundred or a few thousand or maybe — if he was as good as he thought—a few hundred thousand readers.

This is what Dan was thinking as he rode his bike on that beautiful September day when that odd feeling in his chest turned to tightness, then to excruciating pain, then to blackness.

He woke up very slowly in a hospital room, a cardiac monitor beeping out a hiccuping heartbeat. The room was full of light, he was surrounded by a curtain and heard a great bustle of people wandering around outside that curtain. It dawned on him that it must be the ICU, but no one was coming in to check on him.

Calliope was there, sitting in a hospital chair, her head buried in her hands, and her body shivering with wracking sobs.

Somehow she knew he was awake and she looked up at him. "You waited too long," she said. "You wrote a few good things at the end but it wasn't enough. You could have done so much more."

He tried to answer her, but he had a breathing tube in his mouth and could only grunt around it. But that noise, as soft as it was, brought the nurse running in followed quickly by Emily and Ellie.

The nurse started fiddling with settings on the machine and trying to tell him he was going to be okay and to calm down, he was in a hospital. But Emily grabbed his hands. She was crying, saying how much she loved him and Ellie stood on the other side, stroking his cheek.

"Justin's flying in from LA this afternoon, Dan. He wants to see you too. Can you wait for him?" Dan started shaking his head—trying to clear it out, not denying her request—but Emily didn't understand. Instead, she threw her arms around him saying "Dan, Danny, I love you…" but he couldn't answer back.

Over Emily's head, Dan saw Calli with a terrible, rictus of loathing on her face. He saw her raise her beautifully manicured nails then reach through Emily's body and directly into his. "You waited too fucking long," she said again, and he felt her long, red nails dig into his heart like talons.

Times of Life and Death
Canto One in The Lives and Times of Lady Jane

December 1537

Ian strode into the cathedral for the christening, holding a finely-carved decorative wood panel. It was a rich, polished, dark-wood plaque carved with a delicate and complex arabesque of roses and thorns surrounding the words "*Non quia difficilia sunt non audemus, sed quia non audemus, difficilia sunt.*"

When Ian had heard these words almost twenty-five years ago, he knew the phrase would define both this infant's life and death. He didn't know then it would become such a tie to her as a living woman.

He sat in the middle of the nave. The title and the clothes he donned for the christening put him among the wealthy gentry, but not the honored nobility. Ian had chosen a seat close enough to the aisle so he could catch a good look at the child as she was brought forward by her parents. And as he looked into her tiny face as she passed, he fancied even now he could see the mischief already there in her bright green eyes.

Ian Harland was a middle-aged man of forty-seven; gray already streaked his temples and his beard. He was of moderate height for a man when he came from, but rather tall here and now in Tudor England. He was rather proud of the ruffled silk shirt he had purchased yesterday though he desperately kept pulling down his doublet to cover holes in the hose he had scrounged from someone's laundry early this morning.

When the long, tedious ceremony was over and the family sat to accept the gifts, he was able to hand his plaque directly to Lady Eleanor, Countess of Cumberland and younger sister of the girl's mother, Lady Frances. Lady Eleanor ran her fingers over the carving in admiration. She looked up at Ian and smiled. "It is beautiful sir, what do these words mean?"

"They are from the Roman philosopher Seneca," he said, "They say 'It's not because things are difficult that we dare not venture. It's because we dare not venture that they are difficult.'"

Lady Eleanor looked taken aback. "You think these are appropriate words to share with a young noblewoman?"

He smiled back a little sadly. "I believe, my lady, that these words will come to describe a young lady who dares much in her life."

Ian already knew his gift would never end up in the girl's own rooms but because of the beautiful carving, it would hang for many years in the greeting room of Lord Henry, the girl's father. What did surprise him though, was when he realized that he, himself, was the one who commissioned this carving to present at the christening. Throughout all the years he had known her, he never suspected he was the one who had given it to her.

May 1545

The seven-year-old Lady Jane Grey was small for her age and looked to be five or six. She had long golden-red hair desperately trying to escape from her bonnet, and her skinny arms and legs were always in motion.

The servants retained by her parents had learned not to underestimate the child. She had ways of escaping their supervision anytime they took their eyes off her for the briefest of moments.

It was during one such escapade that the young Lady Jane found herself in the stables trying to pull herself up high enough to look over the stall doors at her own pony, whom she dearly loved. She would be caught and brought back inside to her nurse and caretaker, Mrs. Eleyn, in a short while. Mrs. Eleyn would mark down the exact date and time in a letter to Jane's mother, giving Ian an exact time and place on which to triangulate.

Ian Harland was a good-looking young man of twenty-four, dressed as a stablehand but with dark, collar-length hair and black eyes which watched the little girl intently.

When he had been a moody sixteen-year-old boy himself, he had first read about this girl and had been captivated by the story of a smart, headstrong girl who became the first queen regnant of England then, lost her own life so soon afterwards. While his friends played at being space explorers and grew up to be physicists and engineers, Ian imagined himself as her husband, Lord Guildford Dudley, breaking her out of the Tower and saving her from execution. Ian had grown up to be a historian.

He had long forgotten his childhood crush on the girl in the story — he discovered real women were much more interesting than ghosts. But historically and academically, the story of her ascension had always fascinated him, enough that he had written his masters thesis on the role her reign had on the history of the English Reformation.

Lady Jane had always been a ghost to him, a vague idea of a young woman. No contemporary portraits of her remained though one painting made forty years after her death was reputed to be a copy of a life portrait.

Ian wondered what the real Lady Jane looked like and had taken this quick, unauthorized detour from his assigned mission to see her in person for the first time. But on seeing the little girl, he knew he had made a mistake. He felt an unexpected poignancy looking at this bright, happy little girl and knowing her cruel fate.

"That your pony, miss?" he asked her.

Lady Jane turned to regard him suspiciously. "You don't know?" she asked, "are you new here?"

"Very new here, miss," he said.

"You must call me Lady Jane," she said. "It's tiring, I know, but everyone's supposed to do it, or you might get in trouble."

"Oh, I'm sorry, Lady Jane, I *will* try to remember that," he said.

"You talk funny," said Lady Jane, "you have a funny accent. Where are you from?"

Ian was taken aback. He had thought he had the Tudor court accent down pat. "I'm from a place called Leicester, your ladyship."

"'Your ladyship' is for my mother. 'Lady Jane' is fine for me. You don't talk like you're from Leicester. I'm very good with accents and I know lots of people from Leicester and they don't sound anything like you."

"What's your pony's name?" asked Ian.

"I named him Seneca" she said, "after a famous Roman Philosopher I like to read."

"Seneca?" repeated Ian, surprised. "You already know Latin?"

"Of course, you silly, I am very good with Latin and Hebrew and my father says I can learn Greek too."

"Why do you study Latin? At your age, most girls are playing with dolls."

The girl considered his question thoughtfully. "I do love dolls, but my dolls are very smart, and they speak Latin too, in case we have to talk to some Papists."

"I've never heard Latin," said Ian, "can you tell me something in Latin?"

"Of course," she said, "This is from Seneca and my father has it on a plaque in his receiving room. *Non quia difficilia sunt non audemus, sed quia non audemus, difficilia sunt.*"

"That is very impressive, Lady Jane," Ian said sincerely. "What does it mean?"

"It means people don't *not* do things because they are hard, but things are hard because people don't do things." She paused for a moment, thinking about the words. "It's kind of strange. My mother says someone had the plaque carved for me when I was a baby, but she didn't think it was appropriate for a girl's room, so she gave it to my father."

"Well, it does seem an odd gift for a young girl," said Ian, wondering to himself who might have thought such an aphorism would be appropriate for a daughter of nobility.

September 1547

Ian Harland was still in the prime of his life at 40, but he didn't look it today.

Today, his hair was dyed white and he shuffled along with a limp and a bent back. He was carrying a delivery of books to Dr. Michelangelo Florio, Lady Jane's Italian tutor. It was quite a heavy collection Ian had to carry up the long, winding spiral staircase to Dr. Florio's apartments. Had he truly been as old as he looked, he didn't think he would have made it.

At the top of the stairs, he knocked, and Florio opened the door and impatiently waived him inside.

Florio was a short man, also with white hair but his hair was sticking out from under his cap in every direction. His silk shirt and velvet coat were wrinkled and flecked with ink.

Ian smiled to himself. Academics were the same, no matter their time or place.

Ian handed Florio the receipt and asked him to sign and date it for his master. Florio took it, grabbed a quill and wrote down the requested information and handed the bill back to Ian. The delicate-looking girl, who appeared about eight years old, but whom Ian knew was almost ten, kept stumbling over her Italian pronunciation and word choice.

"No, no, no, *no!*" said Florio. "*Attualamente* means 'currently,' not 'actually,' you silly girl. You make silly mistakes like that; you will talk Italian like this English porter here."

"*Io, Signore, sono molto offeso dal tuo commento,*" Ian said, and the young lady tried hard not to laugh but still let out a splutter. Then she smiled that smile Ian already knew so well.

Lady Jane, now and ever, was a small girl, slender in form and lively of face. One might call her comely but not beautiful. But when she smiled, Ian thought, it was an incredible transformation; the proverbial sun showing its dazzling face after a rainstorm.

"*Oh, vuoi il mio lavoro. Sai come parlare latino e francese?*" said Florio sarcastically.

"I do know a little Latin," Ian said. He knew French too but thought he was pushing his role more than enough already. "*Non quia difficilia sunt non audemus...*" he said.

Lady Jane answered immediately, "*sed quia non audemus, difficilia sunt,*" gracing him once again with her smile.

Ian smiled back at the girl, but inside his heart ached both for this little girl whose life would be cut so short, and for his own little girl, also named Jane, well, Lara Jane, whom he would never see grow up.

June 1552

Ian Harland, a strapping young man of twenty-nine, looked dashing in the clothes of a young nobleman. He wore a finely wrought doublet, silk shirt, hose and fashionable shoes. He wore his long hair down his back in a braid held together with a silver ringlet. His hands were elegantly manicured, and he wore a mustache and small goatee, unfashionable for the time, but very popular with the girls.

Lady Jane was such a girl. She was fifteen, still small for her age, enough that she had to wear rising soles to reach five feet. When Ian walked in, she was surrounded by a gaggle of young men while several young women in fancy clothes and ultra-fashionable hair styles—some including live birds and silver tiaras—watched from afar with disapproval.

It certainly wasn't her standing at court that drew the men. If anything, being so close to the succession was more barrier than attraction. It was well known that getting too close to the Tudors puts one's neck in danger. But Lady Jane had that beaming smile and a decidedly unfeminine, full-throated laugh.

Ian was not normally forward with women, even now as a married man and a father, but this would be his one chance. It would be dangerous to show up in her life as a conspicuous young man more than once and he couldn't monopolize her time, especially at this party, where, in about an hour, she would meet her future husband for the first time.

If he were to have his one chance to dance with Lady Jane, this would be it. So, as he walked into the room, he looked boldly at Lady Jane and gave her what he thought was an enticing smile.

She appeared not to notice him, so he was surprised a few minutes later to find her standing close and leaning in to speak intimately with him. "Hello, good sir," she said, "I don't believe I've ever seen you here before. I am Lady Jane Grey." She held her hand out for him to kiss and he did so.

"I have heard of you, Lady Jane, but the descriptions do not do you justice."

"Oh, posh," she said, laughing a little, "you looked like you would be different. I don't need flattery. I'd rather have someone I can talk to intelligently."

"Well maybe I can help there too. I'm not overly good at flattery — though I do tell the truth," he said, smiling. The girl rolled her green eyes at him so he switched tactics. "So, I hear Pope Julius is about to recall the Council of Trent. He was always a man to favor tolerance. Maybe now the Council will be less against our English Church and bloodshed will be avoided."

Now she laughed outright and quite loudly, causing several people to glance over at them. He could feel his ears turning red, but she gently reached up and touched him on his arm and moved her head in even closer to keep the conversation private. "Sir, you come in with overwrought flattery then turn immediately to theological politics. What a way with the ladies you have!" But she was smiling as she said it.

"Pray tell, my lady, what should I talk about with you?"

"Well, if you insist on bringing up Julius, let's talk about his newly raised nephew Innocenzo. Gossip is always good meat for conversation at a party."

Ian scanned his memory for a moment, not immediately picking up on the reference. When he did, his eyes grew wide and his ears even redder. "Is that a proper topic at a fashionable party like this?" he asked.

"Ah, well, we are all Protestants here," she said. "I think the music is about to start. Would you care to be my partner in the first round?"

"I would be honored," said Ian, meaning it more than she would ever know. "I hope it is not too difficult a dance," he said. "I may be worse at dancing than I am with small talk."

Lady Jane laughed again. "An old philosopher once said 'It is not because things are difficult that we do not dare...'"

"*Sed, quia non audemus, difficilia sunt.*" Ian finished for her, then noticed she looked back at him very strangely.

"And how are things in your part of Leicester?" she asked. Ian only smiled, afraid to give away anything more.

In truth, Ian *had* practiced the Pavane over and over before this night and danced passably well but left soon thereafter. It would do neither him nor history any good if he were there when Guildford Dudley arrived.

February 2063

Ian arrived home a little over four months by his own reckoning after he had left to report on the Council of Trent. But it would only be about four weeks by the contemporary world's perception. He walked in, but no little girl came to greet him, no dog, and no wife. Lindy's car was in the garage so he thought at least *she* must be home.

"Hello," he said, into the silence. "I'm home, where is everybody?"

A short silence, then a very icy "I'm in your office, please come here."

Ian tried to understand what could possibly be wrong. He went through the normal things in his head. Nope, not anniversary. Nope, not her birthday or Lara Jane's birthday. He couldn't think of a holiday he missed. He was completely puzzled as he climbed the stairs.

Lindy sat on the floor of his messy office, her long dark hair mussed and her shirt untucked, a very un-Lindy way to look. All around her lay his journals and photo tablets.

"What's wrong, dear?" he asked.

Lindy didn't answer, she just pointed at his journals.

Ian turned his hands out to show his non-comprehension.

"We don't have a marriage anymore," she said, "You're never home and you never see your own child."

"How can you say that? I'm home for weeks at a time..."

"Sure, locked in this office. You still leave me with all the housework, and all the child-raising with Lara. We haven't made love for months."

Ian was stung but he couldn't deny he felt the distance between them too. "Lindy, you know I have a very difficult and demanding job. You knew that when we got married."

Lindy stood up and folded her arms across her chest. "When we got married, you were a historian nerd who hung out in the library and wrote smug treatises on how Tudor wig-making technology affected Elizabethan culinary customs or some such bullshit. We had a life together and I could teach my classes and come home to a husband.

"Ever since your precious Institute recruited you, you're like some secret agent, flying off in a timeship and sneaking into meetings and throne rooms and cathedrals and pretending to be someone else all the time. When you come home, you bring that shit with you. I don't even know who you are any more. You can't or you won't talk about your work. I want a regular life back. I want us to be a family."

"Lindy, love, I can't quit the Institute. I'm on the verge of investigating one of the most intriguing stories of the Tudor era."

"I know, it's you and that damned little girl. No one gives a crap about a five-hundred-year dead teenager except you. But to you, she's like your real daughter. I don't know, is that possible? Is she really your daughter? You seem to care more about her than you do Lara and me."

"What are you talking about?" Ian was genuinely baffled.

"I started reading your journals and looking at your holos and your research. Everything here is about little Jane Grey, it's like you are obsessed with her."

Ian rolled his eyes. "Yeah, sure, I study Jane Grey, she was the subject of my masters dissertation. But she's just a historical figure. I am curious about her but only because I wrote so much about her in grad school and because her story reveals so much about Tudor politics before Elizabeth."

Lindy pulled a small stack of papers and tossed it at him. "Here, here's your report on the coronation of Henry VIII, one of the great landmark events in English history. It's what, six pages? You visit your historical six-year-old *daughter* in a barn and here is twenty pages of meticulous detail, including describing the goddamned shit on her shoes," Lindy said, throwing that report at him too.

"Well, I did the coronation report for work. That's just my summary copy. There's a much longer version I filed at work." He could see she didn't believe him.

"And the description of the cute little girl in the barn is for your own pleasure? It's not marked for work. Do you go visit her in the Institute's machines without telling them?"

"I've never seen you like this. You're bloody crazy right now!"

"Am I crazy? she said, her voice rising. "You named our daughter after her."

"Just her middle name"

"Yeah and what do you insist on calling her?"

Ian lowered his eyes but said nothing.

"You named our dog after her husband, and you named our parrot after her mother," Lindy said. Ian remembered naming the dog Dudley but had forgotten about the parrot.

"You've gone back to meet her now, what, five times, ten times? You spend more time with her than Lara. And you keep going back to meet her as a child, not as a woman."

"She died a child," he said, "It's not possible to visit her as a woman. And this child had a profound influence on our history. For God's sake, she was a martyr of the Reformation."

"How many other people became martyrs during the Reformation, ten thousand…ten million? But it's a pretty little, prepubescent girl that you describe in excruciating detail and go back to meet over and over again, in clear violation of your precious Institute's policies. What are you going to do now, go back and save her from execution so you can have your favorite little daughter?"

"Of course not, that would change history!"

Ian was more scared than he let on. He was petrified to lose this woman he loved, and his truly beloved Lara Jane, but he was also scared that maybe, just maybe, Lindy was right. Was he obsessed with Lady Jane the child? She was smart, witty, and attractive in her own petite way and he felt horribly sad every time he remembered that her head would be cut off at such a young age. He didn't think he was obsessed with her, but he had *dreamed* more than once about rescuing her from the executioner's axe. He would never do it, of course, but the thought had crossed his mind. He knew that someday he would have to attend and record her execution.

"I need some time to think," Lindy said, gathering her coat and purse from the floor. "Lara and I'll be at my mother's house."

"I love you Lindy, and I love Lara" he said to her back as she walked out.

March 1553

It had been a year in his time since Lindy had walked out on him and had taken Lara Jane with her. It took Lindy a suspiciously short time to find a new fiancé and Ian was almost never allowed to see Lara Jane.

Institute policy, of course, forbade his use of the machine to alter the near past of his own life but that didn't mean he sometimes didn't think about it. But he knew he couldn't get away with it. The massive energy signature of his Time Capsule would be detected, and someone would be sent to stop him.

But like his fellow field historians, Ian was becoming disillusioned with the crazy, petty, restrictive Institute rules forbidding any interference with the past. But he also knew that no one could predict what such meddling might do to the time stream. The Institute's Theoretical Chronologists argued for hours over their beers about possible consequences of such meddling but it was Ian and the twenty other field historians who had to live with the consequences of not making these choices in real life.

After Lindy left, the Institute had pulled Ian out of the field until the bosses decided he was recovered enough to handle field work again. No one wanted a field historian to have a mental breakdown where no one could help him and where he might do untold damage.

The team physician was still not convinced that he was ready to go back but the team leader, Dr. Gwilliam, argued forcefully that Ian could be trusted again. So now he was back in Tudor England at a party thrown by the Duke and Duchess of Northumberland to celebrate the betrothal of Lady Jane to Guildford Dudley.

This was the gathering where Northumberland would unveil his plans for his son and the soon-to-be Queen Jane, and Ian listened to the schemes with growing alarm, knowing how soon they would go so catastrophically wrong. Ian was in the role of a hired serving man, having forged his way into the household serving staff to attend on this party so he could hear everything without being noticed.

The span of centuries between 1553 and his wife and daughter only made his heart more melancholic. He felt he was finally coming to terms with the loss of his family, but Ian was suddenly not so sure he agreed with Dr. Gwilliam. He had thought he could handle being back in the field, but now he stood completely frozen, holding the plates of food he was supposed to deliver to the guest tables. Ian was unable to move, to go forward or to go back. It was like his will had been sucked out leaving him an empty shell.

He begged the universe to give him a sign. He could see that the head steward had already noticed his paralysis, and he could only watch as this man stalked towards him.

Then *she* appeared at his side. He was so intent on the steward, he hadn't seen her coming.

Lady Jane looked at him and bestowed her golden smile. "Good sir," she said, "my compliments to the Northumberland staff. This is one of the finest feasts I have ever attended and *that,* my friend, is no light compliment."

Ian quickly regained his composure. He couldn't save her, he couldn't put his own life back together but amid all the pain, it was enough to know that such a magnificent creature existed, even if only for a short while.

He smiled gratefully, then went back to work in both his jobs, serving the gluttonous royals of Tudor England and eavesdropping on their conversations to glean new understanding of this important crossroads of English history.

May 1553

The night was dark, with only a sliver of silver moon in the sky lighting his bumbling progress through the dense woods of the Dudley estate in Northumberland. His window of opportunity was short — if it even existed at all. He desperately searched for the campfire of the hunting party.

He had dressed too lightly for the late-night spring coolness. He was beginning to shiver from the cold as much as from his trepidation at the magnitude of what he was about to do.

It was his own damn fault. He should have started out earlier when it was lighter, when there was more commotion to hide his approach. Ian was fifty two now, and he constantly forgot that he was no longer the young field researcher he had been when the Institute was founded. His eyesight, even with the night glasses, was no longer as good in the dark as it used to be.

He had seen a contemporary letter giving him the time and a place for this encampment, but Institute rules usually required something more specific than "northeast of the big ridge on Guildford's estate" and "long after Guildford and the others had gone to sleep in the tents."

Somewhere out here, Lady Jane sat alone, staring into the fire, trying to decide what to do about the storm of politics and religion that was gathering around her.

It never ceased to amaze him how quiet the past was. In his own time, even in the deepest woods and the darkest hour, there was always some airplane or car or truck or holo making noise somewhere. In 1553, you heard only the frogs, the insects, and the sounds of the forest, nothing else.

Ian tried to be quiet, but with so little light, he was constantly tripping on unseen roots or hitting his face on low-hanging branches. He dared not use his flashlight and dared not utter a sound that might alert the sentries who would surely be guarding the camp.

What he did do — unintentionally, but luckily — was catch the attention of one of the hunting hounds and the dog bayed into the night setting off a chorus of howling from the whole kennel. He finally had a direction for his stumbling, and he soon saw the fire blazing in the night. With a direction and the need for panicked speed gone, Ian was able to go into the stealth mode mastered by all good field historians.

With his infrared-enhancing glasses, he searched for active sentries and found none. He was able to approach the camp undetected. The watch, it seemed, was with the dogs, trying to quiet them down so the Dudleys and their guests could sleep peacefully.

And there she was, wrapped in a blanket and sitting by herself on a camp chair staring into the flames. He guessed that her betrothed Guildford and the other young gentlemen and ladies of the party had made quite merry that evening and were sleeping off their wine.

Ian circled around so that when she did first notice him, it would appear he was coming from the direction of the tents. As he walked towards Lady Jane Grey, he watched the light from the flames dancing across her face, giving her an unearthly glow. In her stillness, there was a powerful combination of serenity and intensity.

He purposefully made noise as he walked so he wouldn't startle her. He spoke softly, "My lady, may I join you for a while?"

She looked up from the fire at him, giving him a wan smile. "I don't think I will be much good company tonight, sir."

"My lady," he said, "I've come to offer some solace in your times of trouble, if you would have it."

She looked at him more closely. "Do I know you sir? Are you a friend of Lord Dudley?" Then she looked closer still. "Do I know you? You look very familiar, but I can't quite place you. I do apologize, I am usually very good with names and faces."

"You do know me, my lady, we have met many times, but not in ways you could easily understand."

"Now you have me interested," she replied, "How would I know you?"

Ian smiled. "The very first time we met — that you might remember — you were a little girl sneaking into your father's stable when you were supposed to be inside. You showed off your newly gained Latin skills to me. *Non quia difficilia sunt non audemus...*" he said.

After a moment, she dutifully answered back "*sed quia non audemus, difficilia sunt.*" A range of emotions swept across her face, and she leaned towards him, peering intently. Ian was sure she was putting things together though she couldn't possibly understand it.

"And you carried the books up to my tutor's tower when I was nine and your son—it must have been your son, he looked so much like you—danced with me a year ago then disappeared before I could talk to him again."

"You need to know something first. I am not a witch, not a demon and not an angel, not any kind of supernatural being, I am a flesh and blood human just like you."

Jane cocked her head at him and flashed her smile. "Well that is certainly reassuring," she said with a hint of irony in her voice.

"My Lady, all of those people were me."

She stared. "You must be sixty now, the man I danced with a year ago was in his twenties. The man who brought the books to Master Florio must have been seventy."

Ian laughed. "You wound me, my lady, I'm not yet fifty-three as we speak now."

"So how did you look twenty-five two years ago and seventy a few years before that? Are you some kind of magician?"

"When I carried the books, it was a wig and makeup. But no, my lady, I am no magician. I am a traveler, I have a ship, a very special type of ship. It doesn't travel on water; it sails in time. I have visited you many times but at different times in my own life but not in the same chronological order as you."

Her eyes widened then narrowed. Ian was pretty sure she didn't know if he was crazy or just joking. "Did my Lord Guildford put you up to this?" she asked warily.

Ian shook his head. "I come from a time when we have machines that do wondrous things you can't even yet imagine."

Lady Jane leaned back on her stool. "Of course, but I suppose you don't have such a machine with you now, right."

"But I do," he said, "May I show you? It is a little, common thing to me. We call it a 'camera,' but it is a very important tool of my trade."

"Pray tell, what is your trade?"

Ian smiled. "I'm a historian. I come from the future and this device paints pictures of things I see to carry back to my own time."

Now she was really smiling at him, "I see, and you can paint a picture of me now, I suppose."

Ian pulled out a small, rectangular device, set it for low-light and said, "My lady, make a face, hold up some fingers, do something I could never have guessed before now that you would do."

Gamely, Lady Jane made a "v" with two fingers, looked through it with one eye and stuck out her tongue. Ian pushed the shutter button and handed her the camera.

She took it from him, still laughing at the joke. But when she looked at the screen, she shrieked and threw the camera into the fire.

Ian scrambled and grabbed a stick to knock it out of the flames. "My lady," he said, "please be careful, it is not fireproof!"

Lady Jane's startled eyes looked back and forth from him to the device. "My God" she said, "What are you?"

A sentry, who had heard her cry out, came towards them. "Is everything all right, my lady," he said. Ian tensed, feeling in his pocket for his taser and wondered doubtfully if it would work through chain mail.

She waved the soldier off, "I am so sorry, a spark flew up on my blanket, I'm fine." After the man walked away, she turned back to Ian. "What are you and what in God's name is that?"

"I am a historian. But instead of reading about people and events from the past, I go back in time and see them for myself, and I use this device to make pictures of what I see to take back to my own time and show everyone what really happened. You'd be surprised how inaccurate reading someone else's description of history is compared with seeing it for yourself."

"How do you travel to times that have already happened. Do you have a special prayer to God or his angels?"

"Ah no, my lady. It is just a very special ship, a mechanical device, a thing made by human hands. We consort neither with angels nor with demons, just humans."

"I don't understand. How can you sail in time?"

"My lady, I can explain all of it but not in the time we have tonight. Our time tonight is short."

"And why is that?" she asked warily.

Ian sighed. "It's because I have to convince you of something now, tonight, before you go back to your tent."

"Ah, I see, you are here to convince me to take the crown. My cousin sent you, right?"

"No, my lady, just the opposite. I want you to choose *not* to be queen. I want you to choose to come with me, to give up everything you know — and live."

"And live?" she asked, sitting up straight now.

"In history, my history, your future, you become queen. You are the first queen regnant of England."

"You think this a bad thing, sir? Women should not rule?"

"Not that, my Lady, not at all. Your cousin Elizabeth was, um, will be, one of the greatest rulers who ever ruled England. She was called Gloriana."

"I see, so what epithet is bestowed on me?"

Ian tried to say it but couldn't.

"Don't flap your lips like a fish, what will I be called?"

"The nine-days queen, my lady."

Lady Jane looked at him for a very long time. He couldn't guess what was going through her mind.

"And how are you going to convince me this bizarre story is true?"

"I have pictures, my lady, in my camera," he said, indicating the device in his hands, "if you will look at them."

"These paintings show me as queen?"

"They are moving pictures, they capture many pictures together, like you are moving, and they capture the sounds too. What I will show you are pictures I took February 12, 1554, just a week ago for me. Your husband has already been executed by that date. These moving pictures show your final moments."

"You want to show me my own death" she asked incredulously, "to convince me to forgo the crown?"

Ian shook his head. "I wouldn't show you that, but these are the moments before when you say your last words."

"Do I grovel and cry then?"

"No, my lady, quite the opposite, you die well, with your head held high and praise to God on your lips."

"If I am queen, who dares order my death?"

"Your cousin Mary Tudor. She will declare herself queen on June 10, the day you are proclaimed, and she will subvert the Council and threaten to march her armies from East Anglia. Your Council will turn on you and Mary will take the throne on June 19 and order your arrest for treason. You will spend the rest of your short life in the Tower of London, nine days as queen, the remainder as prisoner."

"Mary will have me killed?"

"Actually, she will try to save you and your husband but your fath…um, Mary will be forced by events to condemn you."

Lady Jane sat up straighter. "Mary is a Papist. I don't think I can sit by and watch her destroy everything King Henry has done. If you know the future, you can help me keep that Catholic off the throne."

"If you stay here, I cannot do that and I cannot save you. It's not as if you can refuse the throne and it's not as if there is anything you can do to stop Mary. But if it makes you feel better, know that Mary, too, is eventually beheaded and when Elizabeth ascends the throne after Mary, she rules for forty-five years and quickly and permanently brings Protestantism back. This is the history of England viewed from my own time."

"And when is your own time?"

"I was born in 2033."

Lady Jane's eyes grew wide as she did the math. After a moment, she held out her hand for the camera. Ian queued up the video, showed her where to touch to start it playing and sat back and watched her eyes as she watched her own last words in the very first video she had ever seen. Lady Jane did not stop watching after her final words and Ian saw her hunch her neck as he heard the axe fall.

They both stared into the fire for a very long time after the video was finished.

"I don't believe in witchcraft," she said, after a while, "or at least I didn't until now."

"It is a human-made tool like a compass. Or, you know the eyeglasses your tutor used to wear? The camera uses glass lenses just like those to write pictures in a special machine. I can teach you how these things work if you come with me."

"And if I don't?"

"I will leave. I will be sad, but I will leave. I promise you I will not force you, now—or ever—to do anything you don't want to do."

"And if I stay, I will be queen in months and die in less than a year?"

Ian nodded.

"How did you know where to find me tonight?" she asked, suspicion creeping back into her voice.

"Well tomorrow, you will write a letter to your sister Katharine, describing how you stayed up late at night, sitting alone by the fire and thinking about Edward's request for you to take the throne after his death. In five-hundred years or so, another historian I work with finds that Katharine had saved the letter in a box that was hidden away in the Tower for centuries. My colleague knows I am researching you and your life and sends me the letter."

"But if I go with you, I won't write that letter…"

Ian nodded, "Yes, and the future is changed but the past is the past. You will already be with me and I can promise you wonders beyond your imagination and that no one will try to chop off your head."

"Can we save my Lord Guildford too?"

Ian shook his head sadly. "My ship is small, and I can only carry away one person from this time." This was not *strictly* true, but he wasn't about to admit that to her.

She pursed her lips and nodded slowly. "Why do you want to do this, why do you want to save me from this future?"

Ian looked into the fire then back into her eyes. "A week ago, when I watched you face your death with such courage and grace, I realized I have come to admire and care for you greatly.

I know I'm an old man to you and I don't ask anything of you but to travel with me and live."

Lady Jane Grey continued to look into Ian's eyes. "And if this future changes, will it change your time?"

"I don't know what will happen. No one, at least no one that I know of, has ever tried this. We will have to discover that together."

March 1553

Ian walked back to his Time Capsule with a lighter heart than when he had left it. The information he had gained this night from listening to a progressively drunker Northumberland explained a lot of details about Jane's ascension and the betrayal by her Privy Council. He now knew that the seeds of that betrayal had started this night, even before her marriage.

Arriving at last to where he left his capsule, he burrowed through the camouflage to find the entrance and punched his code into the keypad on his device. Calling it a "capsule" was an Institute-inspired misnomer of the highest order. Though it took little space from the outside, it was moderately spacious and at least comfortable on the inside with both a galley, a sitting room and office of sorts and his own bedroom through another door. If one could control the intersection of time and space, it seemed silly to not allow oneself enough space in whatever time the capsule visited.

The entrance code could be typed on his device or a keypad. The code was complex enough that he didn't believe he had to engage any biometrics. No one, particularly no one from this benightedly non-technological time, could possibly break his code or accidentally stumble in and he was certain he had not neglected to close and lock his ship.

That's why, when he literally tripped over women's undergarments as he walked in, he felt the blood drain from his face and the world get suddenly cold. This was utterly impossible and no explanation he could think of had a happy ending.

First was a chemise, then an untied corset and finally the sixteenth-century version of a brassiere laid out in a straight path to his closed bedroom door. He opened the door and leaned down to pick up the dress that had been tossed carelessly on the floor. It didn't occur to him until much later that this was exactly the wrong order for clothes stripped off and dropped carelessly by someone walking from his front door into his bedroom.

Ian never made his bed and didn't initially notice the petite woman buried in the pillows and blankets. When he did finally see her, he dropped everything again and stood there with his mouth hanging open, looking at the twinkling eyes over that smile he knew so well. The face was older than the one on the girl who had restored hope to him earlier this night—now there were laugh lines around the bright green eyes and a few light streaks of grey in the red-gold hair—but there was no mistaking it. She held the sheets up to her neck.

For what seemed like a very long time to him, he stared and made inarticulate sounds while he tried ineffectively to talk, until finally he squeaked out "My lady?"

The woman in the bed laughed out loud then. "Oh, my dear Ian, if only you could see your face now. I knew this would be a surprise to you, but I didn't think it would bring on complete apoplexy. Please, come here and sit down next to me."

He didn't move. She laughed again. "Don't flap your lips like a fish, Ian. I've come back for you."

"Back?" he asked, his voice squeaking again.

"Yes, back. Did you think one lifetime between you and me would be enough?"

"Uhh, do you think you could start from the beginning, or at least somewhere where I might recognize? Why are you here?"

Lady Jane was clearly enjoying herself. "I am here, dear Ian, to completely fuck up your bloody timeline like you did to me so many years ago in my timeline."

"And is that a good thing or a bad thing?"

"For me, it was the best thing you could have done, for you, now, I honestly don't know. But know this, I won't make you do anything—now or ever—that you don't want to do."

"How can you be here as, ah, um, old as you are now. Weren't you, um, executed in 1553? I don't mean to sound callous... I just don't understand it."

"Well, I will-would have been beheaded as a traitor if you hadn't come back for me two months from now in this timeline, some twenty years from now in your timeline and twenty-six years ago in my timeline."

Ian shook his head in frustration. "I'm sorry, my lady, just now, I'm not really able to do math..."

"At age fifty-two, you went to witness my execution. You filmed it, spent a week thinking about it, and you came back to the sixteen-year-old me—about two months from now—and showed me my death on your camera and convinced me to fly away in time with you. Obviously, I decided life as a rogue time traveler was better than dying as a young ex-queen."

"So why are you here now? I'm not complaining, just trying to understand."

"Well, the twenty-five years we spent together were pretty good. They certainly were *interesting*." Lady Jane looked thoughtful, then smiled mischievously, "I do have to say, though, that you were very, very wrong when you promised me no one would try to chop off my head, but I won't hold that against you."

"So where am *I* now? Is the older me here now somewhere? Not that I care much but I think meeting myself is completely against Institute rules."

"Dear Ian, pretty much everything about this is against Institute rules. I never got to visit your precious Institute—your saving me kind of ripped a huge hole in your time stream so it didn't exist when we went back to your time. Just as well, I suspect. Anyway, the you I lived with for twenty-five years passed away at the age of seventy-seven about a year ago in my time. I will be happy to show you pictures of this alternate future you will-would-have-had, but I won't show you *your* last days."

Ian's mind was reeling. This was a lot to process. "Okay, we travelled together for twenty-five years?"

"More or less. We stopped a few times along the way too."

"And we remained friends for all that time?"

"Um, well, no, not exactly *friends*, per se." Lady Jane gave him a wicked smile. "Look, I know this is weird for you to meet your will-would-have-been future wife who wants to travel with you again. It's kind of weird for me too, to meet my late husband before he knows he will-would-be my husband. I do know you are a different person now than the man I married, and I don't know if you will want to stay with me as I am now. I don't know — but I have to find out. I'm older now, maybe an old woman to you now and not the flirty sixteen-year-old you were just talking with in the great hall. But after all we've been through together, I am no longer an ingenue and goddammit, I bloody well love you, or at least the man you will-would-have become so I have to try."

Ian smiled back at her. "My lady, um, should I still call you that…?"

Lady Jane smiled back and nodded. "It means something a little different, but yes, it is quite appropriate."

"My lady," he continued, "I am tired of the Institute's stupid regulations, and I am tired of the Ian Harland who always follows rules. I see you are even stronger and more interesting than I imagined what you would have been like if you lived. Um, well you did live, um would-have-will lived…"

Lady Jane laughed loudly. "The old you and me, we will-would-have had a lot of fun making up new tenses for the English language, and in French too, but especially English. I suspect this game will continue. But," she held up one finger, "I still will-would have set the record with 12 helper verbs back in the Levant about eleven-hundred years ago."

Ian smiled. "Putting that challenge aside for now, I don't know if I can promise anything yet, but I think I would very much like traveling with you. Shall we go together to find what the future brings?"

Lady Jane smiled back, her eyes blinking back tears. "No, dear Ian, we shall go and find out what futures we can create."

Heart's Desire

The president chewed fiercely on her cigar.

She had never been a smoker so it wasn't lit. But it bounced up and down to her nervous internal beat. She was already in a pretty bad mood—third night in the White House and her idiot husband was already on the prowl with his boys, the boys who were supposed to be her people now, not his. They should all be her people now.

Instead, she had a demanding visitor who wanted to play poker with her, a visitor she couldn't refuse.

Her companion sat across from her, shuffling the cards in impossible ways. The cards leapt between his hands, twisting and turning in the air in intricate patterns, changing colors, changing size, flying up, down and sideways. Some left the pack and flew around the president's head. She swatted them out of the air onto the table but they still flew back into his deck.

He was an unassuming-looking man, someone you wouldn't pay any attention to if you saw him on the street. Middle height, middle age, indeterminate ethnicity and wearing a sport jacket with patches on the elbow. You wouldn't notice him at all if you didn't look into the dark, mischievous eyes that darted back and forth when he talked to you. Tonight, he was less innocuous than usual in that he wore a giant handlebar mustache he had grown in the two days since she had last seen him.

He pulled out his own cigar, clipped the end and clamped it between his teeth. A tail slithered out from the back of his pants, and he used the red-hot spade at the end of the tail to light the cigar. Then he sucked hard, inhaling the entire cigar in one giant, continuous pull. He was left with one long ash that finally fell away as he exhaled the smoke in a cloud that surrounded the president's head, sending her into a coughing fit.

"God Damn it, I wish to hell you'd stop doing that," Clinton said, "I nearly fucking lost the election with that coughing."

"My love, there was never any danger of that. We made a deal, after all."

"You made a deal with *him*, too," she retorted, a little huffily.

"Yes, and he wanted to renegotiate—I don't do that. And I did find you that *Access Hollywood* tape. It had been tossed in the garbage six years ago but I found it and restored it. It was a beautiful job, wasn't it?"

"I'm surprised you had to make a deal with him. Didn't you already have his soul locked up?"

"Ahhh, well it's different with people like him."

"Why, because he doesn't have a soul?"

"Oh, he's got a soul all right, every human does; comes with the human experience. It's just that, well, his is so small and black and hard, kind of like a lump of coal. I've already got lots of those in my collection. I like big juicy ones like yours. The more living the soul has done, the more it loves, the more it feels, the more it hopes, the more it hurts, the bigger and juicier it is. Yours, Madam President, will be quite delectable."

"Now," he said, "are you ready to play some poker?" Lucifer dealt the cards, five to each of them. He gave her a stack of chips and put his ante into the middle of the table, and she reciprocated.

There was a knock on the door. "Come in," the president said and one of the White House staff servers walked in. She was a middle-aged women who looked familiar to Hillary, maybe from the first time she lived here.

"Welcome back ma'am," the woman said. She set a glass of wine and a covered dinner in front of the president.

"Do you know where Mr. Clinton is tonight?" The president asked.

"Not exactly, ma'am, he and Mr. Jackson and Mr. Penn and Mr. Bono took a limousine from the pool and went to dinner somewhere on U Street," the woman said.

Then the woman glanced at the table. "It's interesting," she said, "when Mr. Clinton was president, he spent a lot of time in this room playing solitaire too."

The president threw a sharp look at her opponent but he just smiled inscrutably. The staffer didn't seem to notice the exchange.

"Will there be anything else, ma'am?" she asked. Hillary grunted and waved her to the door. The woman looked a little miffed but complied with the dismissal.

"And what did you do with him here?" She asked after the server left. "Share some succubi?" She threw in a blue chip for her first bet.

The Devil smiled. "Nope, we just played poker, just like you and me. Sometimes Dick Morris would join us, and sometimes even The Donald though he absolutely hates cigar smoke, so I would usually make it invisible to him."

"You think I like cigar smoke?" She asked incredulously, pulling the cheroot out of her mouth. "Cigars and I have a really spotty history."

"Oh, I know you hate it, and you really hate it when Bill has cigars, but I'm not courting you anymore. You already made your deal. I just like to come and visit and check on you and make sure you are enjoying my gifts." He looked down and moved some chips. "I'll see your ten and raise you fifty."

Hillary looked down at her cards, seeing she had two pair, queen high. "See your fifty and raise you another."

"Oh my," he said, "you're getting too rich for me. You must have something good. I'll see your fifty and call."

She laid down her two pair and he followed, laying down two pair, king high, smiling beatifically.

They played another hand in silence–other than the sound of her eating and the sucking noise he made with his new cigar.

She had a full house; he had a flush.

Next hand, she had three of a kind, he had four of a kind.

"I'm beginning to sense a pattern here," she said.

He looked mock-offended. "Would I lie to you?"

"Would Bill?" She said, a smirk on her face.

"You wound me, lovely lady," he said, raising his hand to his heart, or at least where a heart would have been if he were human.

"Tell you what," he said. "I have a proposition. One hand, this time for real stakes, and I promise not to make myself win."

Hillary cocked an eye at him. "I don't think I believe you."

"Well, I *am* the Father of Lies, but have I ever broken a real promise to you?"

"That remains to be seen."

"Madam, I do not ever lie. For my contracts to be considered valid by those nit-picky, legalistic, pencil-necked angels in charge of such things, everything I promise by word or in contract must be true."

"Okay, I'll bite, what stakes are you proposing."

"Oh, Madam President, quite straightforward ones. If I win, you give me one Supreme Court nominee. You will have three justices to replace in your first term. Maybe, I shouldn't have told you that, but you will have four. If I win, I get to knock whichever nominee I choose out of the running and you still get to pick the replacement nominee."

"And if I win?" She asked.

"Then I will give you what's inside the locker this key opens!" He said, holding up a small key on a cheap metal chain.

Clinton looked non-plussed. "And what, pray tell, is inside this locker?"

"Inside this locker, my lady, is your true heart's desire. That one thing you have wanted for so long and can never have."

"Monica's heart in a jar?"

Lucifer was taking a puff on his cigar at that moment and he snorted so hard he blew smoke out his ears.

"Dear, you shouldn't play into that evil queen meme so much. Mr. Starr might come back."

"Oh yeah, it *would* more likely be his heart in the jar," she conceded.

The devil smiled at her through his smoke. "No, truly, this would be what you have wanted for many years, something you crave without even knowing it and it won't involve anyone's heart in a jar."

"One supreme court pick, one out of four?"

"Well, I will take only one of your nominees from you—at my discretion. You might very well get the next person you choose for the same spot."

"This seems like a pretty uneven bet for you," said Hillary. She narrowed her eyes at him and leaned forward as if that would help her read his mind.

He blew smoke in her face, pushing her back, blinking and coughing again. "Supreme Court is a pretty big deal. Having the opportunity to remove someone who might really do me some harm could be key to me."

"Couldn't you do it anyway? Even without the bet?"

"Mmmmm, perhaps, but betting like this makes it fun for me. I promise I won't take any of your other picks myself if I lose. Those nominations will live or die without my intervention. I won't even collaborate with my people in the Senate."

"Will you tell me what's in the locker?"

"Nope, you have to win to find out."

"Will you tell me if I lose?"

The Devil just smiled back at her, gently shaking his head "No."

Hillary thought for a few minutes. Yes, she was president now, elected with an historic majority but the damn Republicans still held the Senate and she thought it hardly likely that she would have an easy time with anyone on her list of Supreme Court candidates. Losing just one of her nominees seemed a cheap price to pay for keeping him out of the other nominations.

She didn't really believe the Father of Lies, but damn, she was curious about what he had stored in that locker. She shrugged and simply said, "Okay"

The Devil smiled a broad smile and shuffled the cards again, then he did something he had never done before, he let her cut the deck.

He dealt her five cards and took five cards for himself. Her heart sank when she picked up her cards—a four of hearts, a six of spades, a seven of spades, a two of diamonds and a ten of hearts. Ten high. She turned in three cards but in the end, still had ten high. Her opponent turned in two cards and showed a pair of fives.

She frowned. "I guess I'll never know," she said.

"Double or nothing?" Asked Lucifer, shuffling and again offering her the cut.

"I'm not going to win against you, am I?" She said, more a statement than a question.

"I promise you, I am not making these cards better for myself magically. Same bet, but for two of your nominees."

"What the hell," she said. "It's not like those Neanderthal Republicans will ever approve any of my choices anyway."

The second time, she was dealt a pair of queens. She discarded three and was dealt a pair of twos in her draw.

The Devil pondered his hand for a moment and discarded two. "I win again," he said as he showed his hand, "Two pair, jacks and fours."

The president smiled. "Look again, old Scratch, I've got two pair, queen high."

Lucifer looked like he'd been slapped. "How did you do that?" He asked.

"What's in the locker," she asked.

"Damned if I'm going to tell you," he said and threw the key at her. "If you're going to get help from someone else, I'm not going to play with you anymore." He stood up, blew another cloud of smoke in her face then disappeared.

"Wait, you asshole, where's the locker?"

From far away, she heard him say "basement."

"God damn him," she said to herself, then laughed at her ironic choice of words. She held the key in her hands and it burned her like Frodo's ring. She had to find out what was in that locker. She started heading towards the stairs, but curiosity got the better of her. She stopped and looked at the top two cards in the discard pile. It was a pair of kings.

Downstairs, she went looking for any White House staff member she could find. Going through the empty rooms, opening doors and slamming them behind her. "Mr. Jensen," she yelled. "Mrs. Linesky? Where the hell are you?"

The Chief Usher, Angella Reid, stuck her head out of her office door, curious about the commotion. "Can I help you, Madam President?"

"Yeah," said Hillary, "tell me what lockers are in the basement."

Reid thought for a moment. "Don't know, Ma'am. The basement is where we put the Press Corps, but I don't think they have any lockers. Maybe some of the cameramen keep their equipment in locked trunks, I don't know. Your secret service detail has a locker room down there too…"

"Take me to it."

Reid was taken aback. "Um, yes ma'am. I'll call down and make sure none of the men are down there in the locker room."

"Fuck that, I'm the president, take me there now."

"Yes ma'am," said Reid, finally coming out fully into the hallway. "Follow me, Madam President, we'll take the elevator in the north hall."

As they got into the elevator, the president said nothing more. Her face took on a sour expression as she thought about her security detail. She never liked them, here or in Arkansas. Then she looked down at the key in her hand and snorted loudly, seeing it had the number 666 engraved on it. The first two sixes were professionally punched, the third was scratched in with something sharp.

Leading her through a maze of hallways in the first basement, Reid took her to a pair of doors. "This one," she said pointing, "is for the female agents when we have them. This one," she said pointing to the other door, "is the locker room for the male agents. Let me knock and let them know you are coming."

Hillary pushed past Reid and opened the door. There were a couple of agents just coming out of the showers. Seeing the president, one quickly dove for his towel the other just stood there at attention. Both started to protest but, seeing the look on her face, swallowed their remarks.

"Get the hell out," she barked at them. "Go to the women's locker room, if you want. I'll only be a minute."

"I'm here too, Madam President," said a third man, coming out from a different row of lockers, but wearing far more clothes than his brethren. All three scooted quickly towards the door. When the president spoke, you obeyed.

"Okay," she said to Reid, "we need to find locker six-six-six."

Reid looked like she wanted to laugh but, like the agents, took a look at the President's expression and refrained. Hillary shoved the key in front of Reid's eyes to make her point.

"Yes ma'am," said Reid. "It looks like each row starts with its own number. The first row is 11 through 19, the second row is 21 through 29 and so forth."

They both walked to the sixth row, to locker 66 which had another "6" taped on at the end. On the front of the locker was a cutout of Hillary's face, adorned with horns and a goatee.

Hillary laughed. "He doesn't even have horns or a goatee," she said.

Reid looked sidelong at her. "Ma'am?"

Hillary noted with some disgust that locker 68 was labeled "Party Room" and had a smiling picture of the First Gentleman's face on it with a real cigar taped to its mouth.

The key slipped in the lock of 666 and the door opened. Inside the locker was what looked like a voodoo doll of the President with pins in it and a stained gris-gris bag hanging from one of the hooks but nothing else.

"You have a flashlight?" Hillary asked Reid. Reid pulled out her phone and turned on flashlight mode. Hillary shone it into her locker, moving it around—up and down, side to side—seeing nothing and started to feel foolish. She was probably going to have to fire those agents and Reid so they couldn't tell anyone the story. Then she saw an almost hidden clasp on the back wall of the locker. *Must be a false back*, she thought to herself as she pulled it open.

It wasn't a false back.

When she pulled open the back door of the locker, she saw it was a doorway to a brightly lit street. It had to be somewhere else because the street through the back of the locker was in broad daylight and she felt a warm breeze, not a cold D.C. January night. She could hear Reid gasp behind her but she paid her no attention.

Hillary climbed into the locker. It was a tight fit but she had to know so she pushed herself through. Only the back of her mind seemed to notice that the narrower door at the rear was easier to push her bust and hips through than the front door in the locker room.

For a second, she stood blinking on a street in a city she didn't immediately recognize. The street ran alongside a park filled with bustling downtown office workers, joggers and some homeless men sitting or lying on benches. She seemed to be in the middle of a group of casually-dressed women pulling sandwiches and hot coffee from a food truck and passing them to men on the benches

"Sister Hillary," said one woman, "are you okay?"

Hillary found herself nodding even though she wanted to shake her head violently. She turned around to see where she had come from, and there was no sign of the doorway behind her.

The woman who called out to her, put a sandwich and coffee cup in her hands and waived towards a more wooded area of the park and said "Your turn to go find old Nick in the bushes." Then she walked away, saying "watch his hands, Sister, you know how he is when it's warm."

More obediently than she felt, Hillary took the food along a path into the woods. After a short walk, she came upon an old man sitting on a stone bench. He was wrapped in a blanket, chewing an unlit cigar, and reading a paper. The smell of him was overpowering. He smelled like he hadn't showered for a year.

"Nick?" she said hesitantly.

"Oh, bless you, Sister, you don't know how much joy you bring to my life. Sit here just for a second with old uncle Nick," he said, patting the empty seat on the bench next to him.

She sat daintily, her mind trying to fight her body, but having no effect. As she sat, the end of his cigar suddenly burned bright red and with a mighty inhale, burned to the stub. He blew the cloud of smoke into her face, setting off a huge fit of coughing.

"Oh gosh darn it, I wish you'd stop that," she said, then threw her hand over her mouth. Old Nick started laughing.

"You'll get full control over everything back in a week or two," he said. "Just don't want you acting out like, well, the other Hillary, while you settle in. Want a cigar?"

"I don't smoke," she said.

"Actually, in this continuum, you do. Mostly with Sister Elizabeth when the Mother Superior isn't watching." He handed her the cigar and lit it and she was surprised to find she half enjoyed it. She tried to take a big inhale to blow smoke back in his face but ended up in another coughing fit.

"Ah, cigars, girl, you don't inhale, you puff on them."

She looked a little green but tried to compose herself. "Okay, so my heart's desire is to sit on a bench smoking cigars with the Devil?"

"No, no. On August 22, 1998, you said to a friend–and I quote–'I wish I were a god-damned nun and had never met Bill.' Of all the wishes you've made and hopes you've ever had, that registered as the strongest so now you are one."

"A nun?" She said, looking down at her normal street clothes, a pair of slacks and a modest blouse.

"Yes," he said, smiling wickedly, "a god-damned nun. Our deal still survives your change of lives. But it's a modern order, no penguin suit."

"You promised to make me president!" she hissed at him, her voice slipping higher than she liked.

"I did. I found you that wonderful tape, didn't I? You were elected president but now you've chosen another life."

"So now I'm a nun and I never met Bill? And I spend my days delivering sandwiches to homeless people. I aaaa...was a Methodist. Wwww...They don't have nuns." She couldn't say "am" or "we."

"You'll get all your new memories back over time. You won't forget your other life but you'll remember this one too. Doing it all at once would have been too much of a shock for you and no fun for me. In a nutshell, you converted when you decided to dedicate your life to teaching inner-city kids. You felt yourself better suited to a more contemplative life so you joined a religious order. Frankly, so far, you've found it quite an enjoyable life with none of the pain of your other existence. You deliver sandwiches to the homeless on weekends but mostly you still are that teacher and you actually love doing it."

Hillary was silent for a while, smoking the cigar. *Hmmm*, she thought, *working with kids, never fighting off twenty-two year old bimbos, no one attacking me and my family all the time...*

"Shoot," she said, wincing at the word replacement, "what about Chelsea, I don't want a life without Chelsea."

The devil smiled broadly and handed her his newspaper. The headline read "Two Political Dynasties Unite." The front-page featured a picture of a beautiful, dark-haired girl holding hands with Donald Trump's son, Eric. She looked at the girl's face and it looked somehow familiar. The caption identified the girl as Chelsea Clinton.

Hillary made a choking sound, trying to scream but the new body tamped it into more of a whimper.

"Don't worry," Lucifer said, "she's not your daughter anymore."

"She looks like Lydia, my friend in college."

"Well, yes, veeeerrry good, that was her mother. Chelsea has the same soul, however, in that body. Once a soul is made and assigned, I can't very well make it never exist. You would like her though, she's a lot like your own Chelsea. Too bad about her mother."

"What do you mean?" Hillary's expression retained the look of shock.

"Well, Lydia wasn't as strong as you. She loved Bill as much as you did, but she couldn't take his philandering and she eventually killed herself during Bill's second term."

"What does it mean "Two political dynasties?" She asked. "Why would any Chelsea marry into that horrible family?"

"Oh, that's the beauty of it all. Trump is president now."

"He beat me in the general election?"

"No, no, no. He actually beat 'Lyin' Ted Cruz in the general and frankly, that was a walk in the park for him. Trump's a Democrat now, Tim Kaine is still vice president, Bernie Sander's campaign fizzled out after the first two months and *Fox News* is demonizing Trump and Anderson Cooper is his biggest defender!"

Hillary couldn't make her mouth say the words she wanted to say but the limits on her swearing couldn't stop her from crying.

The devil rejoiced as her soul grew even more delectable.

* * *

Author's Note:

First, this story is satire. I don't actually believe that Hillary Clinton sold her soul to the devil, at least no more than any politician has to balance and weigh beliefs and actions. This story was originally written about three weeks before the 2016 presidential election here in the US.

In case you've forgotten, Hillary had a series of coughing fits at campaign stops and at one point had to be carried to her car for what her campaign said was walking pneumonia. Donald Trump, fair-minded gentleman that he is, used these incidents to claim she was at death's door and unfit for the presidency.

The *Access Hollywood* tape was a late-campaign surprise in which Trump had been recorded bragging to Billy Bush, former host of the TV show *Access Hollywood*, about how he liked to physically assault women because he was just so attracted to them and hell, when you're a celebrity, you can get away with it. It was widely believed at the time that such an ugly admission on tape would kill any possibility of a Trump presidency.

Lydia is completely made up out of whole cloth, any resemblance to a person living or dead is completely coincidental – I just like the name.

"Angella Reid" is the real name of the real White House Usher at the time, but I don't know anything else about her or even whether her office is anywhere near where President Hillary Clinton might play poker with old Scratch. From all real-life accounts I have read, she is very good at her job.

In the original version of this Author's Note, I apologized for getting the election results so wrong. Like almost everyone else, I expected Clinton to win. But after a while, I've started wondering if maybe my story, or some weird reverse variation on it, might not be closer to the truth than I originally thought. We wouldn't actually know, would we?

William Cohen-Kiraly

A Sticky End

"Spider, turn on your recorder please," said the astronaut.

"Yes, boss," replied the robot. The slender human and the multi-armed machine floated gracefully in the center of the airlock with just enough room so they could rotate without scraping against the bulkhead.

"Hi guys." The astronaut's voice cracked a bit before he could continue. "This is Russ and I guess this is my final goodbye to you all.

"I can't believe this, what an incredibly fucked up way to die…

"Here we've traveled 230 million kilometers, half our trip to Io, we're the first humans to go past the inner planets, and I'm going to die because of a stupid glue-gun accident.

"Spidey and I had to do an EVA to fix a couple of damaged hull plates. Looks like it was a small space rock, made a nice hole in the hull and I wanted to make sure it wasn't going to get any bigger or leak our precious air. No big deal, right? I got in my suit and Spidey and I took the high-pressure glue-gun and a hull patch outside, and I fixed the hole and climbed back inside, no problem, no big deal.

"We're in the airlock now, and it's re-pressurized. I've taken off my suit and I am floating here in my skivvies before I see little beads of liquid floating around the airlock and one of them floats by in front of me. I know what it is—Something must have nicked the glue-gun and globs of the Liqui-Weld are floating around. One comes at my face and like an idiot, I try to jerk away by kicking off the wall and I fall backwards against Spidey here.

"Hit my head against him and it hurt like hell. Then I realized my head's not moving away from him and the back of my head is on fire. This shit burns like hell when you get it on your skin and now – and I want you to picture this so I can give you one last laugh – I'm stuck to Spider here along my neck and the back of my head with the rest of my body floating around uselessly.

"I've picked up a bunch more glue drops and some of my fingers are stuck together and I got burning drops of that damned glue on my balls and it's all I can do to keep from screaming.

"When Spidey finally gets in to wake you guys up from your deep freeze, God knows what parts of me will be sticking to him and what parts of me will be floating around this damn airlock, but I don't envy you waking up to the sight of Spider with bits of Russ Hennessy stuck to him.

"And guys, sorry about the mess I'm gonna leave you with in the airlock, but if you're going to survive, I have to get Spidey through that airlock to take care of your machines and wake one of you up. He can just about barely fit through the hatch by himself, what with all those arms flying around.

"It's time to run some of the maintenance tasks that keep you alive and I'm afraid I'm going to have to remove myself from the duty roster kind of permanently. I know Spider can do a lot of the tasks and he can wake the next one of you up. I'm going to ask that he wakes up Meryl because I think he has the strongest stomach.

"I don't think I have a lot of time here. The chemicals in the glue are already starting to make me feel a bit wobbly and since I can see no way to separate myself here in the airlock without ripping — let's not get graphic here — without fatally injuring myself, I want to get it over with without spending any time suffering or starving or dehydrating. This glue ain't gonna be coming off on its own and here in the airlock, there's nothing for me to eat or drink or even try to get myself free.

"So here goes: Allona, forgive me being sexist. You know I respect you for who you are and for your incredible mind but I'm dying so I get to say that you that you make zero gravity look sexier than any female astronaut I have ever flown with and I'll miss your wicked sense of humor.

"Don, remember, I won the last chess game so that makes me the best player even if you used to win more games than me.

"Hiroshi, thanks for teaching me that Japanese guys really can play guitar.

"Meryl, I really did like your cooking on Earth but you suck making lunches from space rations.

"Elysse, thanks for those long, long, philosophy, science and sports debates that made the early months of this flight pass by in fun rather than dreariness.

"Tom, the Browns will beat the Steelers *next* year.

"It has been an honor and a privilege to work with all of you on this incredible voyage. Godspeed to you all and safe travels and watch out for broken glue-guns.

"Thank you Spider, you can turn the recorder off now."

"You're welcome boss," replied the robot.

"And hey, Spider, that goes for you too, it has been a pleasure working with you on this voyage. I'd reach around and pat you on one of your many shoulders but my hand would probably stick there too, and we need you to get through that hatch with as few parts of me stuck to you as possible."

"It is my pleasure to work with all the humans on this ship, thank you for the kind words," replied the robot.

"So big guy, are you gonna miss me when I'm gone?"

"I'm sorry boss, I am not programmed to feel grief. I do not have the ability to feel emotions the way you do."

"Well, you always seem to enjoy being with us. Are you telling me now that's just an act?" asked Russ, smiling a bit. He knew Spider didn't have emotions but couldn't resist the temptation to try to wind him up one last time, hopeless as that may be.

"I am programmed to serve and I am programmed to be as pleasant and polite as possible."

"Well, you know, sometimes you seem kind of human inside that big metal body of yours."

"I am programmed to be human enough to make you feel comfortable working with me but not appear too human, which would also make you uncomfortable."

"I don't know, maybe it's just a human mind trying to see inside your mind, but sometimes, you feel just a bit more than just a machine. I'm not complaining, just noticing that. "

The robot made no reply.

"Okay Spider, we need to figure out how we are gonna do this. I need you to scrape me off you so you can get in through the inner airlock hatch and go wake Meryl. I guess, before you try scraping me off, I'm gonna want you to kill me as quickly and painlessly as possible."

"I cannot do that boss."

"What do you mean?"

"I am not allowed to harm or kill a human. I am programmed to help you and protect you in any way I can. I cannot harm you."

"It's okay Spidey, I'm dying anyway. This glue is poison and it's seeping in through my skin. I need you to do this to save the others."

"I cannot kill you," replied the robot. "I am not allowed to kill or hurt a human."

"But if you don't do it, you will be killing all the other humans on this ship."

"I cannot kill or hurt a human."

"But you are hurting me if you don't put me out of my misery before this poison gets in my mind. It hurts like hell already and it will probably only get worse. That's hurting me."

"I am sorry," said the robot. "I cannot hurt or kill a human. It is how I am programmed."

"Okay, crap. Can you dispose of my body after I'm dead?"

"If other humans are not around to do this, I am programmed to dispose of bodies to prevent infection and other problems associated with corpses."

"Ah, well, you're nothing if not direct. I don't have a lot of strength left right now, but can you turn me so I can reach the outside airlock door."

The robot said nothing but used its flexible arms to rotate the astronaut towards the hatch and within reach of the release.

"Thank you, Spider," said the man. "Now can you do one more thing and sing to me?"

"What would you like to hear, boss?"

The astronaut told him and for a few minutes, Hennessy looked out the airlock porthole at the face of Jupiter already grown in size to nearly fill the round window. Then closed his eyes and pretended to conduct the pounding chords and lilting melody of Holst's *Jupiter, The Bringer of Jollity* as it filled the small chamber.

Russ Hennessy pulled the release to open the airlock to the vast vacuum and cold of space and the music grew softer and softer as the air hissed out into space.

The Singer of Starfish

"You look goofy," Aieai-eei told me.

"What do you mean?" I asked.

"The droopy starfish painted something on you. They painted a big black mark on your forehead." she said, tossing her head in laughter.

I swam over to the place we could see ourselves and looked at myself, turning my head this way and that.

Sure enough, there was a black mark painted on my forehead. They must have done it when they had me out of the water and in that weird haze they can make us feel.

Our whole home was surrounded by hard water but most of it was clear and we could see the pods and pods of starfish that came to see us. But this was a special place where the hard water was dark and shiny and we could see ourselves clearly. We could also dimly see the starfish on the other side. The way they looked at us through the hard water, I think they could see us too.

* * *

I sat in the observation boot with Liam Novotny. We'd been in grad school together at Miami, getting our doctorates a year apart. We had been arguing almost since the first minute we met.

"It's not going to work," Liam said. "I've seen this little trick before, and it didn't impress me the first ten times. I can prove scientifically that dolphins cannot be smart enough to be self-aware. Painting a dot on its forehead won't prove anything. You're just projecting."

"Yeah, I know, you've pulled their brains apart and counted the neurons, Liam" I said, "but you can't tell how smart something is by counting bumps on their head. This is a long-accepted way of determining whether an animal has self-awareness. If it sees itself in a mirror and starts wondering about the mark we add, it recognizes itself in the mirror."

"Sorry, but it's bullshit, Jessie. I don't think any animal without hands and language is self-aware, that's a human quality only, maybe chimps and apes but not these glorified fish."

"You're such an idiot, Liam. Just watch."

* * *

They were watching me intently. One droopy starfish with the long seaweed growing from its head, moved close to its side of the hard water and I could hear its droning words in the water. They talk like calves, one word at a time and no song. I think they have a rudimentary language though. Its funny flat mouth made the weird shapes they always did, and it reached up one of its fins to stroke the hard water near my face. What an odd gesture.

I responded loudly in my own language and the starfish pulled back from the hard water, apparently surprised by my response. They started droning excitedly together as I swam away.

Aieai-eei laughed. "Careful young Eia-clickclick-ina, you will become the 'Singer of Starfish.'"

"And why not Eia-clickclick-ina." said Aiai-ea-whistle-aiai. "She could be the Singer. God knows we've waited long enough for someone to reach out to the droopy starfish," said Aiai-ea-whistle-aiai. "We need someone to tell them to stop destroying our world."

"Aiai-ea-whistle-aiai, you young fool," growled old Aaaa-eaea-a-whistle-a, the ancient male. "Why not Eia-clickclick-ina? Because she's a calf and a prisoner here with the rest of us in the world of the starfish. The Singer will be a great elder, a beautiful streamlined male who can leap out of the water into the starfish world then dive deep back into our world under water. He will be…"

"Hush, old man," said Eeee-aaea-eeii. "We've heard your stories over and over again. Yes, you lived in the wild, yes, you were the Shaper of bait balls. You froze in the Northern Seas and escaped the sharks in the Southern Waters. Squeak, squeak, squeak. Just because you are a male doesn't mean you know everything."

"Do not insult the patriarchs! I know the stories of our people, Aiai-ea-whistle-aiai," said Aaaa-eaea-a-whistle-a. "I know the great prophecy. The Singer will not be a female calf born in captivity. What use would that be to bring our peoples together?"

I had heard the debate before, and it bored me. I continued around the tank, dropping and rising as I swam, thinking and thinking. *Why not me?* I asked myself. The males always thought they knew everything, Aaaa-eaea-a-whistle-a kept telling the same stories over and over again, the great crossing he made across the cold seas, the great bait balls he knew as a child which have now dwindled year after year. He told us the story of how a jealous God had changed one of us into a droopy starfish as punishment for disobedience and how she founded this strange race of beings who lived out of water but looked like droopy starfish.

It gave me the creeps when he described the transformation, how her tail grew longer and split into two weird starfish limbs, how her face flattened into the ridiculously useless, flat, ugly face that these creatures had, how her flippers elongated and grew their own little flippers and how seaweed grew out of the tops of her head. I asked him how they could breath and he described how her blow hole moved from the top of her head into that weird bumpy thing below their eyes.

I still shiver a little every time I think about this, wondering what it must be like to breathe through that funny hole and have seaweed growing out of my skin. Of course I have never really seen seaweed even growing from the ground, I only know the stories from my fellow captives in this little sea surrounded by hard water.

Why not me? I asked myself again. In some ways, I am more comfortable with these strange creatures than my own kind. They raised me when I was little, they feed me every day, they teach me fun games and give me more fish to eat every time I play.

I can look in their eyes and I see something there, some sort of intelligence even beyond their ability to make little seas like the one they built for us and the big floating rocks that Aaaa-eaea-a-whistle-a describes.

I can tell individuals apart when they drone at us and sometimes even by looking at them though their skin below their faces keeps changing color and shape, it is hard to keep track until they make their strange noises.

I was swimming around our sea again for the third time. *Why did they paint me?* I wondered. Maybe they were marking me. Maybe they were choosing *me* to be the Singer of Starfish.

Maybe they wanted to talk to us as much as we wanted to talk to them!

It was a thrilling idea! I was so shocked at this thought that I almost swam into Aiai-ea-whistle-aiai.

"Be careful, little one," she said to me.

I was so excited, I swam to the surface and jumped for joy into the air. I heard loud droning from the starfish as I breached and fell back in.

"Whoa, Eia-clickclick-ina. What's got you all excited?" asked Aieai-eei, the motherly elder female of our little group.

"What if they want to talk to me?" I asked, swimming excitedly around her. "What if they painted me because they chose me to be the Singer? What if that one who painted me is their 'Singer of Dolphins?'"

"My dear," said Aieai-eei, "I think that is reading a lot into the starfish putting a mark on your forehead."

"Maybe," I said, "but what if? What do I have to lose?"

So from that day forward, I tried to talk to the starfish. Most of them ignored me or tried to give me more fish—which I didn't mind at all—but there was one, I think it was the one who reached up to touch the hard water with her weird fin who seemed to be trying to understand. It was smaller than most so I decided it must be a female. I named her E-click-Ea-click like the dolphin that God changed to a starfish.

"Hello" I said to her in my language every time I saw her. And she always droned back a sound to me like she was trying to say 'hello' too. And I listened very carefully and it sounded like it started with the same sound every time.

"EEEoooo," I said to her one morning. It doesn't mean anything in our language but it was what she kept saying to me and it must have been close enough in her language. She didn't respond for a long time but her eyes looked funny as she just stood there looking at me. When she finally responded, it was with her version of the same word.

* * *

At first, I thought it was a joke, someone was playing a trick on me or maybe just a stupid coincidence, little Ellie was just making a noise like me. Then she did it again and I swear she was looking straight at me. I couldn't believe it.

Wait until Liam sees this. He's going to have to throw out his screwed up ideas.

* * *

Later she brought more starfish to see me and she said her strange word and flapped one of her upper fins at me. "EEEoooo," I said back, and they got all agitated and droned at each other.

Aieai-eei popped her head up next to me, watching the starfish.

"What did you say to them, Singer, that got them all excited?" I knew she was making fun of me but I felt proud of myself anyway.

"Say 'EEEoooo' to them. I think it is their word for "hello" I said. "They talk like babies with single words, they don't sing."

Aieai-eei said "EEEEooo" and they all started flapping their fins together and they became even more excited. Everybody in the tank came up and tried it except Aaaa-eaea-a-whistle-a, who would have nothing to do with trying to communicate with the starfish.

They gave us fish but I dropped mine. I wanted to make them understand this was more than jumping through hoops for them. Aiai-ea-whistle-aiai promptly ate my fish that I hoped I could save for later.

This same starfish kept coming back every evening and every day we didn't have to do our games jumping through hoops for fish. I came to recognize the funny shape of her face and the curly seaweed on her head.

Another droopy starfish sometimes came with her to visit us. I had to try hard not to laugh. This one had seaweed growing around his mouth and under that weird thing they breathe through. I'm not sure but he might be the one I saw on the day they painted my forehead.

Sometimes we just swam around together. God must have been pretty angry when he made dolphins into starfish because they were slow and clumsy under water and had to wear big fins on their bottom limbs. But it occurred to me one day that I was even more clumsy in their world of air, and I wondered if maybe God hadn't been so mad at them after all, just practical.

As I spent time with her, I grew fascinated by how they could use those little flippers on their pectoral fins. Everything I wanted to carry, I had to put in my mouth. But the starfish could hold things with their long, ungainly pectoral fins and still use their mouth to drone or make funny shapes. It was unbelievable the things my Dolphin Singer could do with these fins and their little flippers. Maybe these flippers were weak and ungainly but they were almost magical in what they do with little things and even big things.

But learning their language was something else. I could hear and start understanding some of her calf-like words. I soon realized that funny mouth could do things almost as amazing and the weird little flippers. She could only make low sounds and couldn't sing and change pitch to make words and sentences. Instead that funny mouth could only speak in very low tones but within that limited range, they could make more kinds of sounds than I could.

It also became apparent to me that they couldn't even hear most of the sounds I make so she could never learn our language. I had a really hard time with all the unique sounds she made. I could hear the difference sometimes, but I couldn't keep track in my mind of all the changes and certainly, I could never imitate them. No matter how I tried, I couldn't shape sounds like those with my mouth.

It was very slow going. I learned a few of her words, some I could even say or at least translate to my language. For instance her name was Click-Ess-eh-Click-Ah. I wonder if I mangled it as bad as she mangled the low parts of my name.

It took a long time, but I realized they sometimes talk with their fins and flippers too. When it is bent and the knob of little flippers is touching her middle, it means 'me'. When it points away from her body, it means 'you' or 'out.'

The females sometimes joined me when the Singer of Dolphins was with me. They couldn't see what I saw or hear what I heard, at least not all the time, but they were willing to try, at least until they got bored.

But Aaaa-eaea-a-whistle-a grew increasing surly and mean. Sometimes he would come up and bump me when I tried to talk to their Singer. Sometimes he would chase me around the tank, biting me and calling me a stupid little calf but he was old and slow and usually couldn't catch me.

There was one day he really scared me. He came to me after their Singer left and growled at me "I forbid you to keep up this silly game. I am the male here and I forbid you. You will stop pretending you are the Singer of Starfish and act like a proper young female."

"I will do no such thing!" I replied angrily. "I am the Singer. We have already started talking more than ever before."

"You little demon. If you do this again, I *will* kill you. It is forbidden. I will not let our God be mocked like this."

I was taken aback. Aaaa-eaea-a-whistle-a had never seemed all that religious to me. None of us in the Starfish world were. My mother and father weren't. Aieai-eei wasn't., Aiai-ea-whistle-aiai and Eeee-aaea-eeii had both grown up in the real world, not the starfish world, and were believers, but they didn't threaten me like that. It's a male thing I guess.

* * *

What the hell has gotten into Nigel? He was the old male, maybe thirty-five years old, who'd lived in the wild for the first twenty years of his life. We brought him in after the previous male died and until now, he seemed to take naturally to the patriarch's role. But now he was acting crazy, chasing Ellie around the tank, biting at her, pushing her around whenever he could. I had to get him out of there.

Liam and I grabbed the net. It took us over an hour to finally corral him. He seemed wild and upset and he fought hard to avoid us, even biting Liam's hand and my own rear end. Liam even punched him after the bite. "Asshole" I said.

Finally, we caught him and put him into the isolation tank next to the regular dolphin tank.

* * *

It was weird without Aaaa-eaea-a-whistle-a. I didn't miss the abuse, but we'd lived together for so long, it was like something was missing. At night, when the pods of starfish had left, we could hear him crying from across the barriers.

We would sing to him, trying to calm his fevered mind. No dolphin can live alone for very long and it felt like we were losing him. He began to curse me and the starfish and even his god. His wailing and his swimming became erratic and one day, we could not hear him at all. It was sad for all of us.

But I kept working with Click-Ess-eh-Click-Ah and we continued our painfully slow progress. I began to be able to follow some of the movements of her pectoral fins and get a few words out of them. She brought in a rock with straight edges that had something like seaweed coming out of it connecting to big black clamshells she put on what I think were her ears. When she used this rock, she seemed able to hear more of what I sang but it was still hard. We began to name things to each other but even the most basic action seemed hard to convey. The minds of the starfish were so hard to fathom.

That male starfish started to come around too at night, but he didn't try to sing to us. He stood looking down at us, just staring. It was unnerving. I wished I could tell Click-Ess-eh-Click-Ah but I didn't have the words. All I could say in my language was "Night, Night, starfish, there," but I didn't think she understood even with her rock.

* * *

It didn't make sense to me. I knew the words, she kept saying "Night, Night Human there" but I thought I must be misunderstanding. I couldn't understand what she meant. It was crazy, our minds and the mind of a dolphin were so different in how we understood the world.

I tried to talk to Liam about it but he just laughed at me and told me I was wasting my time because these stupid animals weren't smart enough to have a language. It was all in my head, he said. He was getting really annoying. He had based his entire career so far on trying to prove he could determine how smart animals are by measuring their brains. What Ellie and I were doing was amazing, how could he not see it?

I sat there in my favorite bar across the street from Sea Planet, nursing my gin and tonic, trying to guess what she meant when I had a very horrible idea. I grabbed my phone and called Liam. He picked up and I asked him where he was. He said he was at home, but I heard the compressors and I knew where he was. I ran out of the bar so fast, I forgot to pay.

* * *

The male droopy starfish was in the cave with the big rocks that made so much noise but poured out the fresh water with that odd, biting taste. He was flailing around in there, opening holes in the rocks and putting something in and suddenly the water starts burning my eyes and mouth. I hear Aiai-ea-whistle-aiai, Aieai-eei and Eeee-aaea-eeii start crying in pain too. He's doing something to our water and I can't stop him.

I can barely see but I know that droning sound. Click-Ess-eh-Click-Ah is here. She isn't just droning now, but for the first time, I can hear her singing loudly. I open my eyes through the pain. Click-Ess-eh-Click-Ah has wrapped her fins around the male and they are fighting, singing loudly at each other. The male is much bigger and I think he's about to kill her. I cannot let this happen. I leap out of the water and grab his neck in my jaws. Click-Ess-eh-Click-Ah is singing at me, the male is trying to hit me, but I drag him down into the water. As I guessed, the droopy starfish cannot stay under water as long as we can.

* * *

The blood from Liam's neck came to the surface but neither he nor Ellie came up again. At the other end of the tank, the other females were in obvious pain. I jumped in at their end and helped them out of the water one by one, then started hosing them down. Liam must have overloaded the chlorine in the water. It burned my skin and eyes too.

But I jumped in again and tried to pull Ellie up too, but she was too heavy for me. Jasmine, the biggest female, worked her way from the deck back into the water and swam to me and helped me push Ellie away from the worst of the chlorine and back to the other end of the pool.

* * *

I am no longer the Singer of Starfish. I can't see and I can barely sing well enough to be understood. But Aiai-ea-whistle-aiai sings for me. She helped save my life and was permanently scarred too by whatever the male starfish did to us.

After the fight, neither Aiai-ea-whistle-aiai nor I could leap for fish in front of the pods of starfish though our friends seemed to recover fully. Aiai-ea-whistle-aiai and I now live in a new place, somewhere that Click-Ess-eh-Click-Ah can be with us every day. With us are two young calves, a male and a female and Aiai-ea-whistle-aiai is teaching them to sing to the Starfish and understand their weird language.

And Click-Ess-eh-Click-Ah and Aiai-ea-whistle-aiai and the two young ones come to me almost every day and sing the Prophecy of the Singer of Starfish to me and I feel the honor they show me and wish I could still sing.

The Offering

Paris, France — May 1887

The rain tapped insistently on the skylights of Barrias' studio. The sky was grey and he had trouble seeing as he made the final clay for his bronze sculpture.

Barrias didn't know if it was the ghostly light or the tears streaming down his cheeks that blinded him as he shaped the face he knew so well. It didn't matter, his hands knew the shape of this beautiful young girl. He had sketched it and carved it into clay a hundred times.

As he built this monument to his friend, he could feel the delicate neck taking shape under his fingers, the beautiful, playful lips that had smiled so easily. Her face was much like her mother's but her merry, dancing eyes were so like her fathers. Barrias couldn't bring himself to sculpt those eyes, so he left them nearly closed much like his own now.

Bou Saada, Algeria — 1882

They were riding camels through the inhospitable deserts of central Algeria. Camels!

Louis-Ernest Barrias, who had lived in Paris all his life, was now riding camels with his friend, Gustave Guillaumet, the celebrated orientalist painter. He could hardly believe it. How had this laughing man dragged him here with nothing but a promise of paradise? But Barrias followed Guillaumet freely and joyfully, knowing his adventurous friend would teach him things no one else could.

It hadn't been a hard decision for Barrias, despite the backlog of commissions he had. He was feeling his art and his mind growing stale in his Paris studio. Guillaumet, who traveled to Algeria almost every year, said he had just the cure for Barrias's ennui.

Barrias never ceased to be amazed at both the quantity and the vitality of the work that poured from Guillaumet's brushes. Maybe he could bring some of that life back to his own work again but Guillaumet just laughed at him when he said that. "A painting is like a poem," he said. I can dash one off in a day. You have to struggle with writing a huge novel with model and casting and model and casting for months for each babe you birth. Come with me, and I'll show you something new to see and create."

Guillaumet did not work from commissions, but he sold every painting he put on the market. Now that France had an iron grip on the Maghreb, it had become the height of style to decorate one's house with romantic images of the orient.

And Guillaumet – more than any other of the romantic orientalists – rode that wave for almost two decades, spending as much time in Algeria as he did at home with his wife and children.

And now, after all these years, Guillaumet had brought his friend to visit this land he loved so much.

Barrias, so far, was not impressed. Yes, he loved the adventure, but life here in Algeria seemed dirty and sweaty and the amenities they shared so far were not to his liking. Barrias had no trouble with sweating and hard work — he was a creator of gigantic bronze sculptures after all — but he also enjoyed a warm bath and a civilized glass of wine after a long day in his workshop.

In Algeria, the heat was unrelenting, the sand was in everything he ate, everything he wore, everything he slept in. They had been traveling for days on these great stubborn beasts who seemed to hate Barrias with an unbridled passion.

But Gustave said they were close and he told him he would love their destination, so Barrias kept his parched, sand-flecked lips shut for the time being. Gustave, already usually cheery, seemed to brighten more and more as they approached Bou Saada, the town he said was their destination.

It was the biggest town they had seen for days, full of people and camels and horses and donkeys and bustle and a huge market square. They rode through the center of the town and out again to the south without stopping and Barrias grumbled. "I thought you said Bou Saada was our destination. When do we get off these infernal beasts?"

Guillaumet was almost giddy with laughter. "Do you see that villa ahead, on the hill? That, my friend, is this Frenchman's personal paradise. Very soon now."

So Barrias resigned himself to another few kilometers of swaying on the back of this smelly, flea-bitten beast. After what seemed like an hour, they rode through iron gates and the dessert suddenly bloomed into a lush garden. The house was bigger than anything they had seen since Algiers, and it was a fine house, built in the crazy Algerian style they had seen in the north, with the layout of a Roman Villa decorated with the beautiful arches and the geometric tile so common in Muslim art.

A young girl, maybe fourteen, came running from the house shouting "Papa!, Papa!" and Barrias was shocked when he saw Gustave dismount lightly from his high saddle and grab the girl in a bear hug, laughing and crying himself.

"Ah, my dear Meryem, what a pleasure to see you again." He said into her long black hair now covering his face.

Behind her, an elegant woman walked along the path behind the child, almost gliding in her stateliness. "It's about time you finally got here." She said, her own smile belying the sharpness of her words.

Without letting go of the little girl, Guillaumet took this woman into his embrace as well and the small family hugged in contented silence for a few moments. Barrias watched in disbelief and with a touch of horror. He tried to make a graceful dismount from his own beast, but the camel, in a hurry to be finally rid of its burden, stood up before his foot was free and threw him to the ground in a heap.

Gustave must have heard his friend's grunt and let go of his women to help Barrias up. "Barrias, my friend, I want you to meet Sophia Kermali, my wife here in Algeria, and my beautiful daughter, Meryem Kermali-Guillaumet. Sophia, this is my very best friend, Louis-Ernest Barrias. I have told you about him before."

The woman turned her smile on him, her own eyes dancing a bit. "Yes, Cherie," she said to Barrias, "he has mentioned you a *few* times." Her French was flawless.

Barrias sputtered, trying to decide what he should say, finally settling on the neutral and pathetic "It's a pleasure to meet you"

Guillaumet guffawed and clapped his friend hard on the shoulder. "It's all right, my friend, she knows about Charlotte and my family in Paris."

"And does Charlotte know about your family here in Bou Saada?"

Guillaumet still smiled, but a little more stiffly. "No, well, not exactly" he said. "I don't think she would approve so easily as my dear Sophia. Let's get our things off these beasts and I'll show you around."

Barrias was not usually shocked by the things other artists did. They drank, they whored, smoked tobacco and hasheesh, slept with women and sometimes even with other men. Though he was far more abstemious in his own life, he was by no means a prude. But this seemed beyond the pale, this felt less like a little sin and more like betrayal.

Barrias liked Charlotte well enough, though she was a bit conventional for his tastes. The boy, Henri, was very much like

Guillaumet, passionate and irreverent, and the girl, little Charlotte, was the spitting image of her mother, pretty, dainty, fiercely loyal and fiercely judgmental. She treated her older brother much like Charlotte treated her husband, using a sharp tongue to keep the men on the straight and narrow, or so Barrias had supposed.

Barrias' first instinct was to walk away immediately, but he didn't think he could make it back without his friend's guidance. He lay awake that first night, and many other nights that followed. Sometimes he was so angry at Guillaumet that he wanted to steal away in the darkness and ride back to Algiers, hop on a ship back to France, and go tell Charlotte. But they were so deep in Berber country, he wasn't even sure which direction to go to find French officials to help him back — something he was sure Guillaumet counted on.

So in the morning, each morning, he was still there. As he suspected when they rode in, this was a brothel and Sophia was the madame who seems to have retired from the active part of the business when she met Guillaumet.

What bothered Barrias even more, was that over the weeks he was there, he began to understand what his friend saw in Sophia. She was older than Guillaumet and himself by about ten years, but her raven hair showed not a strand of grey—whether by nature or artifice, Barrias did not know. She and Guillaumet were passionate lovers and passionate fighters.

She was an exceedingly handsome woman. Tall, elegant with deep black eyes, a dark flawless skin and a full, ever-expressive mouth.

She found Guillaumet people and places to paint and the painter went further and found even more for himself. He wandered freely in this place that most Frenchmen could not go. Everyone knew he was Sophia's husband and she was both respected and feared.

He watched Guillaumet go into a frenzy of painting he had never seen in their sedate life in Paris. And the passion spread to Barrias too. He found renewed passion in his own work, sketching everything he saw and planning ways to incorporate it into his own sculpture when he got back to Paris.

He drew many sketches of the lovely Sophia, trying to capture her elegance and fire but he never felt he could do her justice. Somehow all his sketches of Sophia felt too tame.

But it was the daughter Meryem that truly captivated Barrias. Not as a woman per se. He could see she would grow up to be a beauty like her mother, but for now, she was on that cusp between innocence and adulthood that he yearned to capture in his own art. Though he sketched so many of the beautiful faces he found there in Bou Saada, it was Meryem he kept coming back to.

One day, he caught Guillaumet sitting in the sunroom they used as an artist's studio, surrounded by the sketches Barrias had made of the girl. Until he saw them laid out like this, Barrias had no idea he had drawn so many.

Guillaumet's eyes were shining. "I cannot believe how well you capture her. I, I am the great painter, but I can't capture her soul the way you do here," he said, pointing to a quick, simple sketch. "In a few simple lines, you capture her as a woman, a child, a coquette, and a deep, dark unknowable sea."

Barrias shook his head. "You know I tried to hate her, I tried to hate them both because of what you were doing to your real Christian family."

"I knew you would try, and I knew you would fail."

"Well, she knew how to get to me. How can a man resist a girl who loves his artwork and wants to be a sculptor just like me."

"Yes, well she wants to be a painter like me too. You don't have girls at home, do you. They can be manipulative little vixens," Guillaumet said smiling. "And this one is so much more powerful than little Charlotte or even, God protect us, big Charlotte her mother."

"She's a little girl, you talk like she is a master manipulator."

"Spoken like a man who has only sons," said Guillaumet.

"But Gustave, how can you do this to your family?" Barrias asked. "If Charlotte ever found out, it would kill her."

"I don't think I could live any other way. I need to be in Paris, I need my family there and I do love them. I love Charlotte very much. She has been a wonderful mother and wonderful companion to me, even in the worst of times. I need to go to Paris to sell my paintings.

"But I have to come here too. When I'm here, when I'm with Sophia and Meryem, I am truly alive instead of just sleepwalking through life. I love Sophia, I love Meryem as much as I love Charlotte and the children, but in a completely different way.

"It's like I'm living two different lives side by side. But if Charlotte never finds out and Sophia is fine with it, who will it hurt?"

It took only two days more for the answer to come. Barrias woke up groggily hearing thunder. Then he woke up some more. There is no thunder in the Saharan dessert.

He threw on his trousers and left the room, finding the house already in panic. There were a few French soldiers who had spent the night and several of the men of Bou Saada, all trying to get their pants on and run out the door. Some of the prostitutes who worked for Sophia also cleared out but many others had nowhere else to go.

"Who is attacking?" Asked Guillaumet.

"Your bastard French Soldiers." Sophia spat out.

"Why would they do that."

"They don't need a reason. Maybe they think we are hiding rebels, maybe we didn't pay enough in bribes, maybe somebody just wants some of our girls. They don't need a reason."

"These are Frenchman, they are not the damn Turks."

Sophia looked at her husband's face and laughed. "You believe this? You are a fool. Do you know how many women your Frenchman have raped? How many men and boys they have killed, how much they have stolen from us? You who come here year after year, yet you are so blind. I do not believe this."

Before the sound of the artillery barrage had stopped echoing, it seemed that French soldiers were marching towards their villa.

Sophia told the remaining women to run, and she grabbed Meryem and told Guillaumet they would be hiding in a priest hole in the basement. It only had room for two, so she begged the Frenchman to keep their secret.

It was too late for the other women. Many tried running out the back, heading away from the city and the soldiers, but were brought back almost immediately at gunpoint.

One soldier — a man who had recently visited as a customer — leveled his pistol at Barrias and Guillaumet and demanded to know where "the old whore and her daughter" were.

Barrias said she had run away last night. But Guillaumet said "Louis, we don't have to lie. These are Frenchman, they won't hurt my family. They are French too because of me!

"Shut up you fool," said Barrias but Guillaumet waived his hand. "They are our brothers. They are Christians."

He took the soldiers into the basement and opened the door of the hidden room himself. As he did so, Sophia spat in his face and called him a murderer.

The mother and daughter were brought up and soon after, the rapes started. For several days, the French soldiers came into the brothel and raped and beat the women of the house over and over. When a woman could no longer satisfy a soldier's needs, she was run through with a sabre and thrown out the window into the horrible pile growing in the courtyard.

Guillaumet tried to get to his wife and daughter, but a soldier smashed his face with the butt of a rifle then tied up both men where they could hear the screaming but do nothing to help. After two days, French soldiers brought Meryem's body out and threw it at their feet, shouting at them, "If you sleep with these dogs, you get a whore for a daughter. You are no Frenchman."

The brothel was destroyed, as was most of Bou Saada. Barrias and Guillaumet were left alive and mostly unhurt, Sophia also remained alive when the soldiers finally left, but she only spat at Guillaumet and left both men tied up when she walked out the door.

Some of the other women also survived the ordeal though many more did not. One of the women finally took pity on the Frenchmen and cut their bonds.

Hungry and shaking, Barrias and Guillaumet walked back to the ruins of Bou Saada to find the newly installed French officials who arranged for their passage back to France.

It took more than two months to arrive back in Paris. Guillaumet was damaged beyond repair. Both his body and his soul were crippled. He sat in his studio, looking at his old paintings, barely talking to his wife and children — or to Barrias.

It was then Barrias did a very stupid thing. He paid a fortune to have someone find Sophia and bring her to Paris. She stayed with a small group of Algerian expatriates in Paris. She wouldn't even talk to Barrias, but Guillaumet went to stand outside her home until she finally let him inside.

Barrias never learned the full story. Guillaumet stayed with her for two weeks, completely abandoning his family but it couldn't have been a happy time for either of them—for any of them. He eventually tried to kill himself with a shotgun and, in fact, he did succeed, but it took him several months of agony to die.

Sophia left him on the street after his suicide attempt and, amazingly, Charlotte and Henri picked him up and carried him back to their house and nursed him through his long decline.

Barrias visited almost every day, but Guillaumet had little to say to him, Charlotte even less.

Guillaumet finally died in his own studio amid his own paintings and in the company of Charlotte, Henri and little Charlotte. Sophia hanged herself a few weeks after Guillaumet died.

Paris, France — May 1887

So Barrias was the one left to grieve, crying for Guillaumet, crying for Sophia, crying for Charlotte and Henri and for little Charlotte, and crying for France.

But most of all, he found himself crying for Meryem. Yes, the sculpture of the girl was for the tomb of his friend, but it was also his love song to that little girl who would never have a tomb of her own.

Author's Note:

This story is a work of fiction based on a very limited knowledge of real historical people. Though the events of this story are partly suggested by some sketchy and intriguing historical suggestions about Guillaumet's death, the story is not in any way a historical account and the people other than Guillaumet and Barrias are completely creations of my imagination.

This story was inspired primarily by the beautiful sculpture at the tomb of Gustave Guillaumet in Montmartre Cemetery in Paris. Louis-Ernest Barrias' sculpture of "The Young Girl from Bou Saada" graces the tomb. The girl in the sculpture is dropping flower petals onto a medallion with Guillaumet's face.

The Big Gumshoes

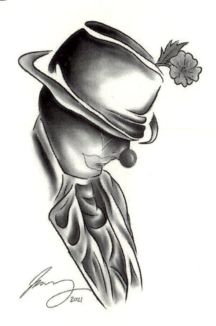

Chicken Cock Whiskey

It was a cold, dreary day. The sky was gray and a sharp, cold rain turned the trailer park roads to mud. It was the kind of spring day I used to suffer through as a kid in Ohio, not something you would expect down here in Florida.

It fit my mood perfectly.

I sat out of the rain underneath my door awning, holding my nose with my left hand and a bottle of Chicken Cock Whiskey with my right.

So the big show was folding its tent after all these years. As always, the men in the top hats were walking away with pockets full of money. The rest of us looked out at bleak futures of not doing the work we loved.

I chuckled mirthlessly to myself. Every night on the news, it seems, you hear about the auto workers and the steel workers losing their jobs to foreign competition. But you never hear about *us* losing *our* jobs to foreigners. The Cirque du Soily—however the hell you pronounce it—the State Circus of China, the Polish Warsaw Acrobatic Team, the Moscow Circus. They all come and tour the country and the TV stations and newspapers fawn all over them while homegrown American circus performers lose their jobs.

So there I was in this black mood, sitting in a broken lawn chair outside my mobile home in the rain, and drinking myself silly with clown water, when I see this big, brown UPS van bounce through the muddy ruts on our dirt roads. This surprised me because we don't get a lot of deliveries in our neck of the woods. It surprised me even more when the van pulls up to my trailer and the driver gets out of his truck holding a big brown box, maybe two feet long. I put my nose back on and stood up unsteadily.

"You Mr. Clumbo?" the driver asked.

"I am," I said, "but I didn't order anything."

"Got something for you anyway," the man said, handing me the box.

My dog Blossom came yapping out from underneath the trailer. Like all little dogs, she was full of spit and vinegar and ran out barking and shaking her little butt violently from side to side. Blossom was a Malshi who was cute as anything, but boy, she had a mouth on her.

The man eyed her warily and said he needed a signature. I signed and he got in his van and drove off.

I took my treasure into my trailer, put it on the kitchen table and grabbed a knife to cut open the tape. On the outside, it was nondescript, a brown box with packing tape and a return address so smeared it was unreadable. The box was not too heavy or too light and it rattled like a lot of little loose marbles were bouncing around inside. '*Jelly beans*,' I thought to myself, and I was right.

When I opened it, hundreds of jelly beans were rolling around in the package. But when I saw what lay among them, my heart sank to a new low.

To most people, all clown shoes look alike but to those of us in the life, they are as distinctive as faces. I recognized the unusual length, the orange fuzzy balls on the toes and the unmistakable red, white, and blue laces. These were the shoes of JellyBeans, my old friend and mentor—the man who taught me both of my careers.

The fact the shoes were packed with jelly beans was overkill. I knew the shoes and I knew the man they belonged to. I also knew that if his shoes were here on my kitchen table, JellyBeans himself had to be dead. They were a part of the man; he would never give them to anyone — not even me— and he would never willingly let them out of his control. I believe he had always planned to be buried in these shoes.

I've been a clown and a detective for thirty-five years so I have a pretty thick skin. I've scared a lot of little kids in my time and upset a lot of bad guys. I have my share of people who don't like me. But seriously, I'm sitting here looking at the end of both my careers. The Big Show, my employer Ringling Brothers, was closing and I had no current cases. Without the circus, who needs a clown PI?

Someone sent me a particularly personal message, but I had no idea who sent it or what they were trying to tell me.

Only master clowns could walk in shoes as long as my friend's and not trip. JellyBeans had taught me to be a master clown and a master investigator. I fully intended to use those skills to find justice for him, even if it was the last thing I did. But as I gazed at the leather in my hands, I was scared I wasn't up to the job. As good as I am, I might never match up to JellyBeans' humor or his penetrating shrewdness. These would indeed be big shoes to fill.

Finding JellyBeans

I put the cap back on the Chicken Cock and stowed the bottle in the little drawer in my little kitchen. The first order of business was to find my friend. Like I said, I knew he was dead, but I had to check out the obvious first.

I pulled out my cell and called his number. Voicemail was full; I expected that. I called his second-in-command, Mr. Teedles, his voicemail was full too. I tried the ringmaster, Leroy Gulch of the Great Atlanta Circus and he picked up. I explained I was looking for JellyBeans and he went silent as death for a moment.

"If you find that son of a bitch and his crew of painted buttons, you tell him he better be here for his next show or the whole lot of them are out on their baggy-pant asses."

That surprised me. "You mean his whole troupe is gone? When was the last time you saw them?"

"Last Tuesday, we were in Wetumpka, Alabama. JB and the boys were going to the Wetumpka Crater to do some private drinking for the night. In the morning, the show packed up for Meridian and we expected the boys to meet us there, but they never showed. Right now, I got some of the laid-up acrobats tryin' to be clowns. I thought anybody could be a clown, but these guys just ain't funny."

Sometimes people just don't take clowns seriously. You'd think a ringmaster, of all people, would know that being a clown was as much a calling as being a trapeze artist. But I guess sometimes I think the same way. I figure it had to be easy being a ringmaster, all you had to do was talk your fool mouth off. I knew better than to say that out loud though.

"Hey, Clumbo, I hear you'll be lookin' for a job soon. If JellyBeans and his crew don't come back tonight, *I* got a job for you."

I thanked him but said I still had a few months left with Ringling Brothers before they closed. Gulch sighed and gave me a few more details. He said JellyBeans and his crew were in a yellow car and had tried to sneak into Wetumpka's famous impact crater outside of town and that's the last he saw or heard of them, He said yes, there was something funny going on with JellyBeans and his crew but no one would tell him what it was. Clowns are notorious for keeping their mouths shut about anything having to do with the life. The last time anyone had seen them was three days ago.

So it was time for a road trip. I packed up my car with a few things I like to have with me and whistled for Blossom to hop into the front seat. I slipped my bowler hat on my head and twirled the little plastic flower for luck, then drove hell for leather to Wetumpka and made the seven-hour trip in five and a half.

I needn't have hurried though. When I got to Wetumpka, it was pretty obvious that something big was going on. City cops, sheriff's deputies and state troopers were all in a big circle near a bend in the Coosa River. Seems some fisherman looking for a secluded spot noticed a car sunk in the river. When the cops pulled it out, they found a badly abused, little yellow VW Bug.

I got to the police cordon on the road and showed them my PI license and said I think I know whose car it was. The trooper went to talk to the deputy detective in charge and came back and nodded to me. I put the windows down for Blossom and the trooper held up the yellow tape for me to go through.

I'm no stranger to dead people. The circus attracts a lot of people who don't live with us for very long. Some die by natural causes, some are killed by the people they are running away from and some are killed by the circus itself.

Still, I wasn't prepared for what I saw. The little yellow car had been pulled out of the Coosa and sat, still dripping, on the riverbank. Laid out in a long row, were my brother and sister clowns.

For a moment, I stood there just staring, clenching my fists to keep myself under control. These were all my friends, every last one of them. But tears can ruin your greasepaint and that does not look good on a PI. I swallowed the sob in the back of my throat and pulled myself together. I could grieve later, right now I had a job to do.

Three days in the river is horrible on maquillage and though I should have known them all, I would have had a hard time recognizing them save for their waterlogged uniforms.

One body caught my attention immediately through the haze of flies; it had no shoes.

The Sheriff's Detective came up to me. "You're Mr. Clumbo," He said rather than asked. "I'm Deputy Detective Andrew Cargill, Elmore County Sheriff's Department."

"Good to meet you sir," I said, taking his outstretched hand. "You know me?"

"Yes sir, every cop in 'Bama knows you. You're the guy who found the elephants hidden in the shoe-box factory. That, sir, was a fine piece of detecting."

I nodded, accepting the compliment. It certainly *was* one of my more memorable cases.

"The trooper says you may know who these clowns are."

"Yes sir," I said. "That one, without the shoes, is JellyBeans. He's the Clown Crew Boss and a longtime friend of mine. He and his crew were clowns in the Great Atlanta Circus that was here last week."

"The gal in the red wig is JollyBelle. She's been a clown for forty years at least. JollyBelle and JellyBeans were good friends for a lot of years."

"Were they lovers?" The detective asked.

"Probably, but I don't know for sure. The life doesn't always leave much time for couples, it's a demanding job."

He nodded like he knew what I was talking about. "Just like being a cop but we all still try."

I named off the others, pointing them out by their distinct uniforms. "Fisheyes, El Marionette, Rambler, Gargles the Gargoyle—one of the ugliest men I had ever met and probably one of the nicest—Miss Rainbow, and Mr. Teedles."

"You find them in the river?" I asked.

"Yep, all of them in the car. All of them *in the trunk of the car*. I don't know how you guys do that and I never will."

I ignored the implicit question. "How'd they die?"

"Don't know, we'll have to get them back to the morgue to find out. We can't tell nothin' with the bodies the way they are."

I nodded curtly.

"Do you know anything about why they're here?" Cargill asked.

"I know what the ringmaster told me. He said after the show in Wetumpka on Tuesday, they were heading up to the crater to do some after-show celebration. That sounds right to me; Jelly-Beans and his crew did enjoy drinkin' a bit. Never while they worked, but after a good show, sure, they liked to celebrate."

The deputy nodded. "There's something you don't know yet and this is not for anyone else to know. Sheriff Jenkins told me to trust you, so I'm gonna trust you with this, okay?"

"You have my word," I said.

"It wasn't just the clowns we found in the trunk. It also contained about twelve purses and twenty-some wallets stolen from people all over Alabama, Florida, Georgia and Mississippi. Money and credit cards were gone."

It's times like this that I'm thankful for the painted-on smile. I couldn't believe what he was saying and if he could have read my expression, he probably wouldn't have kept talking.

"There's been a lot of reports of things gone missing at circuses in Alabama this year. ALEA has been 'looking into it.'" He used air quotes around those words. ALEA is the Alabama Law Enforcement Agency, a kind of fusion of State Patrol and State Bureau of Investigation. We both knew that state politics often meant sweeping inconvenient local problems under the rug. "And," the deputy continued, "there are some on the state level who would love nothin' better than to pin this all on some dead clowns.

I watched his face closely. "But you don't buy it?" I asked him after a moment.

"I don't, I have a brother who's in the life in Texas. I know clowns and I know most of you wouldn't do that shit. Yeah, sure, I know about John Wayne Gacy and all the creepy killer clowns being arrested all over the place, but real clowns like you and JellyBeans and my brother Maximillian, you're not like that. It's not a clown thing to do. Call it a hunch."

"I've known JellyBeans all my adult life," I said, "and I know he'd never steal anything or countenance anyone in his crew thieving from the public. It was his goal in life to make the kids laugh and the bad guys cry. He's the one who taught me how to catch the crooks and protect the circus. I knew JollyBelle too, and she was the same way, honest as the day is long. If they had that stuff with them, they were bringing it to the cops."

"That or it's a setup," said Deputy Cargill.

For a long time Cargill and I stood in silence and watched the crime scene techs imported from Montgomery measure this, weigh that, and dust something else for fingerprints. Then they started zipping the bodies into body bags for transpor to the morgue.

I couldn't speak until the last of my brothers and sisters were loaded into the coroner's van but I finally broke the silence. "So, what are you going to do?"

"It's still an Elmore County murder case. We gotta keep investigating it even if the state wants to sweep it under the rug. Our best lead is the circus. We gotta get someone there on the inside."

I turned to look at him when he said this, and he was already looking straight at me, a little smile on his face.

"Shit," I said.

The High-Tension Dame

I agreed to help, to go back and see what I could find, but I asked Cargill not to let out just yet the identities or the lifestyle of the victims. He said that was no problem—they had to notify next of kin first and that could take as long as I wanted it to. The news that night picked up the story only that a car with eight occupants was pulled out of the Coosa.

I called Gulch and said I had reconsidered his offer. I told my own troupe at Ringling Brothers why I needed a leave of absence before the big top closed and they said they would cover for me while I searched out JellyBean's killer. JB was a legend among clowns.

For the most part, other performers, especially the ringmasters, can't tell what clown is which under the greasepaint. So, if one of us has to be away for a while without the bosses knowing, it's rarely a problem.

I had mixed feelings, though. I had been with the big show for ten years now. I would hate to miss the finale, but it was more important for me to find who did this to my friend and my colleagues.

I joined Great Atlanta in Meridian. Gulch wanted me to train the acrobats to be clowns so he didn't have to hire anyone else. I asked him if the acrobats could easily learn to be ringmasters and that shut him up. I put word out on the Internet and within a day's time, I had five interviews lined up.

The night before the first interviews, I was sitting in Jelly-Beans' trailer. He didn't have the taste to have Chicken Cock whiskey on hand, but his Judge's Preference wasn't too bad a substitute. I poured myself a glass and was sitting out under the awning when a dame walks up and, man, was she a looker. She was a tall glass of water with legs that went on for miles, and dark curly hair hanging loose all the way down her back. She had one of those long, severely elegant faces with high cheekbones and pouty lips.

I offered her a whisky and she accepted and sat down next to me. "I am Uiliana Antonova Espinoza. You are Clumbo the Clown, yes?" Her voice was low and smoky with a strong Russian accent."

"I am," I said, "that's quite a name."

She smiled at me. "Is what happens when a good Russian girl marries a good Spanish boy."

"And to what do I owe the pleasure of your company, Mrs. Espinoza?"

"This dog on your lap, is Blossom, yes?"

I nodded.

"Where did you get him?"

"Funny thing," I said, "she was dropped off in a box on my doorstep. There was a note that said, 'This is Blossom, I know you love dogs, he can't stay with our circus anymore, please take care of him.' Yeah, it was a funny thing, first because it ain't a him. Second, because—though she may look like a circus dog—she didn't seem to know any tricks, at least not circus tricks. But I took one look at that cute little face and couldn't resist her.

Pretty smart too. I've taught her some tricks so I think I'll use her in my show."

"You cannot do this," she said emphatically. "No one here must know you have her. She is very important dog!"

My eyebrows went up at that. I continued to scratch Blossom behind her ears.

The woman pulled a folded-up piece of paper out of her bra and handed it to me—her skin-tight costume had no pockets. I unfolded it and saw a picture of Blossom under handwritten childish letters, saying "Lost Dog" with a number to call and the words "$50 reward."

"Wow," I said, "I love the little pup, it's gonna be hard for me to give her up. How did she get to me?"

"JellyBeans, he sent her to you with my husband Pablo. JellyBeans was great friend, even to us wire-walkers. But he was stupid to send dog with Pablo. Pablo was supposed to deliver message and he couldn't come talk to you."

"Why not, I don't bite."

"He thinks you do. Pablo is scared of clowns."

I laughed, perhaps insensitively, "He's coulrophobic and works in a circus?"

"Once he gets to know you a bit, he is okay. He hid from JellyBeans for a year but later is best friend. But Pablo can't walk up to strange clown and talk so he forgets to give you important message."

"Why would JellyBeans want to send me a lost dog? That doesn't make sense."

"Is not lost, is kidnapped."

"Kidnapped! You're telling me JellyBeans kidnapped someone's dog?"

She must have misread my expression—easy to do with all the greasepaint—because she was waving her hands and saying "No, No, JellyBeans and clowns save dog. It was BabyFace and Cornelia who kidnap little dog. Clowns take dog from them and send to you because they know you will take care of him."

"Her," I said, pedantically.

"Whatever. I don't know how, but clowns hear someone contact girl's rich parents and want ten-thousand dollars for dog's ransom. Kidnapper thinks because parents love child, they pay big dollars to get dog back. JollyBelle say if parents not pay or go to cops, then kidnapper will probably kill dog so clowns kidnap him from kidnappers and send him to you. Pablo is supposed to tell you to hold dog until they find rightful owner. But he tell me yesterday he never give you message."

"Well, Mrs. Espinoza, that explains a lot. How do you know all this?"

"People see us on the high wire, but they don't know we see them too. I see dog stolen while girl in tent. I see BabyFace and Cornelia steal wallets and purses and other things from people."

"And you didn't do anything?" I asked incredulously.

"We are artists, we are above all that. We are here to do show. But JollyBelle and JellyBeans are good friends to us and when they ask us for help, we help."

"So it's BabyFace and Cornelia who are behind all this?" I asked.

"I don't think so," She answered slowly. "Between two of them, they almost have one brain. Someone else is running this racket."

After she left, I thought long and hard about what she had told me. It made sense, BabyFace and Cornelia could easily be ripping off marks in the crowd.

The Great Atlanta Circus was a small circus, and as such, the freak show—now more politely called the sideshow—was actually an independent entity. It was kept around the back of the big tents like it was the circus's unwanted smelly cousin.

I hadn't had the time to go through their show yet, but I knew BabyFace and Cornelia. BabyFace was a little person, but the kind who looked more like a kid than an adult. Cornelia looked like any other attractive dame, but they called her Pretzel Girl because she could tie herself up in impossible knots.

Uiliana said the dog had been left outside the tent with a man who worked for the family, maybe the chauffeur, but

Cornelia put the moves on him and while his eyes were otherwise engaged, BabyFace had grabbed Blossom.

The high-wire people always rubbed me the wrong way, they always acted so high and mighty and usually kept to themselves. But Uiliana was right about BabyFace and Cornelia, neither was very smart, even on those rare occasions they were both sober. Somebody else had to be behind this crime spree and the kidnapping of my poor little Blossom.

Ahh, my little Malshi. Now I know what's behind that sadness I always see in your eyes.

The Dame with the Button Nose

Okay, so I know a lot of you don't know much about the life and how seriously we take our jobs. But here's a hint. If you are interested in becoming a clown, do NOT show up at your first interview dressed in a three-piece suit!

That was my first interview of the day; the second was better. He had some experience, knew how to dress and by my lights, was reasonably funny and seemed like someone I could work with. I was pretty desperate, we had to have a show running within a couple days as per Mr. Gulch. So, I wasn't trying for excellence and artistry as I did in Ringling Brothers. I hired Nimrod on the spot.

It was my third interview, however, that left me speechless and that's pretty hard to do. I'm not one of those mimes.

It was another dame, but this one was really to my liking. She had this cute button nose—which she took off to drink the coffee I offered her. She had red hair sticking straight out at all angles, a bowler with a flower—my type of hat—and an ample figure just hinted at through her uniform. We clowns always like the matronly type. Best of all though, she had a laugh that would make everyone around her laugh with her.

I thought to myself that maybe, just maybe, I'd found *my* JollyBelle. Her name was AnnieBananie and the interview went like this:

"Do you have any experience?"

"I'm a graduate of the Emmett Kelly School of Clowning, 1993. I worked as a local clown for three years, doing parties, company meetings and even some weddings. I earned a Bubbles Award in balloon sculpting three years in a row and I've won several regional tricycle races. I trained my own clown dog, BoJangles, and when we weren't working, we spent a lot of time volunteering for several children's hospitals. I think Bo even pulled off a miracle with one of the kids. I can't be sure, but she was supposed to be dying. Bo would climb into her hospital bed and lick her face every time we came to visit. The girl came back to visit me in 2004 to show me her own baby. I cried then, good tears, never took to the sad clown motif.

"Anyway, Bo and I got a job with the Chicago Three Ring where we worked for almost five years. But in 2007, Bo passed and the Chicago Circus closed. I met a guy after one of our shows and when the circus closed, he asked me to marry him on one condition—I had to give up the life. He didn't want to take some clown home to meet his parents.

"So since then, I've worked at the Chicago Stock Exchange where I did pretty well—better than my husband in fact—and he couldn't stand that, so he left me six months ago.

"With my money, I've endowed a permanent BoJangles Clown Residency at Chicago Hope and I miss the life, I miss it every day. If you give me a chance again, I'll..."

I stopped her there and hired her on the spot.

After Annie, there were a few more I passed on. One mime, one sad clown and one really scary clown dude with fangs. Mimes and scary clowns don't belong in a circus, and while I appreciate the skill of a sad clown, he wouldn't fit into the act I was just starting to put together in my head.

Then there was a brother and sister act called Mumbo and Tumbo. I didn't like that their names were so close to mine, but actually, they were pretty good. And five clowns was what the Gulch wanted so that's what I gave him.

Putting on a Show

The next day, the five of us got together to plan our act. If I was going to be undercover here, we had to have a respectable show. Gulch was going to give us two fifteen-minute sets a day and wanted us to work the crowds when we weren't in the ring.

First off, I've never seen acrobats more relieved than when they got to give up their clown costumes and go back to tumbling. I suppose I'd feel the same way if I tried acrobatting.

When my new troupe got down to business, we came up with a pretty good couple of sets almost right away. It was the usual stuff with the little car, the fake cannon shoot, the clowns pretending to be elephants and ringmasters. Nothing that creative to start off with, but a good, respectable show.

Working with Nimrod and Mumbo and Tumbo was okay. They were decent enough, right from the get-go, I could tell Nimrod had a thing for Tumbo and Mumbo wasn't all that excited about it—and Tumbo didn't like the idea any better than his sister. But that was okay, Nimrod wasn't too pushy about it.

I was sorry as hell I couldn't bring Blossom into the act. I'd trained her for it, and she didn't really like being left alone all day but after Uiliana's warning, I couldn't take any chances.

Working with Annie, though, was a dream. Just when the other four of us were going to go with an okay show, she came up with a series of unique gags, sometimes just little tweaks, sometimes whole new avenues, and she turned our "okay" show into one we could be proud of. And she wasn't kidding about how good she was with balloon animals.

Balloon sculpting is something I'm good at. I can make rocket ships, and a cat-dog from the old cartoon. When I really want to impress, I've got a series of movable hats of all kinds.

But Annie could actually make a peacock with individual feathers, Dory, Sebastian the Lobster, Ariel the Mermaid and every Avenger, including Dr. Strange with a removable cape.

Between the two of us and a lot of popped balloons, we got Nimrod who was already passable, and Mumbo and Tumbo, who needed a lot of extra help, up-to-speed sculpting some pretty impressive figures. Every once in a while, I tried to show off. I did a duck billed dinosaur and then Annie did the scariest T-Rex I've ever seen. I tried to do a funny Minion and she did the three girls from *Despicable Me* holding hands. Whatever I made, she did me one better and blew me out of the water. I like that in a woman.

The next day, we were already doing our sets then milling through the crowd between performances, doing magic tricks and giving away balloon animals. It was a great setup for me because it gave me the chance to keep an eye on BabyFace and Cornelia who…

…did absolutely *nothing* out of the ordinary.

After the evening show, I took Annie out for dinner and a couple of drinks. We talked about everything, growing up as clowns, learning the business, how she left the life and how empty she felt in civilian clothes.

I talked about my long climb from the salt mines of Cleveland to the biggest of the big tops. I told her a little about working with JellyBeans in the circus, but I mentioned nothing of our investigative work together. I still didn't know who I was dealing with, and I was afraid if I let anything slip, I could be putting her in danger. Whoever killed JellyBeans and his crew wouldn't stop at killing my crew if they thought any of us knew something.

We ended up in a country-western bar and for a short while, I was afraid the local toughs were going to start with us. But Annie and I hit the dance floor and showed everybody what turned out to be some amazing moves together. I, for one, did not know I could actually two-step in size 24 shoes. Instead of getting thrown out, we had the crowd surrounding us, and stomping and clapping while we danced.

I was falling hard for this dame.

BabyFace's Sticky Fingers

We had a show in the morning, so Annie and I walked back to the circus complex about midnight. I put my arm around her waist, and she not only didn't push it away, she leaned into me for warmth against the evening chill.

I'm not a mover. I'm a bit shy with women and I'm a clown. Generally, those of us in the life are not used to dames, even clown dames, falling for us on the first date. I was going to walk her to her trailer, but we had to pass JellyBeans' trailer—well, my trailer now—first.

It was Annie who suggested we go into my trailer for some coffee, and I had to fake a cough to cover my own surprise. Needless to say, I didn't turn down the request.

When we got to the trailer, my poor, much-neglected Blossom started crying behind the door. Though I had paid a couple of kids to look in on her and feed her and take her out when I couldn't, she had grown very attached to me.

I opened the door and she bounded out. She ran circles around us, first sniffing Annie's shoes then jumping up on me. I tried to pet her on the ground to say "hi," but she virtually climbed up my body in her excitement, whimpering with joy, licking me everywhere then just rubbing her face in mine, knocking off my nose.

When I finally got her down, I looked over at Annie, wanting to introduce them. But Annie had an odd expression on her face.

"So, you have a dog, hunh? A cute little brown and white dog?"

I nodded. "She's really a loving dog," I said lamely.

"I can see that. How did you come to have a dog but not use her in your show?"

"Well, I can't actually tell you that right now. Soon, I hope…"

"I'll bet you can't. Goodnight, Mr. Clumbo, I've had a very nice time, but I think I need to go home now," and she walked away.

I stood there dumbfounded, holding the still wildly-squirming and face-licking Blossom, wondering what had just happened. Did she hate dogs? Well, no, not from the stories she told. Did she love them and think I was neglecting Blossom?

I sighed, walked the little Malshi in the dark and went back inside for the night.

The next day dawned bright and slightly warmer. When the gates opened and the people started pouring in, me and my clowns were out with the milling crowds, entertaining the kids, folding balloon animals, or in Annie's case, balloon masterpieces. You could see the parents were really impressed with what she made, and the kids were over the moon with their new toys.

Annie was pleasant enough with me and seemed to stick within seeing distance of me, but she wasn't particularly warm.

Even Nimrod noticed. Under his breath as we were folding some more animals, he asked "What the hell did you do to her last night. She really liked you yesterday and now she acts like you're Pogo the Clown. Hope you're not getting arrested. I like this gig."

I didn't dignify that with an answer.

We did our matinée show and were soon back out working in the crowd. Annie stayed watching me as I tried to watch BabyFace and Cornelia.

This time, I hit pay dirt. BabyFace was dressed in what looked like kids' clothes and he walked up to women standing by themselves. He was always holding a big stick of cotton candy. He'd ask them something or talk to them for a few minutes then gave each one a big sticky hug. While the women were trying to disentangle themselves from the overly affectionate boy and wipe off the sticky residue, I saw his hand slip into their purses and come out with a wallet.

I was pissed. You don't treat paying customers that way. I dropped any pretense of folding animals and moved like a thunderstorm towards BabyFace. He saw me coming and started running. Then I heard Annie scream my name, but I wasn't going to drag her into this now.

That's when the lights went out.

The Really Big Dame

The sideshow had an ancient, out-of-tune, out-of-rhythm calliope that played all the time the circus was open. The sound was bad enough across the circus complex. When I woke up, I was in what must have been the storage tent right next to the calliope. That distressing noise, along with a horrible pounding headache, made me want to knock myself back unconscious.

I was tied tightly in a chair, back-to-back with someone else also tied to a chair. Worse, I knew who it was. I don't know how, maybe her scent, maybe something else subtle, but it was Annie.

It was a smallish tent, there was one electric light bulb hanging above us and a lot of boxes scattered around. On one of these boxes, sat BabyFace smoking a cigar with one hand, holding a pistol in the other. Despite the encumbrances, he was also holding a magazine with an unfurled centerfold. The lucky bastard had a pair of earphones. I tried to shout some insult at him, but Annie answered me, screaming at the top of her lungs "He can't hear you. I already tried."

I tried to yell back "I'm sorry" but I'm not sure she heard.

It was a very long time later—I can't tell you how long—but with my headache and the endlessly repeating music, it seemed to be a *very* long time—the calliope finally started slowing down and getting softer, like a wind-up toy running down its spring.

BabyFace still had his earphones on so I quickly said to Annie "I'm so sorry for getting you involved in this. I didn't mean to."

"You didn't get me involved. I got me involved. Now we gotta figure out how to get away from your friends here. I can't undo any of these knots."

"I wonder if the CIA knows about the torture potential of a calliope?" I asked.

"I don't know about the CIA, but Momma knows, I can promise you that." It was BabyFace, he had pulled off his headphones. "And before I joined the sideshow, I was Merchant Marines, so I know how to tie a knot."

"Who's Momma?" I asked.

"I am", said a very sweet, light voice. I turned my head expecting to see the lithe and slender Cornelia but instead, I saw a behemoth of a woman, maybe five hundred pounds. I looked at the door behind her that she must have just come through and thought to myself, *no way.*

"Now," she said, "who the hell are you and why did you have our little bitchy hostage in your trailer?"

"You didn't kidnap the dog?" asked Annie.

"What? No! What the hell kind of clown do you think I am?"

The fat lady kicked one of the wooden boxes hard and it split apart with a loud crack.

"Look at me, you clowns. I'm asking the questions now."

"My name is Clumbo, this here is AnnieBananie, and she has nothing to do with this, she doesn't know anything, I just hired her a couple days back."

"And why Mr. Clumbo, did you have my dog?"

"He's not your dog, you witch," Annie spat. "I was hired by the Marks family to find him and bring him back."

Okay, so this was a shock to me.

"I'm a friend of JellyBeans and JollyBelle," I said, "JellyBeans sent me the dog. I didn't know why until I got here to take his place. He sent the dog with Pablo to my house in Florida."

It was disturbing to hear a light, feminine, tinkling laugh come from such a big woman.

"Pablo? Hahahaha (*tinkle tinkle*). He's scared to death of clowns. I bet he couldn't even talk to you when you opened the door."

"He didn't try. Blossom was left in a basket on my doorstep with a note. It said to take care of her. I didn't even know about Pablo until Uiliana told me the story the day I got here."

I heard Annie catch a bit in her throat. I took that as a good sign—if we ever got out of here alive...

"You have him now?" Annie asked the woman.

"Yeah, we've got the little shit back in the cage," said the fat lady, "The thing just cries and cries. Who would ever want a little bitch like that is beyond me but if he pays the $10,000, Mr. Marks will get him back. If he doesn't, I got a bag and a rock and a lake."

Just like you did to JellyBeans I thought, but didn't say it out loud.

"Now, we have a problem," the woman said, settling down on one of the sturdier boxes. "Momma's show has a little side gig going on here. I think our time is up with Great Atlanta, but we need a few more days to get the ransom and then we'll be gone."

"I guess we have to hold miss prissy clown here since she knows everything but you, Clumbo, I need you to keep your act going and keep quiet or I'll do to you what I did to JellyBeans and his pack of meddlers.

"They stole my doggy captive and they were going to tell the cops about the other ways Momma's little freaks make some extra spending money."

"By ripping off the paying customers," I spat back, "the families that come here to see the circus and have a little fun? They don't deserve that."

"They do deserve it." The pretty voice was gone and a low and dark growl more appropriate to the woman, was in its place.

"You see them as sweet little kids playing with the clowns and *ooh-ing* and *aah-ing* at the horse riders, the acrobats, and the elephants. We see them for what they really are. The little monsters stand outside our cages and tell us how ugly and disgusting we are. They throw peanuts and popcorn at us. Teddy, the Wolf Boy, had bubblegum thrown in his hair yesterday and it took us an hour and half to get it out and we still had to cut off some of his precious fur.

"Then the mommies point at me and tell their kids 'This is what you'll look like if you eat all that cotton candy.' I have a glandular problem. No one gets like me from too much cotton candy…

"So go ahead and live in your little dreamworld about these 'nice' people who come to the circus. We know better. We live in cages not to keep us *in* but to keep them *out*.

"Now that I know who you are, I can do the same thing to you that I did to JellyBeans and JollyBelle."

I blinked in my confusion. *Now that I know who you are?* "Wait," I said, "so, you didn't know about me and JellyBeans? You're not the one who sent me his shoes?"

"Wait, what?" said Annie.

"I don't know you from Ronald McDonald and why would I send you JellyBeans' shoes? He loved those shoes, maybe more than he loved JollyBelle. He's going to be buried in those shoes.

"They were a great act, but I got them fired and I can get you fired too. Gulch and I are very, *very* good friends."

"Wait, what?" I said, now completely confused.

"What, you think a woman like me doesn't have admirers and lovers too?"

Okay so that was a picture I didn't need in my head. When not sober or in his glory in the ring, Gulch was an ugly, wrinkled, skinny, old man who looked like a skid-row bum.

"So you don't know about JellyBeans and his crew?" I asked.

"What do you mean?" It was the fat lady's turn to look nonplussed.

"You heard about that car in the river in Wetumpka last week?"

"I don't listen to the news," she said. "Most of the time it's too depressing."

"That car had seven bodies in the trunk. It was JellyBean and JollyBelle and the whole crew."

"How do you get seven bodies in the trunk of a car?" asked BabyFace. "Even me and seven clones of me couldn't do that." he said.

"Professional secret," I said.

BabyFace rolled his eyes.

"I'm a PI too, a clown PI, working with the Elmore County Sheriff's office to see if we can find out who killed them."

"And why did you bring the little bitch with you?" asked the fat lady.

"I told you, I just hired her a couple days ago."

I felt the tied-together chairs jerk a bit. "And I was just starting to like you again," said Annie.

"I meant the damn dog, you idiot." Said the fat lady.

"I thought she was calling you names," I said to Annie, "I don't think of you like that…"

"Why did you bring the *dog* bitch," boomed the fat lady.

"Because I didn't know. I thought I could use her in my act. Everyone loves a dog act and she's pretty smart. I've taught her a bunch of tricks since I got her.

"Look," I continued, "I think we have a much bigger mutual problem here. If you didn't kill JellyBeans and send me his shoes, who did and are we all still in danger?"

"Who else knew about the kidnapping and the stealing?" Annie asked. "Does all of Momma's Sideshow know?"

"I think some of them suspect, but it's only me, Cornelia and BabyFace who actually know—and Leroy Gulch," said the fat lady.

"And the meddling fools in the high wire act, they seem to see everything," said BabyFace.

"But they don't deign to stoop down to our level. No, my sweet little boy, I think we need to bring Mr Gulch here too for a little chat. Can you go wake him from his stupor and bring him here. Take your little friend."

"You know how you don't like it when I call you Big Momma and laugh at your thunder thighs?" asked BabyFace.

"Yes, why?" asked the fat lady.

"Never mind," he said sulkily and left the trailer pointing his gun at the floor.

He came back a few minutes later hauling a still half-inebriated Gulch behind him.

Gulch came into the tent and saw Annie and me in our chairs.

"Oh, there you are," he slurred. "You didn't do your evening show tonight, so I think I'm going to have to fire you."

Then he seemed to register the ropes around us. "Oh no, Adeline, not again."

"Leroy," she said, "what happened to JellyBeans? What did you do? I just wanted him fired and sent away."

Gulch couldn't meet Adeline's eyes. "I didn't do that," he whined.

"But you know what happened?" she asked, but he didn't answer. "Leroy, what happened to JellyBeans and his crew?

He actually fell to his knees in front of her, grasping for her hands but she pulled away. "I had to tell the owners," he said. "JellyBeans and JollyBelle were going to the cops, and it would be all over. You'd be in jail, and I'd be in jail. The owners were trying to sell Great Atlanta and if word got out that we had a theft ring here, no one would ever buy the circus."

"So you had them killed?!" She thundered.

"I didn't," he whimpered, "I was just trying to warn the owners. I had no idea they would do something like that. I liked JellyBeans, he was the funniest clown I've ever worked with. But the owners sent me his shoes and I knew what had happened. JellyBeans always told me if anything happened to him, I should contact Clumbo, so I sent him the shoes, knowing he would come. I filled them with jelly beans so he would know they were JellyBeans' shoes. What are we going to do now, dear?"

"Well, Leroy, we can't just let them go," said Momma, "We'll have to leave them tied up here for a few days until we can get away."

"I can't go." Gulch said, "I've still got my job, at least for a while. The owners say they'll take care of me."

"Like they took care of JellyBeans?" I asked helpfully. Gulch just put his head in his hands.

Babyface started playing with his gun again, twirling the cylinder, flipping the latch back and forth, and shifting it from hand to hand. "I don't want to go back to prison," he said. "It ain't a very good place for someone like me."

"Not so good for me either," said Momma, "but we aren't killing them. Where can we hide them for a week?"

"Momma, you're not gonna do that," said a new voice, deep and booming. "We're gonna let them go."

I turned again to look at the door. The smallish tent was getting pretty full now. Herbie the Strong Man and Teddy the Wolf Boy stood inside the doorway. Cornelia stood just behind them.

"It's time to end this, Momma," said Herbie. Teddy and Cornelia nodded their agreement. "I don't want to be part of a family that does things like this."

Cornelia added, "It's not like we can blend in with the rest of the world. Even if we did take off, the cops are gonna find a plus-sized woman and a minus-sized man and a pretzel girl pretty easily. I'm tired of living like this."

"We're still family," said Teddy, "whatever happens, we'll take care of you."

Nobody tried to stop Herbie as he walked up to us with a very large knife and started cutting the ropes. *"Sorry about hitting you,"* he said under his breath as he was freeing us, *"I didn't know."*

"No problem," I said, still eyeing the knife carefully.

Blossom Goes Home

One of the basic rules of undercover work is to have a regular check-in with the outside world. If you don't check-in, your allies know something is wrong and they come and find out why. It seems both Annie and I had such arrangements.

When our friends found out neither of us was there for the evening show, they got worried and started asking questions. Uiliana and Pablo had seen enough of what had happened to lead them to the sideshow and they rushed in to save us just as we were walking out of the storage tent. There was actually a pretty funny scene when Annie's people and my people were all running at us with guns drawn without knowing that the other side were good guys too. As we watched them try to figure out who was who, I knew I had a great new routine for the next time I had a crew of my own. Adeline, Gulch, Babyface and

Cornelia were not really hardened criminals and they gave up right away. I doubt they would have even killed the dog.

Like Momma said, the rest of the sideshow was clueless about the theft ring. When Herbie hit me from behind and grabbed Annie on Adeline's orders, he just thought he was protecting his friends. He wasn't necessarily all that bright, but he was a great showman. He convinced the crowd the capture of the two clowns was part of the show.

Once threatened with a very long prison sentence, Gulch—who was just a weak man caught between powerful people—sang like a canary. Two days later, it was my privilege to be with Deputy Detective Cargill in the offices of Joseph Agate and Associates—the owners of the Great Atlantic Circus. Like so many others, they wanted out of the business because all the circuses were slowly going broke.

Mr. Agate was a big, powerful man who wasn't taking kindly to being accused of murder by me.

"You're a real Bozo, you know that," he said.

"Compliments aren't going to get you out of this," I replied.

Cargill read him his rights and pulled out his handcuffs. Agate looked like he was thinking about putting up a fight.

"Allow me, "I said, and I pulled out a long balloon and started blowing it up. Agate watched me, more puzzled than anything, until he saw me fold them into a giant pair of balloon handcuffs. He started laughing at me and said, "Okay, I'll bite," and he put his hands through the latex bracelets.

With a quick flick of my thumbnail, I popped the balloon and the handcuffs tightened hard around his wrists. He stopped laughing very quickly.

Sometimes when you're a clown, people just don't take you seriously.

Later that day, Annie and I drove Blossom back to the ritzy suburbs of Montgomery. Annie wasn't lying about most of her history—she had just left out the part about getting a PI's license after she got bored playing with other people's money.

You could see it in Blossom's eyes when she finally understood where we were taking her. She started whining and squirming and running all around the back seat of the car. She could barely contain her excitement.

We pulled up the long driveway and Annie got out of the car to open the door for the dog. But Blossom ran around the back seat about five more times, leapt into the front seat and jumped in my lap while I still sat in the driver's seat. She licked my greasepaint one last time and gave me a long soulful look to say goodbye. Then she bounded through my open window straight for the little girl who was herself balling with joy. The dog hit her and knocked her down—which is pretty impressive when you're only about twelve pounds of pooch—and they rolled together in mutual ecstasy.

We got out of the car to talk to the parents and collect Annie's fee. They were incredibly happy with the outcome.

"What *is* a Malshi?" Annie asked me as we walked back to the car, "I never heard of that breed before."

"It's one of those designer mixed breeds. It's a Maltese-Shih Tzu. But it's more than that," I said. "For that little girl, It's the stuff that dreams are made of."

We walked back to the car holding hands.

A Day in the Life of the Great Space Explorer

Jeffrey Tripplethorn woke up aching.

His neck hurt, his back ached. When he tried to pull his feet from under the covers, they got tangled up in the sheets. He had felt fine when he went to bed the night before, but not now. A shiver of panic and confusion darted anxiously around his mind.

"Lieutenant Tripplethorn," said a deep, booming voice, "please don't be alarmed. I know this must seem strange to you right now but I assure you, there is an explanation and things will be better soon."

"Who are you?" Jeffrey asked, looking around but seeing little as his eyes seemed much worse than he remembered them.

"This is Dr. Horn of the Starship Encounter. We picked up your ship floating in deep space and you had been in suspended animation for 300 years. I'm afraid you've aged quite a bit since the last time you remember."

"Dr. Horn, I've heard of you. What do you mean I've aged?"

"Do you see the mirror next to the viewport? Go take a look."

Jeffrey looked around his room and saw what looked like a window on the wall. Though his eyes seemed to be playing tricks on him, he could see stars slowly moving across the view. A few feet away on a dresser was a small mirror. He got unsteadily to his feet and went over to it. He bent down—painfully—to look and started screaming at what he saw.

"Lieutenant," said the voice, "Please calm down. I know what it must look like but remember, we have regeneration pods. Once we get you up and well, we can put you in one of the tanks and poof, you'll be twenty-five again in no time. You just have to give us some time and patience."

Jeffrey sat down heavily in his chair. He was in utter disbelief. He tried to remember how he got here. He didn't remember being on any kind of starship. Mostly, he just remembered getting drunk the night before.

Then he remembered flying and then all kinds of flashing lights. Maybe that was the starship. He remembered the IVs and the mask and being put into the big tube. That must have been his suspended animation tank. And the noise it made, the big, loud, scary humming. Then nothing.

"Oh my god, I remember now," he said softly to himself but Dr. Horn seemed to hear.

"Yes, Mr. Tripplethorn, it will be all right. I'm in another part of sickbay but I'm going to send my orderly in to give you an assist. This will be André, he's a Medical Special Operative."

A moment later, a man walked into the room. Jeffrey could only stare at him. He was maybe four feet tall, with a very dark complexion, and a rolling gait. The man smiled and waved at him and said cheerily he was going to help Jeffrey get dressed.

It seemed odd to Jeffrey that the dresser drawers in a gleaming new spaceship like the Encounter would look like they were made of cheap plywood. But maybe they did that to add a homey air to the super-sleek modern design. A man could feel at home here.

André talked with Jeffrey as he helped him out of the pajamas saying cheerful, meaningless pleasantries. But as he helped Jeffrey into the silver space jumpsuit, he whispered into his ear "I am not André the MSO, I am Rugar and I am from the planet Garfon and I'm here to pay you back for what you did to my people."

As the strange little man said this, Jeffrey looked at him again and could see the subtle little differences that identified him as a Garf, the pointed teeth, the lumpy spine, and the reptilian skin. He knew he would never see the regeneration tanks.

Jeffrey moaned but was too scared to say anything. Somehow, he would have to let Dr. Horn know he had an alien imposter in his sickbay.

* * *

"Oh great, André, what did you say to him *this* time? Now I gotta go clean his pants again."

* * *

"Commodore Tripplethorn," said the young woman, "please follow me to breakfast in the Captain's Dining Room. There has been a murder."

Jeffrey looked at the woman, her short bobbed hair, her pretty face, her white starched uniform. It took him a moment but he finally placed her.

"Ensign Pennysworth. Yes, of course. I'll follow you."

"Your disguise, Commodore, is wonderful. They will never suspect that this doddering old man is the young, virile Captain Tripplethorn."

"Ah, yes, it is good, isn't it?" said Jeffrey, straightening a bit. "Now what's this about a murder on a starship?"

"Captain Ensworth will explain. It is vital that we keep this to ourselves. No one else on the ship can know."

"Of course, Ensign. Haven't I always been discreet?"

She sat him down next to an old, grizzled veteran with a captain's hat. They brought him a plate full of eggs, bacon and toast and a damnable good cup of coffee from a replicator. They were surrounded by a room full of officers.

"Captain Ensworth, it shows an extreme lack of discipline that your officers are not in uniform."

"Ahh, it's alright sir, we just got back from planet leave. We'll have everyone ship-shape for your inspection by lunch."

"Very well sir, I will be watching them very closely for my report to the Admiralty. Now what is it you want to talk about?"

"Commodore, there has been a murder of a human officer during planet leave. I suspect one of the MourMouri rebels. After breakfast, I want you to go down to MourMour and see if you can weed out the bastard who did this to my officer."

"Can you give me details?"

The captain raised an eyebrow. "Didn't you read the files? I sent them to your console this morning."

Tripplethorn was momentarily confused. "Well yes, but I had a busy morning. I didn't get to read my document inbox. Give me the rundown."

The captain leaned back in his chair "Not much to tell, really. Lt. Sparks and several friends had dinner at the Herefords Restaurant, you know Herefords?"

"Yes, of course I do, best steaks in the galaxy, go on."

"Well, after dinner, the Lieutenant went for a walk in the garden alone. He still held on to that ancient custom of smoking cigars. His friends say they saw a blaster flash and heard Sparks scream. When they ran out to check on him, he had a fist sized hole in his chest. But blasters never leave blood. They are efficient that way."

"Oh, yes, of course, I've said that many times myself," said Tripplethorn.

* * *

The MourMouri rebels were given their blasters and bandanas and told what to expect. They went into the garden, hid behind trees, sat out on the benches, tucked into niches in the garden wall. The atmosphere was festive. It was a beautiful warm spring day, a delight for people who hadn't been outside for many months.

* * *

The Commodore was led to the transporter. The doors slipped open and he and the woman who escorted him to breakfast stepped in and the doors slid closed behind him.

"Your blaster sir," she said, handing him his ray gun. She held one of her own.

There was that peculiar lurching feeling as the transporter took them down to the planet surface. The doors slid open again and they walked into a glass atrium. The woman led the Commodore to a sliding glass door, tapped her pass against a card lock and they walked into the garden.

The Commodore immediately fell into a tactical stance and looked around suspiciously.

"Be very careful," said the Ensign, "These rebels are masters of disguise. They can look like anybody."

"I know, ensign, I have dealt with them for years." But he seemed not to notice the woman in a wheelchair as he walked right by her until she pulled her bandana over her face, screamed a bloody war cry and started shooting at them with her blaster.

"You bloody witch." He yelled back, taking aim and shooting her where she sat. The woman screamed in pain, clutched her chest and yelled "The Commodore has killed me! Avenge my death my brothers and sisters." Then she dropped her blaster and lay still, her head lolling to the side.

Another man came out from behind a tree, yelling "I am Darlok, the leader of this rebellion. How dare you bring your foreign ways to our planet? We have lived in peace under the great Mauronna for thousands of years and you Earthlings come and destroy it all. We will drive you from our planet." His pistol made a curious whirring noise, sending sparks flying out every which way as he shot at the Commodore and the Ensign.

The Ensign howled in pain, dropped her pistol. "He got my shooting arm, Commodore, It's up to you now."

The Commodore reeled around and shot Darlok nearly point blank, sending him around the bench and onto the ground. It was like blinders came off the Commodore's eyes, he saw all the rebels, at least a score of them. There were young men behind trees, old women on benches, a middle-aged woman in white uniform in one of the brick lined niches in the wall, all had their bandana's covering their faces and all were aiming for him.

Like he was in a slow-motion ballet, Commodore Tripplethorn weaved and dodged through the garden, hitting every one of his intended targets. Some died spectacularly, others just seemed to fall back where they were. He was so caught up in his battle lust, he didn't see the woman who had just come in the gate and stood firmly in the garden path until he turned around and whirled straight into her. She was an immovable rock. Tripplethorn dropped his blaster and fell ignobly on his ass.

"What the hell is going on here?" Growled the woman, looking not at Tripplethorn but at Darlok who was picking himself up off the ground, still holding his blaster.

"Ms Donnally, such a surprise to see you here on a Saturday."

"Yes, Derrick, it apparently is. What the hell is going on here?"

Tripplethorn was looking between the woman and Darlok/Derrick, his mouth hanging open. "How can you be standing there, I just killed you! You damned alien animal."

"Ensign, can you take the Commodore back to the transporter and tell him about our training exercise?"

"You'll do no such thing Meredith. I want to know what's going on," said the woman.

Meredith tried to help the Commodore up but he fought her every inch of the way to his feet. You could see the panic rising in his eyes. He kept trying to pull out of her grasp. His breathing was getting rapid and heaving and he started making inarticulate noises.

"Ma'am," said Derrick, "let us take him back to his room and I promise I can explain. It won't help anything if he has a meltdown out here."

The woman nodded curtly and Meredith led Tripplethorn back to the doors, trying to explain to him how they had faked a training exercise for him. "You didn't. I know all about the MourMouri rebels and Darlok and that is Darlok. What are you trying to do to me? What is this place?"

Another one of the corpses, a bigger man, got up and grabbed his other elbow and helped Meredith lead the complaining Tripplethorn back towards the elevator in the atrium.

Back at the gate, Derrick was trying to explain things to the nursing home's new director. "Ma'am, um, well, it was his daughter's idea," he said.

"Really," she said dubiously, staring down over her glasses at him.

"You know about him right? He has Korsakoff's Syndrome. He can't remember anything that happened since 1987. Everyday he wakes up and can't understand why he is thirty years older than when he went to bed.

"Every morning, he used to go crazy. He would yell and scream and throw himself against the door. We had to put him in restraints and that just made things worse.

"We called his daughter, Sarah, and she had an idea."

"Is she here? Does she know what you're doing?"

"I think she's visited him maybe twice in the last ten years. It seems he was a mean drunk when she was growing up. She doesn't want anything to do with him. But she brought us all his old manuscripts."

"His manuscripts?" Asked Donnally.

"Yeah, well it seems he fancied himself a science fiction writer and he wrote like six novels and twenty or thirty short stories. They all feature a guy named Tripplethorn and they are all really, really terrible stories. Even I can tell that. His daughter said he never got anything published.

"So we experimented a bit and found out he remembers his stories really well. So every day when he wakes up, we convince him he is the great space explorer Tripplethorn who aged somehow or other and we tell him we'll put him in a regeneration pod and he's okay with that. We put a TV in his room with a star video and told him it's a porthole. They didn't have flatscreen TVs in the '80s so he thinks it's a window.

"Then we act out scenes from his books and he thinks he's the Commodore and we have some fun and he gets to live the life he always dreamed of. On days like this, all the residents from the Friedlander Pavilion like to join in and it's kind of a party and everyone gets to be outside and the Commodore gets some exercise.

"As long as we can keep him engaged in the stories, he stays with us for the whole day. If he sits down to rest or loses the train of the story, we have to start all over again. And we always have to start all over again every morning."

"Was Mr. Brightman, my predecessor okay with this?"

"He knew it happened but didin't want details"

"And the State?"

"Well no, we don't tell the state inspectors or even the board of trustees."

"Everyone else is okay with it?"

The MourMouri/residents and staff all nodded. One woman said "This is the most fun thing we get to do here. Better than those stupid painting parties or wheelchair aerobics."

"I'm not sure about André though. He plays along but in Tripplethorn's books, the really evil guys in his stories were always dwarves so I think André sometimes says stuff to wind him up."

"And what about Mr. Tripplethorn? Have you ever asked him when he's not caught up in one of your stories?"

"Not me, ma'am, but Dr. Gareth did once. He was the psychiatrist before Dr. Martinez. Dr. Gareth said he explained what we did every day and that Tripplethorn said he actually liked the idea."

"But that had to be almost ten years ago"

"Yeah, I know, but every day Mr. Tripplethorn wakes up, he's exactly like he was the day before. We can predict almost to the letter every word he's going to say when we give him the same information. I doubt he's changed his mind about what we're doing."

"Honestly, Derrick," said Ms. Donnally, "I have no idea what I'm going to do with you all…"

Something That Will Not Let Go

A shadow from another time
Is waiting in the night
Something happened long ago
Something that will not let go

October Project
"Bury My Lovely"

Chapter 1

    The little girl looked out the yellow-crusted attic window at the woman trudging up the long path to the house. Even from afar, she knew it was Junie returning after so many years. Junie had put on some weight in the intervening years and her hair looked scraggly even from this far away. But the girl could feel it was the same person, her long lost friend and companion finally returning.

Junie carried a ripped backpack across one shoulder and pulled a cheap, wheeled suitcase behind her. The wheels kept getting caught in ruts in the dirt road leading up to the old farmhouse. She walked slowly, frequently stopping to pull the wheeled case out of the ruts. Twice, she sat down on the case to smoke a cigarette.

Chapter 2

When June finally reached the door of the house, she knocked but got no answer. She knocked a little louder—she knew he was home; his pickup was in the drive— but still she got no answer. Finally, she balled her hand into a fist and pounded on the door with all her might.

She heard the old man walking through the house, banging things as he moved towards the door.

"Don't know who the hell you think you are but I'm warnin' you I got a .45 and I ain't afraid to use it," she heard him say through the door. Then he pulled it open and, for a moment, just stared at her.

"Hello Junebug," he said finally.

"Hey Poppa, how you doin'?"

"I'm alright but you sure look like shit."

"Love you too, Poppa, I need a place to stay for a couple weeks."

"I know, Junie, there was a deputy here askin' 'bout you a few days ago. She said some Nashville cops wanted to talk to you about some drug dealin'. I told her I ain't seen you for fifteen years and you'd never come back here."

"Yeah Poppa, but I got nowhere else to go now and I don't think they'll come back here. If they do, I won't make no trouble, I'll go with them peacefully and say I made you take me in."

"Aw, Junebug, I don't give a shit about that. You can blow away any cop who comes here if you want, I'll even lend you my guns. It's just I don't got any money to take care of anyone anymore."

"I got some money, and I can earn my keep if you need something done around here. Just for a few weeks 'til all this shit blows over."

"You got any extra cigarettes?" he said as the stepped aside and held the door open for her. "I'm nearly out."

Chapter 3

The house was the same as she remembered—falling apart, messy, smelling equally of mold, stale smoke, and stale beer. Her father, Lester Bailey, hadn't changed much in the intervening years either. He had a little more grizzly stubble and a little more beer belly sticking out from his otherwise wiry frame. His hair was a little grayer and thinner.

June Bailey cooked dinner for the two of them. He had some rabbit in the icebox and a few veggies from the garden. She ate at the dining room table. Lester grabbed his plate without comment and ate in front of his TV. After dinner, she washed their dishes along with the pile of unwashed plates and forks from the sink. She spent a little time cleaning up the beer cans and empty cigarette packs that were strewn all over the kitchen but ran out of motivation pretty quickly. Her head was hurting, and her stomach was already roiling.

The old room in the attic seemed smaller than she remembered it. Her bed stood against the wall, covered with moth-eaten yellowed sheets, probably the same ones that were there when she left seventeen years ago. The attic floor was slanted but the brick she put under the bed's legs to lift it was still there. A cracked dresser with drawers that pulled out crooked easily held the small collection of clothes and the handful of personal keepsakes she was able to take with her when she left Nashville.

She started to clean here too a little. As a kid, she spent most of her time up here—as much as she could—trying to keep out of Poppa's way.

She changed the sheets and started to scrape the years of yellow crap coating the windows.

Incredibly, she had found a bottle of cleaner under the kitchen sink and used it to mop the layers of dust off the floor in her room. For a moment, after finishing, she looked down at it and enjoyed the clean, then the smell of the cleaner broke through her stuffy nose and she threw up all over the freshly mopped floor.

"Fuck" she said to herself. Her brain knew it was coming, but somewhere in her heart, she hoped that this time at least, it would pass her by. But now it hit her like a truck. It had been three days since her last fix and right on schedule, the goddamned super flu.

June ran down the stairs, nearly falling onto the second floor and into the only working bathroom in the house. She just barely made it without soiling herself. When she finally was able to crawl back upstairs, she dragged a trash can with her. June was feeling the wooziness and sick haze that always came from withdrawal.

Her father saw her stumbling up the stairs. "You alright, Junebug."

"Sure Poppa, just got a bad case of the flu."

"Can I get you anything?" he asked. "I got some ginger ale downstairs if you want."

"Naw, Poppa, I don't need nothin' right now."

It was all she could do to try to scrape up the puke from the floor into the trash can; she couldn't even finish that simple task. June was already getting the shakes and finally had to crawl into the bed where she pulled the sheets up to her neck, but the shivering wouldn't stop. She closed her eyes and felt the shame and the fear and the anger and the pure disgust of having her withdrawal here.

Chapter 4

Two men walked the fence in companionable silence. Lester drank a beer and smoked a cigarette, the other man walked with his hands in his pockets.

"My little girl is back" said Lester. "She's a fucking junkie and she's throwing up all over the place."

"Yep, kids are a pain in the ass. She gonna be here for a long time?" asked the other man. The man had shoulder length hair, a scraggly beard and mustache and actually wore a bandana on his head. Lester thought he looked like an idiot but had never said so out loud.

"Don't know," answered Lester, "I ain't got any extra money to feed her. Right now, she's sick as hell, so I'm taking care of her like I had to when my wife was sick. So she'll be here for a while, I guess. Maybe I cain't take as many of these walks with you and maybe you have to keep a low profile 'cuz I don't know what she'd do if she knew you were livin' here too."

"That's okay, it's getting harder for me to come out here with you. My little girl needs me to stay inside with her now. I can't go up in the attic anyways so I won't get in your way."

"I don't know why the hell you don't just get the hell out of here," said Lester. "You can leave your little bitch on her own. Sounds like she can take care of herself. Just go through that gate over there and walk off. Town's only about five miles away."

"I can't leave here," he said. "My body's buried somewhere out near where the girl is. I'm tied to that body. I know I keep asking you this but please, can you move my body somewhere, anywhere but here? Then maybe I can go on where I'm supposed to go."

Then the man stopped and closed his eyes and leaned his head back. His face looked like he was fighting something inside himself. "I'm sorry, Lester, I have to go back in the house now. My little girl is calling me."

Chapter 5

For two days, June tossed and turned in her bed. For two days, she didn't sleep, didn't eat, didn't get out of the bed. Every time she started to nod off, her legs started twitching so bad the bed shook violently.

She used the trash can for all her bodily functions. Her father did bring up the ginger ale and—wonder of wonders—he actually did finish cleaning up her floor and took her trash can down to empty and clean it when it got too full.

"No more'n I had to do for your mother," he said. But he didn't stay much to comfort her which was probably a blessing.

The weirdest part for Junie was the flashback to her childhood. While she lay there, shivering and feeling her mind go in and out of crazy, she thought she felt and heard her imaginary friend from childhood sitting next to her, stroking her forehead, and saying "It's gonna be alright Junie, It's gonna pass and then you're gonna be alright again. Everything's going to be alright." June hadn't thought about Mari since the day she left home at sixteen.

On the third day, the shaking and the mind sickness finally started letting up and she was able to sleep for two more days and nights. After that, she still felt like crap, headachy, lethargic, and depressed. She wanted a new fix more than anything, but she knew she didn't have enough money and she didn't know where to get shit in this crap town anyway.

But at least she was able to crawl out of bed and go downstairs.

Food was a revelation to her. She hadn't eaten anything but junk food and alcohol in a very long time. But now, with the drugs out of her system, real food actually tasted pretty good, even the crap her father kept around.

He watched her eat for a long time before he finally said. "Girl, you gonna eat me out of house and home. Shit, every other junkie I know gets skinny. You're the only one I ever seen who got even fatter."

June closed her eyes for a moment to hold back the tears—more pissed at herself for almost crying than at him for his words.

That night, when she went back up to her room, she took a look in the mirror that stood in the corner and studied at her haggard, junkie face, crooked and drug-stained teeth and her bloated body. She threw her spare blanket over the mirror to hide the reflection.

Lying in bed, June let the exhaustion spread over her. Though the dope-sickness was easing a bit, she still felt sickly. It had been a long day, a long week, a long month. The bastard boyfriend had betrayed her, but that wasn't a big surprise. She always figured he would screw her over someday. The cops were after her again and that wasn't much of a surprise either. She didn't have a lot of choices for making money and most of them were against the law.

Seventeen years ago, she vowed she would never come back here. But then, she was younger, she had a body men would pay to rent, and she didn't have a drug problem. She could get and take anything she wanted without the shakes and sickness she got now every time her supply was cut off.

Staring up at the ceiling, she watched the dust motes drift in the moonlight. She lay there for a long time, unable to close her eyes or unclench her hands. But she must have fallen asleep because she felt the little girl take her hand, unclench the claw, and put her little head on June's chest.

"I'm so glad you came back, Junie, I missed you for such a long time," the little girl said in June's dream.

Chapter 6

On the morning she finally came downstairs, Lester Bailey was pouring himself a shot for breakfast.

"Want some," he said, pushing the bottle towards her.

June just shook her head and poured herself a bowl of Cheerios. She went to the fridge to get some milk but there wasn't any behind all the beer. After she took a closer look at the cereal, she dumped that out too. At least he had coffee and a working coffeepot.

"You gonna live here, you cain't throw away good food like that," he snapped.

"Poppa, it had green fuzz growin' on it."

"Well, you're a grown woman now, if you're gonna stay here, you gotta earn your keep."

"How 'bout I start by cleanin' this pig sty up."

Lester just looked over his glass at her and took a couple of sips. "Alright. I'm gonna go hunting. You want boomer or rabbit?"

"Can you get some milk and cereal from the grocery?" she asked.

"You got any money?" he spat back at her, "'cause I don't. The sonofabitch at the feed store fired me and the government check don't go far."

"I got some money, a little bit. I can go to the store for milk and some other stuff when you git back."

After his old truck rumbled and backfired down the long driveway, June started in on what she could only think of a monstrous task. Just starting with the living room, she picked up three paper bags full of trash, old papers, used bottles, cigarette butts and a few sticky things she didn't care to identify. There were dirty plates underneath piles of fast-food wrappers that must have been sitting there for months.

Opening up all the windows did help clear the staleness in the air a bit. She gathered the dishes into the kitchen and washed them in all the lukewarm water she could coax out of the faucet. She was surprised to see he actually did have dish soap and a sponge, neither of which looked particularly well-used.

Mostly, this squalor didn't really bother her much. She and the bastard hadn't lived much better in the squat they slept in for the last few months. But somehow, taking care of the old man seemed like the right thing to do, if only to rub his nose in the idea that she had somehow escaped his life and lived a better one. She didn't believe it herself but maybe he would.

Then she went upstairs to the second floor. Her Momma's sick room was just the way it was when she left seventeen years ago except for seventeen years of new dust and rot. Nothing had been moved, nothing had been cleaned, in the nearly twenty-five years since her mother died. This didn't surprise her much either. Her father never went into that room after her mother went to the hospital.

The bathroom was a mess, with half-cleaned piss and puke on the floor and walls, pretty much the same as she remembered it. But for the first time in her own life, she got down on her hands and knees and cleaned it until it didn't stink. She wouldn't say it was clean but it was a hell of a lot better than it had been.

It was his room that really puzzled her though. It was obviously used and less decayed than the other rooms though calling it clean or tidy would be a long stretch. It was the master bedroom of the house and still had a king-size bed. When she lived here before, he always slept on the far side from the door but now both sides were mussed. Who the hell was sleeping here with him?

After Lester got back with his catch, she took the truck and made the trip down to the Piggly Wiggly. It felt surreal going back in there again—nothing had really changed except that a couple of the girls she had gone to high school with were now the women at the cash registers and the boys from school were now the men stocking shelves. Fortunately, nobody seemed to recognize her. It took most of her sparse remaining cash to buy milk, cereal, rice, some apples and a few other staples like coffee, sugar and cigarettes.

She had to hand it to her father, he always came home with game. Between freshly butchered rabbit, some rice, and a few shots of her Poppa's whiskey, she finally had something in her stomach that seemed to ease the lingering withdrawal a little bit.

They didn't talk much, he watched his TV shows during dinner then they went out on the porch to smoke in silence for a while before she climbed back into her attic.

When she got there, Mari was sitting on the edge of her bed, her legs dangling over and swinging back and forth.

"Hi Mari," June said. "I guess I didn't expect to see you here again."

"Why not?" asked the little girl, cocking her head in a coquettish way,

"I guess 'cause I thought you were my imagination."

Mari laughed at that. "Where'd you get a silly ideal like that? We've been playing together since you were a little girl."

"I dunno," said June, "I guess when I went away and you weren't there, I figured you couldn't possibly be real, and I must have imagined you to escape my Poppa for a while."

"Sweet Junie," said the little girl, "I've always been here for you and you were always here for me."

June took a long look at the girl, drinking in the visage of her old friend. Mari still looked the same as she had seventeen years ago. She looked maybe about twelve years old with mouse brown, unevenly cut hair, a long face halfway between angelic and homely, and beautiful brown doe eyes. She was wearing the same knee-length frayed dark blue jumper with ripped pockets that June had always seen her in.

The little girl smiled at her. "I don't think you know how much you help me, Junie. Anytime you want to come back home, I'll be waiting for you here. I miss you when you're gone."

Why don't you come back to Nashville with me? I can take care of you. I'll even like go straight and treat you like a little princess. We can be together all the time. We'll get an apartment together."

The girl smiled back, but sadly.

"You know I can't leave here. I gotta take care of my Daddy." Suddenly, June thought, her smile looked just a little bit feral.

June thought back on all the midnight talks the girls used to have. Mari's Daddy had been as cruel and nasty as her own Poppa. "Your daddy's here too?" she asked.

"Yep, he lives with your Daddy now. I can't leave him alone, he needs me." Mari said, looking down at her hands.

"Does he sleep in my Poppa's room now with him?" asked June.

"We don't really sleep but he keeps your Poppa company sometimes at night. They like to talk all the time."

"What do they talk about?"

"They talk about how all the women in their lives screwed everything up for them. How they would be so much better off if they never married or had kids. They just like to feel sorry for themselves."

"They used to take long walks out around the farm, but I won't let Daddy do that anymore" said Mari, "not since you came back. I keep him in the house now. A lot of times they go down to the room."

"In the basement?" asked June, stunned.

Mari nodded her head, June stared at her in disbelief. "Why would they stay in the room?"

"It used to be my Daddy's favorite room."

June thought about that for a long time. "Anytime I want to imagine what Hell is like, I think of the room."

Mari nodded gravely. "Me too, but for my Daddy and your Poppa, I think it was their happy place."

"That's a horrible thought," said June.

After a long time holding each other for comfort against the memories of their long dead past, June finally fell asleep.

Chapter 7

In the morning, June woke up to Mari shouting at her and shaking her.

"Junie, we gotta go downstairs to the room."

"I don't wanna go there," said June, still half asleep.

"Junie, we gotta go down there now and take your suitcase."

"I don't ever wanna go down there again," said June, trying to wave the girl away.

"It's the cops, Junie, the cops are coming up the road. If you stay up here, they're gonna find you. If we go to the room, they'll never find us."

Junie grabbed her rolling case and followed the girl down to the second floor. Junie found her father alone on his bed.

"Poppa," she said, shaking him now. "It's the cops. They're coming. I'm gonna go down into the basement room."

"Oh fuck," he said, "somebody must have recognized you at the Piggly Wiggly. I'll go take care of them."

June and Mari continued down into the back of the family room. June lifted the rug and the trap door and climbed down the rickety steps. June felt the same terror in the pit of her stomach that she always felt when Poppa dragged her down here as a child.

The steps led into a short, dirt-wall tunnel with one electric bulb hanging from a loose wire. The wires continued down the tunnel and disappeared just above a wooden door which opened into a crudely finished room with a wood plank floor, wall-board walls and a completely unfinished ceiling. One more bare bulb hung from the cord running across the ceiling.

The room was just the way she remembered it, smelling musty and vaguely like sour human sweat. It was a small, claustrophobic room, maybe ten feet by eight feet. The air was cloyingly still. It took every ounce of her strength to walk in this room and close the door behind her.

The big heavy metal bed still stood against the back wall covered with a stained mattress but with its handcuffs hanging loose.

June and Mari sat down on the bed. June placed herself right in the middle, but Mari sat on the very edge of the metal frame. The girl was giggling.

"What are you laughin' at girl?" Asked June.

"You're sittin' right in the middle of my Daddy, and I don't think he likes it very much."

From upstairs, they could hear a pounding on the door. "Lester, I know you're in there," a man shouted, "It's Deputy Hodges. Open your damn door."

"You got a warrant?"

"Yeah, actually, this time we do, we're here to talk to June Bailey. Open this door or we're gonna kick it down again."

"I'm comin', I'm comin'."

They heard the door open and the sound of booted feet tromping in. "I got a warrant for June Bailey's arrest here, Lester. Best you tell us where she is so nothin' bad happens to you or her."

"I ain't seen her in fifteen years, the little whore went up to Nashville."

"She was at the Piggly Wiggly yesterday, drivin' your truck."

"She's a junkie, I wouldn't let her near my truck."

The deputy laughed at that. "You're a fuckin' drunk, Lester. How many times we picked you up and driven you home this year already? She couldn't be any worse than you."

"My, my, Lester," said a woman's voice, "looks like you did a lot of cleaning since I was here a couple weeks ago."

"I got sick of livin' in a pig sty."

"Shit Lester, I don't think you ever washed a dish in your life," she said.

"Never too old to start," he replied sulkily.

"We got an arrest warrant, Lester, and we're not leavin' here without your junkie daughter."

This was followed by the sounds of boots tromping upstairs and doors being opened and cops calling her name over and over. They went in and out of the front and back doors, probably searching the shed and the old decrepit barn too.

June was sweating profusely. She kept watching the trap door but it never opened. After what seemed like an eternity, she finally heard them leave with the male deputy pushing Lester against the wall, saying he was gonna keep an eye on him.

Junie breathed a sigh of relief and Mari looked up at her brightly. "You know, it was my Daddy who built this room."

That got June's attention."I didn't know that," she said. "Did he build it for you?"

"No, my parents were protestors, my Mommy said. They were fighting the government to get us out of a big, awful war. My Daddy built the room so they could hide from the FBI when they came." She paused a moment, "but I don't think they ever came. But that's why the room is impossible to find if you don't know it's there. They used to keep cans of food and a wind-up radio down there. Mommy said they were "flower children," that's how I got my name."

"I thought Mari came from the Bible."

"My name is Marigold Poppy, like the flowers, and my Mommy was Chrysanthemum but everybody called her Chris and my Daddy was Blu Wolf, he wasn't named after a flower."

"So your Daddy didn't build the room to punish you. That's what my Poppa used it for," said June.

"When the Government never came to arrest them, I think my Mommy forgot about the room, but my Daddy didn't. He liked to bring me down here too, just like your Poppa. I think my Daddy may have told your Poppa about the room.

"My Daddy took me down here to do things he said Mommy must never know about. He said it was 'free love', but that Mommy didn't understand how important 'free love' was. He used to give me some of their drugs to make me enjoy it more, he said, but it didn't work. I hated the room just like you did."

After a moment, Mari added "But your Poppa is the one who put handcuffs on the bed. My Daddy never did that."

Chapter 8

When June finally came back up the rickety staircase it was like coming up for air after nearly drowning. It was already well into mid-morning.

Lester was waiting for her. He had made her a cup of coffee, something she didn't remember him ever doing for anybody before.

"Hey Junebug, I just saved your ass so I'm gonna need your help today," he said.

"You want me to do some more cleaning?'," she asked suspiciously. Lester was not usually a man for anything but giving orders to his daughter.

"Naw, you know where that little girl is buried out back?"

"Sure Poppa."

"I want to dig up the grave next to her."

"There ain't but only one grave out there, Poppa."

"There is someone else buried out there. I don't know which side of the girl he's on but he was buried in an unmarked grave somewhere next to her."

"What?" asked June. "Why do you want to dig up someone's grave, that's sacrilegious, ain't it?"

"I think he needs our help."

June laughed at him. "You're talking about Blu Wolf, right?"

Lester looked up at her in surprise. "You know about him?" he asked. "He said I was the only one he ever talked to."

"No Poppa, I never talked to him but I know his little girl. His daughter is here too. She helped me through all the shit you put me through when I was little."

Lester's face clouded over into that look she had always feared. June took a small step back from him.

"What the fuck are you talking about, what 'shit' did I put you through?"

"Hell, Poppa, it's all done and gone. No need to fight about it now. Why do you want to dig this sorry bastard up?"

Lester looked down at his hands again. "Cuz he's stuck here. He says as long as his body is in this grave, he cain't leave the house. If I can dig up his bones and move him somewhere else, he can go on to the next life or somethin'."

"I'll make you a deal, Poppa. I'll help you dig him up and move him if you help me dig up the little girl. Maybe then I can take her back with me to Nashville."

"You want to take a little girl ghost back to Nashville with you? Damn, Junebug, you're still a sick little shit."

"I love you too, Daddy," she said, turning to go out to the shed to get some shovels.

Chapter 9

It was a hot Tennessee day and neither father nor daughter was in particularly good shape for the difficult task of un-digging graves. Both had to stop and rest frequently, smoke a cigarette or go into the nearby trees and pee.

The difficulty of their task was made much worse because, while the girl's grave was marked with a handmade painted cross and a few porcelain saints, it wasn't clear where the man was buried. They first dug a deep trench on the left side of her grave. It took them what seemed like hours to dig down several feet.

When that yielded nothing, they dug another trench on the right side. Here, pretty close to the surface, they found a metal belt buckle, a rotted shoe, one gold tooth where the head ought to have been and a small round white stone which Junie declared looked like a kneecap.

Lester had brought a big wooden box lined with cloth to carry away the body and he put these relics gently into it and closed the lid.

"That's a sorry lot of body pieces," June said, lighting another cigarette. "Don't think movin' his kneecap is gonna free his spirit to go to hell."

Lester just glared at her. "I cain't dig no more, if you still want the little girl's body, we gotta do that tomorrow."

June nodded her head. She was near to exhaustion herself though her Poppa had definitely taken the worst of it. He couldn't even stand straight. "Let me carry that for you Poppa," she said, taking the box from him and handing him her shovel.

Silently, they walked back to the house.

Up in June's room, she found Mari sitting on the edge of the bed, laughing.

June smiled back at her. "What are you laughing about now, girl?"

"I told my daddy that he had to stay here because his body was buried outside. I told him he had to find somebody to move it so he could move on."

June looked at Mari more closely. "But that's not true?" she asked.

"His body was carried away by coyotes. My Mommy didn't bury him very deep."

"Was that his kneecap we found out there?"

Mari shrugged. "Maybe, I didn't watch his body too closely. But I told him that to make him go crazy trying to get your Daddy to dig him up."

Despite her own painful exhaustion, June found herself smiling at Mari's bizarre little joke. "So why did your Mommy bury your Daddy out behind the barn?"

"Cuz my Daddy killed me, and Mommy finally figured out what he was doing to me. He gave me too much drugs and I couldn't breathe anymore and he carried me upstairs and told my Mommy that it was an accident but she didn't believe him.

"She went and got a gun from their bedroom, and she killed him."

"Did you see her shoot him?" asked June.

"Yep, I was already standing there outside my body watching this, but my Mommy couldn't see me or hear me no matter how much I cried.

"Even though he died the same day I did, it was like a month before my Daddy came back so he didn't see what Mommy did with his body or when the dogs came to dig him up.

"Mommy left a few days later cuz she didn't know I was still here. She came back though, a few years ago, after she died too. She was much older, but she came back to say she still loved me and that I had a brother and sister in Chicago. When she saw how I had to stay here to take care of Daddy, she kissed me on my head and said she had to go but someday we would be together again."

"I'm so sorry Mari," said June, not knowing what to do to comfort the girl or if she even needed it. Mari looked back at her with that feral smile back on her face. "It's okay Junie. I like taking care of my Daddy now."

"You don't still have to do free love with him anymore do you?"

"Nope, and now he has to do the things I tell him to do."

"How do you do that?" asked June.

"I think things at him and now he has to do what I think at him. It's like my mind is stronger than his. It took a long time to learn how much I can control him—It's like using his own needs and wants against him."

Chapter 10

When June came downstairs again, Lester was sitting at the kitchen table, holding his head in his hands. He didn't look up when she came in.

June pulled out a couple of frozen dinners which didn't look too far out of date and cooked them in the oven. The microwave probably hadn't worked for years.

Lester grabbed a bottle of whiskey and started in drinking straight from the bottle. June knew from long experience that this was never a good sign.

She ate her dinner but he only toyed with his, taking a few bites then mixing up the various sections of food and continuing with his whiskey.

After a very long silence, he slammed the bottle onto the table and growled at her. "What the hell do you mean all the 'shit' I put you through."

June looked at the sorry-ass scrawny little man who used to terrify her and this time she answered.

"You mean like locking me in the room every time you got drunk and got pissed at me?"

"You were a fucking ornery-ass little bitch, I tried to teach you manners. I tried bein' nice but even as a little girl you fought me every step of the way."

A huge guffaw burst from June, almost making her choke on her beer. "You! Teaching me manners? You're the biggest fuckin' nastiest piece of shit I know. Learnin' manners from you would be like learnin' manners from a rabid raccoon!"

"You fuckin' little slut," he spat back at her. "I'm still yer daddy an' you cain't talk to me like that. Not while yer stayin' in my house."

A lot of emotions swam across her face. Fury for the years of abuse, hatred of this nasty, ugly, sick, waste-of-skin. But he had a point, she had nowhere else to go now. With her lips trembling against the lie, she said "Sorry Poppa" and turned away to try to keep her fury in check.

"I never did nothin' to you that you didn't ask for or deserve. You were an ornery little cuss and a little slut. When your Momma died of the cancer, you threw yourself at me."

June whirled around back at Lester, taking a step towards him, making him teeter back. "I was eight-fucking-years old, and I hated it every time you raped me."

"I didn't rape you. You made yourself all pretty and cute and climbed in my bed next to me."

"My Momma just died, and I needed my Poppa to comfort me. I wasn't tryin' to get you aroused, for Christ's sake. Besides, you used to play grab ass with me before Momma even got sick."

"You came on to me. I'm a guy, when a pretty girl comes on to me, that's how we act, dammit."

June stood looking at him, not knowing how to answer such shit. Tears were streaming down her face and her fingers were clenched into claws just like they did when she was a child.

"I don't know what the hell happened to you, you fat ugly pig," he continued. "When you was little, you was a pretty little thing."

June advanced on him, only half-noticing in the back of her mind that this time, he moved back instead of her.

"You raped your own goddamn daughter every chance you got. You came into my room and you fuckin' raped a little girl over and over and over. You are a fuckin' pervert."

"You don't call your daddy names like that, you little slut" he said and he slapped her as hard as he could.

Yeah, June realized, it stung. But suddenly she knew the measure of this man and she knew she wasn't a scared little girl anymore. She pulled back then swung a fist at his face.

Lester was old and unsteady from his years of drinking. She outweighed him by at least 50 pounds and for once, she was mad, and he was scared. Her punch literally lifted him off his feet and sent him flying into the wall behind him. He grunted as he hit the wall and slid down it, leaving a small stripe of blood from where his scalp had split.

Chapter 11

Mari and Junie sat in the attic room, looking out the window at the moonlit path to the house.

"Why can't you leave here Mari?" asked June. "Is it like a wall when you get to the gate?

Mari shook her head. "It's not a wall, it's just like I don't have the will to go any further. I don't want to and I can't make myself want to."

"If I took your body with me, could you come with me?" asked June, already suspecting the answer.

"No, Junie, I want to stay here. I want to stay here with my Daddy."

"Why do you want to stay here with him? He hurt you. He made you do things no little girl should ever have to do"

Mari nodded her head slightly in thought. "Yeah, but now I can make him do things."

June looked at her sharply. "Do you make him do those kinds of things?"

"No," said the little girl, "I just control where he goes."

"Can anyone but me see you and talk to you?" asked June

"There's been like five families that have lived here since I died, and they all had kids. All the kids could see me but none of the adults."

"Did they believe in you or were they all like me and thought you were imaginary?" asked June.

Mari smiled gently at her and touched her arm. June thought it was like feather brushing her skin. "You really believed in me, at least while you were here. And they all did, in some way or another. Some knew I was a ghost, one little girl thought I was a fairy. Some of them told their parents and none of them believed them except for the one man and his wife. That little boy was named Joey and his sister was a three-year-old named Adele.

"I got to sit with all the kids when their parents read to them, and we'd play in the attic and sometimes when we were outside. My favorite game was always hide and seek."

"Why," asked June, "because you knew all the good hiding places?"

"No, silly," She said and she disappeared and June could hear her giggle. Then she popped back, laughing even more.

"Did all the adults see your Daddy?" asked June.

"No," said Mari, "only two of them. One was Joey's dad and the other was your Poppa.

"Joey's dad got really scared listening to my Daddy, and one day he told his wife they had to get out of here and they moved away the very next day.

"I think Daddy could only talk to people who understood what he wants, and Joey's dad maybe felt the same things but couldn't really go through with it.

"But your Poppa and my Daddy used to take long walks around the house and into the woods as far as Blu could go. Your Poppa used to drink out there, away from your Momma and they would talk and talk about us.

"I don't think your Poppa really believed my Daddy was real though, not for a long, long time. He thought he was a hallucination from drinking but that didn't stop him from talking about you and your Momma to Blu. He used to say terrible things and Blu would keep encouraging him."

There were silent for a very long time until June asked, "What's it like being dead?"

"It's a relief, really. I don't need things the same way I did before.

"When you're alive, you need things. You need food, you need water, you need to go to the bathroom. When I was alive, I went through what you did when you first got here. My Daddy had given me drugs so many times, I felt like I needed them.

"When I died, all of those needs went away. I could play, I could walk anywhere I want, I could come and go from existence as I wanted.

"But when my Daddy came back, he still needed his drugs and he still wanted to free love me but even at the beginning, I was stronger than he was.

"I only wanted one thing, to make him feel the pain he put me through when I was alive.

"I think when you're dead, you only need the most important things you needed when you were alive.

"He couldn't touch me, and I couldn't touch him anymore but I could use my desire and his needs to make him cry, to make him plead.

"And since you've come back, I want more than ever to hurt him because he made your Poppa hurt you. But he made me too, like your Poppa made you.

"When you first got here, I started making my Daddy stay in the house. Then I made it so he has to stay in the room, like they did to you and me. Now I made it so he has to stay in the bed, and you made it so your Poppa has to stay in the bed too. I think that is beautiful."

"Could I do that to my Poppa if we were dead?"

"I don't know," said Mari, "but I want you to stay with me and maybe your Poppa will stay too."

Chapter 12

It was probably an hour or two later when Lester regained consciousness. He opened his eyes and was nearly sick. He lay there looking up into the one single bulb hanging from the ceiling. He was back in his room—"the" room—lying on "the" bed. When he tried to shift to ease the headache, he realized he was cuffed to the bed with the handcuffs he used to use on Junie when she wouldn't do what he wanted. Even worse, he was sharing the space with the ghost of his friend Blu Wolf. He could feel him flowing through him.

He tried to talk to his friend, but Blu didn't answer. Instead, he could feel the dead man like a liquid mist flowing in his ears, out his nose, through his stomach. It was like a smell, he couldn't smell, a touch he couldn't feel, a sound he couldn't hear, all enveloping him in swirling eddies.

He lay there for hours. His head was bursting with pain from the concussion, and his arms were stiff and sore from being stretched out. He tried to pull on the cuffs but they just cut into his wrists. He hadn't had a cigarette or a drink for hours and he was really feeling the lack of both.

When June finally did come down, she offered him a drink of water and a few drags on her cigarette.

"Remember when you used to lock me down here" she asked. You never brought me water. You made me lie here for hours or sometimes even days with no food and no water."

"You were a little girl. You could handle it. I'm an old man. Please, for Christ's sake, let me go. I cain't be like this for very long or I'm gonna die."

"Ohhhh," she said with teasing in her voice, "we wouldn't want that now, would we?"

"Please, Junie, please," he said plaintively.

"I remember saying 'please, Poppa, please,'" she said.

Lester started crying.

Chapter 13

He lay there in his own mess. His arms were on fire from the way he was cuffed. The bulb was off but he felt like he could see things anyway. It was like watching a movie of his life. When he was young, he swore he would never be like his own son-of-a-bitch old man. When he was young, he could handle drinking. He could see when he was young and in love, he could see June's mom when they were both nineteen. He had a job, they had a house, they had a beautiful little girl. And he could see how beautiful this little girl was and how his wife stopped wanting him and how good all that whiskey tasted.

When the bulb turned on, it was like the world exploding in his mind. He hadn't even heard her when she came down into the room.

"Junie," he said, surprised at how dry and raspy his own voice was. "Are you gonna let me go, baby?"

"I don't know yet what I'm gonna do. Me and Mari are talking about it."

"That little girl," he croaked, "you gotta be an example for her. If you let me go, maybe she will let her daddy go. You gotta show her what true Christian forgiveness is for your soul and her soul too."

June laughed at him. "She's not a little girl anymore. She looks like one, but she's lived here for nearly fifty years now."

June sat down on the edge of the bed and gave him water and some food and some tobacco. Then she pulled his soiled pants off and washed him and gave him clean underwear, throwing the pants in the corner. He wanted to kick her but found his legs were like pieces of lead that he could barely lift.

"Baby, can you get me some whiskey, please?" he said.

"Already thought of that" she said, smiling at him. She pulled a flask out of her pocket and winked at him. "Got it right here." Then she started drinking it herself.

"Oh Junie, please, just a mouthful?" he asked, ashamed of the whine in his voice. She relented and poured from the flask into his mouth.

"I was just lookin' at that picture on the wall in the living room of you and me and Momma."

"It's a nice picture, ain't it?" he said. "You and your Momma look so pretty there."

"Yeah, we look like such a happy family."

"We were, baby, we were. Until your Momma got sick, we were a happy family. Don't you remember the good times before your Momma got sick?"

"Yeah, Poppa, I was thinkin' of all the good times when you was drunk and yelling at us. I remember when I couldn't go to school for three days cuz you gave me a big black eye. I remember Momma holding me when I was crying but she never really did anything to stop you. Hell, sometimes she would just start screaming her head off at me too."

"Oh, God, Junie, surely you must remember something happier than that."

"I just burned that picture in the fireplace, Poppa."

He felt tears running down the sides of his face because he couldn't remember any better times himself.

"Hey Poppa, I remembered another really happy time. Remember when I was six and you burned me with your cigarette?" June lit herself another one.

"It was an accident, you walked into it."

"The hell it was, you grabbed me and held me down and yelled at me. I don't even remember what for now."

"I'm really sorry, baby" he said, watching the glowing tip of hers as she took a long drag then dropped her hand to her knee.

"Please Junie, don't do that, let me go, please. I promise I will never hurt you again. I promise I won't ever tell anyone you did this. Fuck, I'll even give you my truck. Just, please let me go."

"I guess I'm gonna think about it," she said, Then, with a quick jab, she put her cigarette out on his crotch and left him there writhing and sobbing.

Chapter 14

Two days more, she visited him once a day, at least he thought it was once a day. Time was starting to blur for him.

She fed him and cleaned him but didn't do anything for his wound which was starting to puss up. He felt himself getting weaker and more brain-fogged. He begged and pleaded but she just kept saying she was thinking about it.

On what he guessed was the third day, she came down the stairs carrying a big pitcher.

"Please Junie, I need a doctor, I need some medicine. It hurts so bad." He was whining again but he couldn't stop himself.

"Okay, here's some medicine" she said, grabbing the pitcher and pouring liquid on his wound. He screamed in agony and even more in fear when he realized it was gasoline and it burned the suppurating wound into unbearable pain.

"Oh, poor baby. Let me make you feel good like you wanted me to before." And she grabbed his member and started rubbing. Much to his dismay and horrible pain, he felt it stiffen. The wound screamed and so did he.

"No June, please God, no. Let's talk about this. Maybe I can help you. Let's go upstairs, please, no." But June sloshed gas all around the little room, soaked his mattress and soaked him.

"Want a cigarette, Poppa, want one last cigarette before we go?"

He shook his head back and forth violently, feeling gasoline spray out of his hair.

"Well, I'm going to have one and she sat down on his stomach, driving all the air out of his lungs and lit one up and blew smoke up toward the ceiling. His eyes watched the glowing tip go up and down and up and down again.

"Mari and I have decided we're going to destroy this horrible house. Maybe you and me are going to join her and her Daddy and be a happy family for ever and ever or maybe we'll put an end to this little corner of Hell and we'll all be set free. Either way is okay by me."

Then she casually flicked her cigarette into the puddle of gasoline on the floor and closed her eyes.

Lester screamed as the flames followed the gasoline around her and lit him up. She sat there calmly and quietly inside her circle of flame until it caught her too and put an end to all her pain and desires.

Pea Soup

I'm not a big a man — not a tough or scary guy — so new roommate day is always an anxious day. My last cellmate, Peter, was a putz, but at least I wasn't scared of him. He was an obnoxious little shit who thought Taylor Swift was sending him love notes in her lyrics. Yeah, sure, he kept singing the special lyrics under his breath and talked about her all the time, but he was never going to rape me or shiv me because I looked at him wrong.

But I couldn't help worrying all day who I was going to get this time. Somebody like my first roomie, Elephant? Elephant wasn't such a bad guy except that he took up most of the cell when he stood up and the fucker wanted the top bunk, and every night I watched it sag down until it was three inches above my face.

Or maybe it would be one of those bastards from the Vice Lords or Gangster Disciples from Milwaukee — one of those guys who make you their bitch from the moment they walk in. I guess that was what scared me most.

All day, my thoughts went round and round, thinking of all the worst possible cellmates I might get. I did my shift in the kitchen, walked around the yard at exercise, all the time wondering whether my life was gonna be made hell or, well if not great, maybe at least bearable, for the next few years.

So imagine my joy when 3:45 p.m. came around and in walked Brady Skenendore.

"Brady, man, it is a pleasure to see you again." I was actually sincere when I said this, but he looked at me blankly.

"Do I know you?" he asked, looking into my face.

I laughed. I get this a lot from lawyers and don't take any offense.

"Sure you do, we've been in court twenty or thirty times together but nobody ever paid any attention to me."

He cocked his head and looked at me more carefully. "Holy shit, you're the court reporter, Judge Abbott's court, if I'm not mistaken."

"I'm impressed," I said. "About half the lawyers don't even recognize my face *after* I've told them who I am. Tom Dantoin," I said as I extended my hand.

"Brady Skenendore," he replied, shaking it heartily. "I'm glad to meet you. I had visions of being put in a cell with one of the bastards I defended as a public defender. That thought scares the crap out of me."

"You always did okay with the PD work," I said. "I woulda thought you'd be more worried about being in a cell with one of the Hockers brothers."

Brady narrowed his eyes at me. "Why would you say something like that?"

"No big deal, but I know what you did to them with that will. Old Hockers was a real bastard and his grandsons didn't fall far from the tree. I actually saw one of them when I got sent up to Oakhill for some medical stuff a year or two ago. I don't remember which one was which, though."

"What do you mean, you 'know what I did?' If you're some kind of prison rat…"

I just laughed at him. "I was the court reporter, I got to hear everything every attorney said; I got to look at every piece of evidence. I'm a smart guy and I know the scam you pulled on them. It's that same trick Irene Dempsey used to use all the time in her probate cases, but you were always much better at it. I hear she ended up in Taycheedah for a couple of years and lost her license then she bought a diner in Fond du Lac. So, what are you in for?"

Brady seemed not to like my answer very much but after a moment, he relented and spoke. "They claim I recruited people for Worker's Comp claims who weren't really injured. I'm the victim here, how would I know they were lying to me? They took away my license and gave me five years."

"Oh, you mean like the Cady case and the Debraske case?" I said, regretting it a second later. I always let my mouth run when I shouldn't.

Brady glared at me for a long time. I think he wanted to punch me or something, but thought better of it. I was younger and not so fat as he was and, well, we did have to bunk together for the foreseeable future.

"Yeah," he said, "those two and a few more. They all scammed me though. I had no idea they were lying to me." He started unloading his things and we started divvying up the space. New guy always gets the bottom bunk.

"Okay," he said after the preliminaries were done, "so we both know a lot of folks in *my* profession should be here, but what in the hell is a court reporter doing here?"

"Second Degree Intentional Homicide," I said, "twenty to life."

Brady whistled. "What the hell did you do?"

"Trusted a prosecutor and grabbed the wrong can of peas."

Brady sat down on the bunk and looked straight at me. "Okay, so now you gotta explain that," he said.

"No problem," I said, "I've confessed anyway so I got nothing to hide. You remember Sam, the assistant DA?"

"Sure," Brady said, "I think any guy who ever walked into the Marshallville County Court remembers Sam."

"Yep," I said, "she isn't beautiful, or even particularly well-endowed, but she knows how to use her stuff. She's sure not my type, not usually anyway. She's kind of 'ridden hard and put away wet' as the judge used to say. She works out for two hours every morning then chain smokes and drinks whiskey the rest of the day. But she sure can wrap most guys around her little nicotine-stained fingers.

"Me, I usually go for the brainy type, maybe even a little sexy-nerd type like Grace, judge Abbott's secretary. I always thought that she was really cute. But I was too scared to ask her out."

"Yeah, she's sort of cute," said Brady, pursing his lips thoughtfully, "but Sam is probably more *my* type, I did sleep with her…"

"…during the Zachary case, yeah, we all knew. She really wanted that conviction."

"You bastard," said Brady but without any animosity.

"Well, you weren't exactly subtle." I said, snorting a bit. "Anyway, Sam wasn't my type and I figured I was immune to her wiles. I thought I could see right through her and figured, as a lowly, invisible court reporter, it wouldn't be anything I'd ever have to worry about. She seemed to like lawyers and judges and cops.

"Boy, was I wrong. When Sam wants something, Sam gets it. I think Abbott himself is the only guy she couldn't get into her bed, but he's a true believer.

"And Sam's really, really good. She started working on me a month before the Mancheski brothers' trial. First, she started visiting me in the cafeteria at lunch. She sat down and told me she liked detective novels and we started talking. I turned her on to Ruth Rendell, my favorite, and she got me reading Stuart M. Kaminsky. Then she said she likes puzzles and we did the Sudokus together. I don't know why anybody does those, it's like playing solitaire—something you do when you're bored and need something easy.

"Sam actually had to write down numbers to solve them. Can you believe that?"

"I'm not much of a puzzle guy," said Brady, "I wouldn't know."

"Well, she starts trying to convince me I'm the greatest puzzle guy she's ever met. Then she gets me to take her out to dinner and eventually we end up at her place.

"I knew, I just knew, that it was all wrong when I got to her place. She had all these games and mystery books in her living room. All the games were out of the plastic wrap but there wasn't a banged corner or ripped box among them. Who has Deluxe Scrabble without a ding on the box? There were a bunch of mystery books, and I don't think she ever even bothered to crack the spines, and as far as I know, she reads everything on her iPad.

"But by this time, I wanted it so much to be true that I ignored all the signs. I thought maybe she was so attracted to me, that she was trying to impress me."

"You're a fool, just like the rest of us, eh?"

I smiled and nodded back. "You betcha. So when the trial finally starts, I'm sleeping with Sam every night and lying to the judge. When she talks in court, I get down every word she says. When it's anyone else, my fingers get clumsy because I'm watching her. Fortunately, we'd just introduced tape recorders in the court so I was able to go back every evening and fix up the transcripts.

"I know you're not from Marshallville, but do you know about the Mancheski brothers?"

"Drug dealers or something, right."

"Right, they were big dealers in Madison and wanted to expand out west so they moved into Marshallville. Within a month, they took over all the business at the high school and junior college but they made a really big mistake when they beat the crap out of their major competitor who happened to be the assistant police chief's son.

"Now these two brothers didn't look anything like brothers. I don't know if they were half brothers or one was adopted or what, but one was like 6' 6" and built like a brick wall and the other was 5' 3", wore skinny-rimmed little glasses and looked every inch the accountant. And that's what they were like in real life. The big one, François — Frankie — was the enforcer, the muscle, the front man, the guy you'd go to see to buy or sell. But the little one, Evan, was the brains, the strategist, the guy who controlled all the money.

"The cops were pissed and went after them full force but they couldn't seem to hang trafficking charges on them. They got Frankie on assault charges and eventually got Evan on tax evasion in separate trials. They were able to keep them apart for a long time and by the time Evan's trial rolled around, Frankie was already out on parole. Problem was that Evan hid the money they still had when Frankie was in jail, but the cops got everything from their home, put their old, crooked lawyer in jail, and monitored every conversation. The court ordered that Frankie couldn't visit or write to Evan while Evan was being held for trial.

"The investigator figured they had several million dollars hidden somewhere, probably in cash, but no one knew where. And that's where Sam started working me like a little finger puppet.

"'Tom,' she says to me one night in bed—and mind you — I don't regret that part one little bit — 'Tom,' she says, 'we need your help. I know Evan needs to tell Frankie where the money is. This new lawyer is costing them a fortune and Evan knows he's not going to get out anytime soon. You're the best detective we've got at figuring out these puzzles.'

"'I'm sure he's trying to tell Frankie where the money is. Frankie can't see his brother in jail but he can come to the trial so I think Evan will try to tell him in some kind of code. That's where we need you. Do you think you can figure out when he does this?'

"So every day, I go in and watch. If Judge Abbott knew I was aiding the prosecution, I would have been fired on the spot.

"I've got one advantage I figure. Old Frankie is not the brightest lightbulb in the hallway and Evan knows he's got to be pretty obvious. I listened for anything and everything out of the ordinary. I watched Evan and tried to pay special attention when he tried to catch his brother's eye.

"Finally, I noticed that every time he looked at Frankie, he tapped his pencil or his finger and he tapped out the same rhythm every time *tum-tumtumtumtumtum-tumtumtumtumtumtum-tumtumtum*. I asked Sam if the digits 1-5-6-3 meant anything to her and she got very excited. 1563 Hunters Rest is the address of an old farmhouse they owned just outside of Gratiot. She said the cops had searched it twice and not found anything.

"Evan kept doing that for like three days until I finally saw them looking at each other and Frank was nodding vigorously then raising his hands like this." I demonstrated what Frank had done, raising his hands just a little bit in a sort of hidden query gesture.

"Because of my angle, I couldn't really see what Evan signaled back but it must have been some kind of 'wait' message.

"Evan took the stand in his own defense. Sam said she was shocked he did that, there wasn't any reason he should. She didn't think it mattered since she pretty much had an open and shut case against him. He was going to jail for sure.

"He tried to make excuses for everything Sam questioned him about everything that the cops claimed he did, and most of these excuses sounded pretty lame. But he kept using this weird expression over and over again. I never heard it before, but he kept saying it like it was some kind of normal expression. 'What are you trying to do, pee in a can?' he asked Sam when she cross examined him. Or 'that was nothing, I was just trying to pee in a can.'

"It sounded weird to me, but I didn't understand. Sam and I were sleeping together that night at her place. We're lying in bed when I suddenly sat up and whacked my head on the headboard. She had one of these water beds with lots of shelves. After I stopped swearing, Sam asked me what was up.

"I asked her if there was a kitchen there with canned food."

"'Of course,' she said. 'It was an old farmhouse. We know they owned it but we never found anything illegal there so we had to leave it alone. There was some guy living there. I suppose he worked for the Mancheskis but we couldn't prove it.'

"I asked her if the food in the farmhouse was still there, and she said she supposed it was.

"The money is hidden there in a can of peas.

"She asked me how I knew that, and I looked at her for a minute until she finally said, 'Oh shit' and I saw the light dawn in her eyes.

"'Let's go get it', she said, 'right now.'

"'What about the guy who lives there?' I asked her.

"'Oh, he's gone now, we've been keeping tabs on the place since you broke the code. But we gotta go now. You think Old Frankie boy is going to wait to pick up his money?'

"Okay, let's call Chief Villain, I said, but you got to leave me out of it. If the judge knew I was sleeping with you, he'd kill me — then he'd fire me.'

"She cackled at that, you know, that wicked-witchy cackle she does when she's really happy.

"'You know,' she said, 'they don't know exactly how much money is in there. There might be $5 million, there might just be three. The forensic accountants say they are only sure that about $2 million is missing. If we go there, we can take anything over $2 million for ourselves and you'll never have to type another day in your life. You can write that novel you want to write, and we can make love on the beach anywhere you want to live.'

"I said, 'We can't just go steal money like that' and she reminded me we were stealing from drug dealers. Then she rubbed her breasts against my back, and I started picturing beaches and the stupid part of me took over completely.

"Okay, I said. But how do we get in? She opened her nightstand drawer and handed me a key. Then she reached in again and handed me a pistol. 'Take this, lover,' she said, 'just in case.'

"Stupid part ruled. I put my pants and shirt on, put the gun in my jacket pocket. Sam suggested we drive separately so we could split up later and not be seen together. At 3 a.m., we arrived at the farmhouse just outside of Gratiot. The house was at the end of a long driveway just off Hunters Rest which is some numbered state road so it's not completely off the beaten path.

"She pulled into some trees near the beginning of the driveway, I pulled all the way up the driveway. I looked around to make sure no one was coming up the road, then I went up to the door and used the key and walked down the hall into the kitchen.

"I didn't turn on any lights, just used a flashlight Sam gave me. I went to the kitchen, started pulling out all the cans in the cupboard. I don't know whether it was the Mancheskis or the guy who lived there, but somebody really liked canned peas. There were like twenty-five cans of them — the really big cans, not the little cans most people usually buy. I finally found eight cans that didn't seem to slosh like the others and I put them in my bag and carried them outside to Sam's car.

"She pulled out a can-opener and started opening them up and dumped wads of curled up thousand-dollar bills onto the passenger seat. It was more money than I had ever seen in my life. One of the cans still had peas in it and she threw that one out the window.

"She didn't open the last two cans, she handed them to me and told me to put them back and she would call the cops and let them know to come check. She said if they found money there, they wouldn't suspect we took any of it.

"Still dreaming of beaches and Sam's breasts, I did what she told me. I took the cans back into the kitchen and started trying to put everything back like it was. I heard footsteps behind, and the light came on. I started to say something to Sam and turned around, but it was Frankie Mancheski. He grabbed a huge frying pan from the rack and roared and started coming at me. I shot him three times and ran for the door.

"Then I heard sirens and I figured I better get the hell out of there. I couldn't imagine why they were coming so fast, but I didn't want to find out, so I ran out to Sam's car.

"The fucking bitch was gone. She'd set me up.

"Across the street was my car. I got into my car, and I started driving away as fast as I could go but I didn't get very far. The Lafayette County Deputies are pretty good at stopping runaway Honda Fits. I loved that car too. Did you know that if you wreck your car fleeing the cops, the insurance company doesn't pay?

"Anyway, they arrested me, found the body, matched the bullets to the gun in my pocket. Hell, I even still had two cans of peas in the bag over my shoulder. Turned out to be just about $1.3 million in hundreds and thousands.

"I told them about Sam, but it seems they had phone records that proved she was in her house in Marshallville when she called the cops. I don't know if she rigged it up somehow, had someone call for her on her own phone, or just slept with one of the forensic guys.

"You know, the cops love her and would do anything for her, and not just the ones who she slept with. All the cops love her because she always treats them well in court."

"People saw us together in the cafeteria and she testified that I had approached her and pumped her for information about the Mancheski case. Since I was a member of the court, she said, she didn't think too much about it until after I appeared to go crazy.

"God damn," Brady said, "I knew I liked that girl. Maybe if I hired her, I wouldn't be here."

"Dream on," I replied, "if you hired her, you would have been here years earlier."

It was call to dinner and I told Brady I would show him the way to the cafeteria and explain Jackson's special seating nuances.

As we were walking, Brady said to me, "Yeah, you're probably right about that. She didn't prosecute me in my case because we worked together on several cases but I did see her at the courthouse and she was looking pretty happy and well dressed."

"I bet," I said.

"Nice brand new Jag too," he added. "I'd love to take a ride in that."

"Beats a Fit, I suppose," I said ruefully.

The Severed World
Canto Two in The Lives and Times of Lady Jane

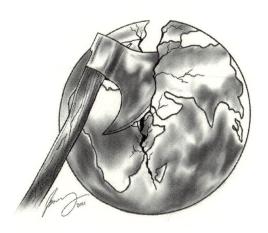

March 1553

By the Blood of Our Savior, Jane thought to herself, *what am I doing?*

This wasn't the first, the second, or even the third time tonight she ran these words through her head. A few hours ago, this escape had seemed an answer to her paralyzing fears. But the quest had not worn well over the long, meandering trek through the woods.

Now she could hear the baying of Lord John's hunting hounds.

"Do you not hear the dogs, sir? If we don't find your ship, we're going to die!"

Ian looked panicked himself but pointed forward and said "I know where we are now, the ship is just through this clearing, over there in that copse of trees. Run! We can make it."

Lady Jane ran with all her might and despite her long dress, she easily kept up with the older man. But she stopped short when she saw they were headed for a tiny shed sitting between two large oaks.

"*This* is your time ship?" Jane asked, spitting out the first word in disgust.

I'm going to die following this warlock, she thought. *If I had become queen, at least I would have had a nice, dignified beheading. Now I'm going to be run down like a wild pig.*

"My lady, we will be safe in there. Remember I promised you wonders…"

"True. Well, this would be a good time for you to deliver." She could hear the dogs just behind them, the clanking of the soldiers' weapons and the hoofbeats of horses.

Ian got near the door of his shed, and did something with that damned box he carried and the door made a hissing sound like a giant snake and slid aside into the wall.

"God's Wounds," she whispered, frozen in horror as she looked inside. Though the shed appeared no bigger than a horse's stall on the outside, the room through the door was much larger. Jane was sure she was about to enter the Hell-Mouth and for a moment she stood paralyzed, tears running down her face.

Then she heard sweet Guildford Dudley's voice, that shy boy who really *did* love her in his own, useless way. "Jane, stop, we will save you from this whoreson," he yelled.

She turned around to see him riding into the far side of the small clearing where he pulled his horse short. His father, Lord John Dudley, came barreling into the clearing behind him and slammed his son's chest with a casual back-fist in passing. The blow knocked the boy off his horse.

"You sodding idiot, this whore will never be a part of *our* family," Lord John shouted as he drew his sword. Behind him, the ten men of his family guard, the men who had been on sentry duty with the hunting party, started running into the clearing.

"Now, you ungrateful harlot, prepare to meet your *precious* God. I should have known better than to trust any of you filthy Tudors." He started forward and Jane felt Ian's hand grab the back of her cloak and pull her roughly into his HellMouth. The door hissed shut just as Lord John hit it with a thunderous clang of his chain mail shirt against the outside. There was no seeming effect on the shed.

Moments later, pounding noises surrounded them, echoing through the strange ship.

She gazed around. It wasn't a huge room, but it was as big as her father's study with a desk and chairs on one end. There was no fireplace, and the ceiling and walls were smooth and flat, almost like they were made from metal or stone. There was the strange door they had come in through and another smaller door on the other side of the room. All over the room were little doors in the walls that must have been cabinets. And strangely, there were what looked like handrails all around the room, even near the ceiling.

She turned around to look at Ian, he was still bent over, holding his knees.

"Sorry about grabbing you like that," he said, still panting a little. "I don't think Lord John had your best interests in mind."

"What are we going to do? They'll stay out there until we have to come out."

Ian straightened. "Why would we ever come out here? Don't you want to visit my time?"

Jane stared at him for a moment, not sure what to make of any of this. Was he insane, or a warlock, or was he what he claimed to be? Only the first two made sense to her, but the seeming sincerity of this crazy old man still made her want to believe the third option, that he was a time traveler who had come from the future to save her from her execution.

"All right," she said, "what happens now?"

Ian smiled at her. "Well, I thought I would have had a little more time to prepare you, but I guess you're going to have to learn a few very strange things very quickly. Please, sit down here," he said, motioning her to one of the chairs at the large desk at one end of the room.

The desk and chairs looked quite odd to her. The desk seemed to be growing out of the wall and the chairs were on posts but looked like thrones with padding behind the head and even the legs.

"Now" he said, "use the harness to buckle yourself in. Put the flat tongue into the slot on the other end." He tried to demonstrate, but when she couldn't seem to follow his instructions, he unbuckled himself and secured her, apologizing for the necessary intimacy, then he sat down again in his own throne.

Running his fingers across a dark area full of small lighted squares, he brought forth more moving paintings that showed on the wall above them. They were like the little one he had shown her at the campfire which had seemingly showed Jane her execution a few months from now, but these were much bigger.

Lady Jane gasped. She could see in these paintings Lord John and his soldiers around the outside of the shed, banging the walls with their fists and their swords. The painters, or what had he called them? — *cameras?* — seemed to look down from the roof of the shed, clearly showing the walls and the men surrounding them on all sides. Because of the wide angle, she could also see that Guildford still sat splayed on the ground in the distance, holding his head in his hands.

Ian spoke to these screens and the people in the paintings looked around as if they could hear him. "Lord John, please move your soldiers away from my ship. This could get painful for them."

Jane could hear John growl back a response but couldn't understand what he said.

Ian tapped some more on the raised squares and Jane saw what looked like little bolts of blue lightning come from the shed and climb up their bodies and around the metal of their swords. Men yelped and shouted, some fell down, others dropped their swords and ran backwards away from the shed. Only Lord John, his face still contorted in rage, kept pounding the door with his pommel.

"Lord John, please, I don't want to hurt anyone," said Ian. More of the blue lightening, bigger and brighter now, came from the ship, then even Lord John had to back away.

Ian looked at her. "My lady, hold on, we are going to fly to get away from these sword-swinging idiots."

"We are going to…" was all of the question she got out before there was shaking and a loud rumbling. She could see in the paintings what looked like steam or smoke or dust coming from below the shed.

She saw Lord John and his soldiers crawling backward to escape the smoke and heat. Then more astonishingly, she watched as this shed seemed to levitate. Ian truly *was* a very powerful warlock. Maybe she was about to die and go to hell but it certainly wasn't going to be boring. She knew it was a sin, but she found that thought comforted her more than it repulsed her.

"Hold on tight," said Ian. In a few moments, we are going to have to move very fast. It's going to push you back in your seat very hard, but there is no danger. It may be very uncomfortable and it will scare you, but you will be safe." He looked at her. She thought he was trying to smile reassuringly but it didn't work.

After a moment, he said "Then it's going to get really weird…"

Jane yelped as her chair suddenly tipped back. There seemed to be a handgrip just right for grabbing in terror. She found herself staring at the ceiling which was now also covered with the moving paintings, some still showing the sides of the shed and looking down over the treetops. They seemed to be rotating gently as they hovered. Another painting showed the clouds above them in the early morning sky.

For a moment more, they continued to hover. Then there was another roar and she was pushed back hard against the thick padding of the chair. She let out a low moan of surprise and anguish as she felt herself pushed back harder and harder and watched in the paintings as they seemed to zoom towards the clouds and leave the ground behind. Her bladder loosened and tears filled her eyes then dribbled down her temples towards the back of her head. Adventure, she decided, is not always dignified.

She tried talking but couldn't draw enough breath to shout over the roar. Jane tried closing her eyes but quickly opened them again to watch the lovely and terrifying images on the ceiling.

She had learned in her lessons that the world was a globe and now she saw an actual curve on the horizon. One painting showed the tops of the clouds now quickly receding from her and she realized she was looking *down* on the landscape of Heaven.

After a few moments, both the roar and the pressure started to ease and Jane found herself gasping for air and still clutching wildly at the handgrips but at least the pounding of her heart started to subside. She looked over at Ian and saw he was watching her closely with what looked like empathy.

"I am so, so sorry. I had planned to warn you about what was going to happen but I needed to get them away from the sides of the ship. It is pretty tough, this ship, but there are some delicate and very necessary things out there that I didn't want them to damage.

"So," he continued, "you know the world is a globe, like the moon, right?"

Jane nodded, wondering where he was going with this.

"The very first part of our trip is that we have to get so high above the Earth that we are orbiting it, that is, we are going around it like the moon goes around the Earth."

Jane looked back at the paintings on the ceiling and saw that their ship was continuing to climb higher and higher and the curve of the horizon was becoming more prominent as they rose.

"So the next thing I need to prepare you for is weightlessness. As we get high enough, we get so far from the Earth that we weigh less and less, and you will begin to float through this ship. It is a little disconcerting at first, but you will get used to it…"

His words didn't help as much as he probably intended. Jane looked at the paintings on the ceiling and started to see the curve of the Earth arced against blackness, then she saw the earth as a globe floating in blackness. She felt herself moving up against the harness when she pushed back on the throne with even the lightest touch. The roaring was gone, replaced with a steady, quiet vibration.

Ian came around to her, floating through the room like a ghost or an angel might, and he released her from the harness. He told her to try to hang on to the chairs and table or to the rungs built into the wall, especially while she was first getting used to it. He said that after a while, it actually becomes kind of fun.

Jane pushed away from the throne and found herself floating. She grasped desperately for the arms of her chair and missed and felt like she was falling up. It was a good thing Jane had not eaten much in the last few days. Everything still remaining in her stomach came out and floated in little balls in front of her.

Ian laughed gently. "That happens to a lot of people their first time," he said as he cleaned it up with a net.

She had to smile to herself. Adventure, it seems, takes away *all* your dignity.

Transit 1553 to 2085: Jane's Diary, Day-Cycle 1

The warlock has given me a magical pen that does not need to be dipped in ink and a pile of paper bound together with a metal coil. He says I should keep a diary like he does on one of his machines. He says it might help me cope with all the things I will need to learn.

Ian was right, weightlessness is fun but so very strange. So many things that seem normal to him are so very strange to me.

First, Ian gave me new clothes to wear. I wish I could show these to my ladies-in-waiting. They would just die. Instead of big formal dresses over my small clothes and girdles, I am wearing something very similar to what a male acrobat might wear in a performance. It fits close to my body and it stretches in the strangest ways. I have never seen cloth like this.

It is not lady-like at all but wearing my skirts, even my close-fitting hunting dress, would be very ungainly here where nothing holds them down. So I am in this jongleur outfit and truth be told, it is incredibly comfortable and, I think, shows off my womanhood in ways far more flattering than frilly dresses. I can see Ian watch me out of the corner of his eyes. Maybe this is something I can use.

He is nothing like Guildford. Guildford was sweet and tentative and so very young. This Ian is not so young in looks or temper, but he is handsome for a man of his age and, so far, has shown me nothing but courtesy and respect. I don't yet know what to make of him, but it is too late, methinks, to turn back.

I am more scared than I have ever been — and more exhilarated. My mind and faith tell me my mortal soul is in danger of the magic that surrounds me, but in my heart, I cannot be anything but entranced.

This ship and this time traveling have to be devil's work but Ian says the ship is nothing but a machine built by the hands of very smart men. I don't know what to make of what he tells me.

Here is what he has explained to me so far:

To travel in time, we must also travel in space, we must travel much farther than numbers can even express, at least the numbers I know. He says that not only does the world move through time but that the world and the sun and the moon and the planets are also moving through space and to get to his time, we must also get to the place the world will be when we want to stop.

He says that when we travel through time and space, his machine bends time and space around us so we can travel very, very fast. I do not understand this part at all. He calls this part of the trip the "Transit."

He also says that even though we travel faster than anything I can imagine, it still takes time for us to travel because the journey is so very long. This journey, Ian says, will take the equivalent of about fifteen days. On the ship, he calls these cycles.

This is where he said something weird that makes me very suspicious.

When we started flying, we could look at "monitors" which are the paintings that show pictures from outside the ship. They are much like his little camera which had the pictures from my execution — there are more cameras outside the ship which make paintings or pictures immediately. But now that we are traveling to his time, in this special mode where time and space are "bent," we cannot use these monitors and there are no windows or portholes. I wonder what it is he does not want me to see.

Transit 1553 to 2085: Jane's Diary, Day-Cycle 2

Ian is a very funny man. On one hand, he is very direct, he talks to me like I am a man and not some silly girl. He seems to expect me to understand and does not condescend to me because of my sex or my age.

But he is so awkward when talking about human bodies. I noticed this when he first went looking for clothes I could wear. There is a small store of clothes in a closet here in many sizes and shapes because sometimes Ian travels with other historians — or perhaps other demons — I don't yet know which. But he seems loath to touch me in even the most innocent of ways.

And God's Blood, when he tried to show me how to use the privy, he turned positively red. He said he knew how a man could use it to pass water, but he had never travelled with a woman and never knew how it fitted. I had to figure that out by myself.

Using the privy while weightless is a wonder. Since nothing goes "down" in this weightlessness, you have to use a machine that sucks everything into a hose. It is so strange.

Sleeping in weightlessness is strange too. The sleeping room contains beds to lie on when the ship is on the Earth but which fold up when the ship is in Transit. For sleeping in weightlessness there are padded bags held fast to the walls and a privacy partition that Ian pulls down between us. Off this room is the very small privy with its strange fittings.

I couldn't eat for about a day — a cycle — after we became weightless, much like the first time I went on a water ship. Food on this vessel is actually very good but it is strange too. It is stored in a cabinet in a kind of flexible glass that Ian calls 'bi-o-de-grade-able-plaz-tic.'

Anyway, the food tastes wonderful after he puts it into a what he calls a "my-crow-wave" which is another one of his strange magic machines. This one makes food hot without fire.

Since we cannot put the food into dishes without it flying around the room, we have to scoop or squeeze it from this 'plaz-tic' directly into our mouths.

Transit 1553 to 2085: Jane's Diary, Day-Cycle 3

I have been so obsessed with the machines that cook and act as privy and that fly through space and time, that I hadn't yet paid any attention to the machine that Ian spends much of his time with. This machine may be the most wondrous of them all.

Today, he showed me how he uses it and started teaching me how I too, could use it. It is the most amazing thing I have ever seen.

It uses a "monitor" like the ones I have described before which can be shown on the wall or on a flat board that can be placed in front of you.

The desk table has what Ian calls a "keyboard." When turned on, you can see every letter in the English language in a box shown in dark black against the desk. And when you touch your fingers to the 'keys,' the letters appear on the monitor.

You can also talk to the "computer" and it hears your words and writes them out on this monitor. And you can move your fingers across the desk with different numbers of fingers and the computer moves things on the monitor following your gestures.

This is how you use it, and it is pretty easy. But it is what it actually does that is so incredible. He showed me how to bring up words and pictures on this monitor. The language and writing are odd, but I can read them, and they become easier as

I practice. I can "type" words onto this monitor and it searches for any word I put there and brings me definitions, words, and pictures — even moving pictures — and sounds about anything I want.

It is very strange to read about oneself in history. When I ask Ian why his computer still says I was executed, he says he is not sure, that he has never changed history before. He assumes it is because when the computer was made, I had already been executed, and that maybe, changing history doesn't change things that travel with us.

According to the history on his computer, it was my father's fault that Mary had to kill me. She would have let me live if he had not led a rebellion to free me. My father was always a hard man. It is strange to me how reading about him and my mother in history books makes me feel like they are already dead, and I can never see them again. I do not know for sure what I shall see when we get to "Ian's time."

Transit 1553 to 2085: Day-Cycle 4

Ian lied to me today. I don't understand why, it is about such a simple thing.

Today I asked Ian the name of his ship and he said the ship was officially called KLI-2439 but that he calls it Klieo after the Greek Muse of History. He said there is an official plaque inside an "access panel" near the back of the galley. He said the official designation is written inside this door. But he makes log entries like any ship captain and he just speaks his into the 'computer.' I have overheard him several times clearly calling the ship "The Seneca."

I went to the door he described and was able to finally figure out how to open it. Inside was a small crawl space filled with long round cylinders that bend in many directions. There are glowing cylinders and flashing lights in many colors and a lot of noise that disappears when the door is shut. This crawl space would be big enough for me to fit into but I don't dare as I don't know what all these things are. On the inside of the door is the plaque Ian described and it does have "KLI-2439" inscribed but the name is crossed out with what I guess is one of Ian's magic pens. Below it, "Seneca" is clearly written along with the phrase from my father's sitting room: *"Non quia difficilia sunt non audemus, sed quia non audemus, difficilia sunt."*

I remember asking my father about those words when I was young, and he said they mean "It's not because things are difficult that we dare not venture. It's because we dare not venture that they are difficult." He said the words were written by the Latin philosopher Seneca and I liked those words so much that I named my very first pony "Seneca" — much to my father's amusement.

I didn't know who he was then but the very first time I remember meeting Ian was when he was a young man, and I was a child of six or seven. I told him those words from my father's plaque.

As I put the panel back, I saw Ian watching me from the other end of the galley but he said nothing.

Transit 1553 to 2085: Day-Cycle 5

Jane had spent an hour unsuccessfully trying to figure out how to open the door to the outside and had ended pounding on it with her fists in frustration.

Now she pulled herself from corner to corner to corner to corner in the main room of the ship. Though there is no up and down in Transit, the ship itself was designed with a floor and ceiling and she pulled herself along the ceiling, sometimes looking "up" at the ceiling wall, sometimes "down" at the room.

Her pulse pounded in her ears and her hands shook as she grabbed each of the hand pulls across the walls. Jane's teardrops floated in a long thin cloud that defined her path. Her hair and face grew wet as she passed through them over and over again.

She had to get out of this ship. The walls were closing in and her soul was in mortal danger. She was defying God with her cowardice. God had ordained her death and now she was traveling with this demon to escape God's holy will.

Ian came out of the sleeping room, rubbing the sleep out of his eyes. Jane saw him and propelled herself straight at him.

"Get me out of here," she said. "Get me out of here *now*. I can't stand this anymore."

"My lady?" Ian said. She could see fear and confusion in his eyes, but he didn't back down.

"I can't stand being closed up in this room anymore. You have to stop this ship and let me out or take me back to my time. I'd rather be executed than live in that malignant and Godless time you come from."

"Ah, you've been reading history, then."

"Ian Harwood, tell me this. Do *you* believe in God? I see nothing on this ship to tell me you do. There is no chapel, no cross, no Bible."

"No, My lady, I do not."

"Then how can I trust you? Atheists are worse than the Christ-killer Jews. If you don't believe in God, you are an agent of Satan."

"Yeah, well, I don't believe in him either," Ian said.

"I just read a short history of the twenty-first century. I don't understand much of what happened but so many people died. So much of the world was destroyed by floods and fire. People roasted to death in the heat while other countries sent soldiers to kill them. I can't even comprehend the number of people who died."

Ian closed his eyes. "About 1.8 billion in wars, heat, flooding, and storms, almost all before 2067. Almost four times the number of all the people alive in the world in your time."

Jane pulled her face closer to his. "It is because you abandoned the great chain of being and decided you knew better than God. I don't want to go there. I cannot live among such people. I cannot live in such a world."

"Lady Jane, not everyone in my time is as godless as I am. And as awful as the world became in the 2060s, we have been able to turn the tide, at least somewhat. There are still six billion people who, almost every one, live better and freer and richer than *anyone* in your time."

"In my time, we recognized God's will and people lived as *He* decreed," she said, her face floating inches from his.

Ian's face clouded. "In your time, *you* hung people for being poor. *You* burnt people at the stake for believing different things than you. Most of *your* subjects, *my lady*, lived a week away from starvation. You, yourself, were going to be executed because you didn't believe crackers turned into Jesus's body when you ate them at church. Don't tell me how much nicer it was in 1553."

Jane slapped him hard, and it sent them both rotating away from each other in an alarming spin until he was able to grasp on to a handhold and she spun into the bulkhead. Still, she said "God is not to be trifled with by sophistry. I never cared whether the papists believe in transubstantiation, I do care if God's will is done.

"God has laid a plan for all of us and I have betrayed Him by not doing His will. You must stop this ship and take me back. If it is God's will I be executed, then I must die with my head held high." She grimaced at her poor choice of metaphors. "I know why your history books still say I was executed, because you will turn this ship around and take me back."

"My lady, I cannot do that," Ian said.

"I want to go back. You said you would never ask me to do anything I didn't want to do."

Ian looked away. "It is not in my power. I can't stop the ship; I can't reprogram her mid-Transit. I will take you back if you wish but we'll have to go back to the Institute first, to my time, and recharge before I can take you back. If this is what you still wish then, I will take you back to the exact time you left and you can resume your life — and your death — as if this had never happened."

Jane cried her tears for so many things. She did not want to die; she did not want to give that wonderful speech before Mary had her head cut off. She did not want to defy God's will. She was scared of all she read about Ian's time and thought it would be a horrible time to be alive.

She hated this man for who he was but somehow couldn't hate him personally and she buried her head in his shoulder as they floated near each other. "Why would God do this to me? Why would he send me to such an evil time as yours?"

She felt him gently stroke her hair. "Maybe, my lady, He has a different plan for you. I'm no expert on what God might want, but maybe he chose that you not die, but that you bring God back to England."

This was a new thought for her and she felt herself become very still.

Transit 1553 to 2085: Day-Cycle 6-8

Jane knew of no other way to understand what she should do except by praying but kneeling before God in weightlessness was a challenge.

The only place she could find to stay still enough to pray was strapped into her sleeping bag and she stayed there for two days, trying to understand what God was willing her to do.

Ian considerately respected her privacy and spent his sleep cycles in the other room. He brought her food and drink but otherwise left her alone. His only warning to her was that she should be exercising to keep her muscles toned but Jane argued that exercising was not something ladies did.

After two days and two nights, she had no better answer to her fears and found that her claustrophobia was so much worse in the small sleeping room.

Nor, she realized, not for the first time, did she ever handle boredom well.

Transit 1553 to 2085: Day-Cycle 9-11

With a quiet truce between them, Jane came out of her prayer retreat and began working on the computer again, this time focusing on the programs Ian had used to learn the English of her time.

Going through the tutorials, Jane understood some of the odd parts of his accent and the sometimes very funny words he used. It wasn't Ian's fault, he had learned what this computer had taught him, and that wasn't always strictly accurate though, she had to admit, most of it was passable.

She wondered if the mistakes were a problem with the voice from the computer and finally asked Ian what he thought.

He seemed pleased she was talking to him again. "I think," he said, "it's because when those lessons were being put together, there were no recordings from your time, some of it was guesswork. I did not even hear some of the mistakes that amuse you so much. Maybe you and I can work together to make lessons for other historians that are more accurate."

Jane had to admit to herself that this idea intrigued her. She already spoke seven languages. It would be fun to use that knowledge to help others.

While Ian exercised or worked on his own journals or cooked and cleaned for her, Jane buried herself in reversing Ian's lessons in Tudor English to learn his twenty-first century English. It would be best to be prepared, she thought. Many of the concepts in Ian's English were hard to understand. They assumed a knowledge and view of the world she did not share but she persevered. Instead of Ian sleeping in the work room now, it was Jane strapped in the chair and listening to the computer speak in twenty-first century English for as long as she could keep her eyes open.

On Day-Cycle 11, Ian came in from the sleeping area and bid her good morning. He still looked a little fuzzy with sleep. She had come to understand he was not a quick riser, needing something called "coffee" to start his day.

"Good morning, sweet Ian," she said. "Would you be a dear and fix me a cup of tea while you're making breakfast?"

"Of course," he said, turning towards the galley. Then he stopped and slowly turned back toward her in amazement and Jane felt herself smiling broadly. She had spoken the phrase in an almost perfect 21st Century accent.

It gave her pleasure to surprise this man.

Transit 1553 to 2085: Day Cycle 15

The past fourteen days of Transit had been eye-opening, life-changing, fascinating, scary and shocking for Jane.

In a few hours they would be dropping out of Transit. Now, provided Ian and his computer have been telling the truth, she would see her new world for the first time.

Ian pulled himself down into the chair across the desk from her, but he didn't look at her. Jane wondered to herself that maybe she was too hard on him, but she had always been told that Jews and atheists were the most evil of humans. It was hard for her to meld her idea of what an atheist was with this man who seemed to honestly care for her, who had a sense of humor and who, after all, *had* saved her life.

"We've been decelerating for a few days, uh, slowing down, but once we drop out of transit, you will start to feel the deceleration, much like we felt the acceleration when we left your time. You'll need to strap yourself in tightly like we did then too. I'll bring the cameras online as soon as I can and we can take a quick tour around the Earth before we need to head back to London pretty quickly. Our power is running lower than I like. Once there, you can do what you like. I hope you'll want to visit the Institute but if you don't want to meet more atheists, I can take you to my home or put you up with someone else I think you will like if you prefer."

"Ian, I am sorry, I don't mean to hurt you. It's hard for me; I don't know what to think right now."

Ian smiled sadly at her, "I can only imagine. Whatever you need, whatever will help you through, let me know."

"Thank you, good sir. You have been nothing but kind to me."

When the timeship dropped out of Transit, Ian turned on the monitors.

And gasped.

"What is it?" Jane asked.

Ian brought up another monitor side by side with the view outside the Seneca. "On the left are images of the world taken in

2082," he said, and started pointing out the differences. "In my 2082, only a little of the southern polar ice cap remained. Where and when we are, both ice caps are bigger than they ever were in my lifetime. The islands of Indonesia and the Maldives are still above water. Look, the city of Venice still exists. These are the cities in my time in the New World. In this time, they are completely different. So is Africa. There are several mega-cities in Africa."

Jane looked at the comparisons. She could see the differences he pointed out but both were so incredibly different than even her imperfect knowledge. Why did the New World or Africa, places full of illiterate savages as far as she knew, even have cities?

Ian kept calling out differences that surprised him but meant little to Jane. The lands of what Ian called "Australia", "California," "Pantanal," "Brazil," and "Siberia" no longer showed great swaths of blackened forests and the Great Barrier Reef was alive and visible again, even from high orbit. North and South America had great cities but many were in completely different places than those of Ian's time. Africa had most of the same cities as before but now Lagos, Cairo and Johannesburg were megalopolises, at least five times as big as they were in the photos Ian showed from his time.

Ian became very quiet after a while. Jane asked, "What else did you lie to me about?"

Ian glanced her way and back towards the screens without answering. He piloted one more orbit then navigated towards London.

As they flew over the city, it was Jane's turn to gasp. "It's huge," she said in awe.

"It's half the size it should be," Ian said. The Thames is like it was in 2000… And the Institute isn't here now anywhere. I can't find it visually or by radio beacon." They were both silent, sailing above London for a few moments. Ian said "I will go to where the Institute would have been, but everything has changed."

Jane noted quietly, almost to herself, "It has changed a bit for me too."

Ian looked at Jane, this time smiling broadly. "My lady, Your Royal Highness and Queen Regnant of England and Ireland, I think your nine days of reign may have been a little more important to history than I originally suspected."

Outskirts of London, April 8, 2085

Jane thought she would be thankful to be back in gravity. Instead, she found her arms and legs felt like lead weights when she tried to heave herself out of the seat she had been strapped into. She could hear her heart pounding and found herself breathing hard by the time she crossed the room — it was like clawing her way through molasses. Ian had told her to exercise, and she regretted not having followed his advice, especially watching him moving *almost* normally. He smiled ruefully at her but refrained from saying *I told you so.*

But gravity did allow her to kneel and pray for the first time in many weeks. It was Sunday here and now in London and she needed His guidance now as much as she had sitting by the campfire before the start of this strange adventure.

"Dear Christ," she prayed, "I pray you let me know what you want me to do. You have sent me to a strange new world, and I do not understand."

Ian sat at his terminal looking at monitors and listening with a device that covered one ear. He looked perplexed. "My lady, if it makes you feel any better, I'm as confused as you. This is no more my world than it is yours."

"Sir, I am praying, what I ask is between me and God."

"Sorry," Ian said. "I didn't mean to interrupt."

After a few moments, she pulled herself heavily to her feet. "I am sorry too," she said. "When you convinced me to come with you, it seemed so simple. I didn't want to die, and your camera videos made a very good argument that I should join you. But what have we done? What do we do now?"

Unknown Location Near London, April 9-15, 2085

Jane was as sick as she had ever been in her life. For the first two days, she couldn't keep food down and she could barely crawl out of bed to relieve herself.

But Ian pushed her. He made her get up and walk, first around the Seneca, then outside in the woods surrounding the Seneca. Feeling the cold, spring wind and occasional rain in her face gave her the first hint of normalcy she had felt in weeks.

Ian showed her how to use the exercise equipment and he kept coming back in to sit by her bedside and take care of her needs when she had to go back and lie down. Sometimes he even read to her from his little handheld device which apparently contained stories and poetry as well as gruesome pictures of her execution.

He had pulled the bed down from the wall for her and it was infinitely more comfortable than the zero-gravity suspended bags.

On the third day, he said, "I think you will like this. Since we are back in gravity, you can use something called a 'shower.'" He got up, packed the zero-gravity fixtures into the bulkhead and showed her the controls, grabbed her a fresh towel and left her alone.

She had to admit that this 'shower' was like heaven. Maybe sorcery could have a place in her life.

After drying herself and getting dressed, she sat down to dinner. "Sir, why didn't you warn me about this awful sickness?"

Ian looked at her over the top of his reading glasses. "My lady, I *did* warn you. You said you didn't think exercising was lady-like."

"Did you know I would be this sick?"

Ian grimaced. "The Institute warned *us* and we all followed their guidelines. I guess I didn't really know how bad it would be if we did not."

"Have you had any luck contacting your Institute yet?"

Ian shook his head. "The Seneca is sitting exactly where the cafeteria would be if the Institute existed. London itself doesn't extend out to where we are in this 2085. I doubt the Institute exists anywhere when we are now."

Day by day, she began to regain her strength and each day they walked further through the woods. The Seneca was hidden in a stand of trees but there was a small paved road and many trails crisscrossing the area around their landing site.

On the sixth day after their landing, Jane was able to walk the mile and a half to the spot Ian had told her about. They were on a ledge in the forest which dropped off sharply in front of them, revealing a vista of a busy, collective farm. There was one large building, a church by the looks of it. This church was surrounded by a handful of low buildings, some of which had chimneys with smoke pouring out, others that looked like barns and grain storage.

In the fields between them and the church, twenty or so men looked like they were planting. Ian handed her the binoculars and she was surprised. They were monks, complete with tonsures and robes.

"Christ's Blood" she said. "I guess Henry's dissolution of the monasteries didn't last."

Ian chuffed. "Even in my time, the monasteries had long returned."

They walked back to the Seneca in silence. Jane refused to complain that he walked too fast for her in her still-weakened condition.

This shower thing, though, worked magic on her. When they got back, the sun was hanging low in the sky and Ian readily agreed to cook dinner while she showered. She had enjoyed the feel of warm water on her skin and was luxuriating in the feel of the soft, warm towel when there was a knock on the outside door of the Seneca. Jane felt herself let out a small gasp.

Ian must have been equally surprised, he let out an obscenity. She couldn't fault him for that.

"You stay in there," he said through the door, "I'll send the video to your bulkhead."

A second later, a picture from the camera at the ship's entrance appeared on the wall.

On the bulkhead in the sleeping room, an image appeared showing the ship's entrance. Outside the ship was an elderly priest, wearing a collar and cassock. He had shoulder-length gray hair, a well-wrinkled face with a kindly expression and a small smile.

He was pounding the metal head of his cane against the door.

"Come on, amigo, I know you are in there. I just followed you here. I mean you no harm." He spoke with an accent somewhat like Ian's but with an odd lilt and rolling of his r's that reminded her of the Spanish Envoys who used to meet with her father.

"Stay in there," Ian repeated to Jane.

"Sir," he said to the man out front through his speaker system. "I will open the door. Please do not be afraid by what you see. I mean no harm either."

Jane could see the old priest chuckle in the video feed. She heard the whoosh of the door and Ian changed the picture to the view of the door from the inside.

The priest stood there, leaning on his cane. The red light of the sunset illuminating him from behind, causing his hair to glow orange. He had a large canvas bag slung over one shoulder.

After a moment, the priest asked "Aren't you going to invite me in, Señor?"

Jane could see the surprise in Ian's profile. He seemed to be expecting the reaction she had shown the first time the door opened to a room so much bigger inside than outside.

"I am so sorry," Ian said. "Please come in. I am Ian Harland, I'm from Leicester."

"Yes, *ciertamente* you are," said the priest, smiling rather too broadly. I am Father Mateo Adler, and I am from Plymouth." A quick smile passed over his face again. "Truly, *I* am."

"I'm sorry, I guess I expected more of a reaction when I opened the door."

"Ah, sí, yes. You are not the first person from your planet to visit us here at St. Rumwald's."

This took Ian quite by surprise, she could hear it in his voice. "You've met *other* travelers like me?"

"There have been several and they all seem to like to come visit St. Rumwald's. Most don't even open their door but some do but they try not to say much, only ask a lot of strange questions. But the last one was quite talkative and invited me in like you have. He said he was from a planet called *Tralfamadore*, so I assume you will say that too. His ship was similar to yours but perhaps a bit better at hiding in the woods."

"Tral-fam-a-dore?" Ian repeated slowly, staring at the priest in disbelief.

"Yes, *mi hijo*, you have heard of it, I see?"

"Um, yes, you could say that. Who was he?"

"He said his name was Jacob Patel."

Jane had finished dressing quickly and chose to ignore Ian's instructions to stay hidden.

Ian looked like he was trying to collect himself and didn't notice her entrance from the sleeping quarters.

"Ah," said the priest, "this must be your wife. Jacob said you would be traveling together — from Tralfamadore." The priest's eyes danced.

"Can you describe him?"

"He was dark-skinned, short, bald, looked like a Hindu, I don't know if they have Hindus on Tralfamadore, do you?"

"We certainly do. Almost as many as there are in London."

It was Fr. Mateo now who looked non-plussed. "There are very few Hindus in London. Why would you say that?"

"I, um, must be misinformed," said Ian.

"Perhaps you can introduce me to your lady," he said, smiling at Jane.

Ian shook his head, apparently trying to clear it. "Um yes, this is my traveling companion, not my wife. Her name is Jane, um, Goodall. Um, Jane, this is Fr. Mateo Adler."

"Pleased to meet you," said Jane, taking his outstretched hand and dropping a quick curtsy.

"*Jacob* said we would be traveling together?" Ian pursued.

"Yes, he was here several months ago, looking for you. He said he thought you might be coming and waited for about a week. We saw him come, much the same way we saw you come in. You Tralfamadorians make quite a splash on our communication network. When you land, your ships break up our wireless transmissions for miles around.

"But he grew impatient and said he didn't know where or when you would arrive. He gave me something…" Fr. Adler rummaged in his jacket pocket and pulled out a small paper. "He said you would understand it and that I should give it to you if you came. He said to tell you that the Great Institute of Tralfamadore wants to see you and you should use these numbers to meet him so he can take you back. He seemed quite insistent."

Ian's hands shook a little as he took the paper from the old priest.

"What else is in your bag," asked Jane and the priest smiled at her.

"Ah my dear, I'm glad you ask. This Jacob fellow wouldn't leave his spaceship but since you two have already been walking around, I thought you might be more willing to discover more about our Earth or at least our little corner of it here around St. Rumwald's and London. We have been watching you since you arrived, and it looks like the lady has recovered from her weakness. I would be happy to take you on a tour of London, our greatest city, but you can't go out in the silly clothes you have on." Adler made a face, "they look like pajamas. I brought you new clothes more fitting for sightseeing."

Jane felt her excitement growing unexpectedly. She had thought she was over her claustrophobia but realized now just how much she wanted to see more than these four walls and the little bit of surrounding woods. "I think we would both very much like that," she said.

Ian looked like he still might not trust his voice but nodded.

"Good" said Adler. "Is tomorrow morning too soon?"

"Ian?" Jane inquired, slightly concerned by the look on his face.

"Uh, that would be great," he said. "I can't wait to see London close up."

The priest handed the bag to Jane and nodded pleasantly to them. "Bueno, I will take my leave of you now and see you bright and early tomorrow morning. Please join us where the path crosses the paved road when the sun pokes its face over the hill. I think it will be a very interesting trip for all of us. Buenos Noches," he said with a bow.

After he left, Jane turned to Ian. "Fine, good sir. Which question will you answer first?"

Ian gave her a wry smile that disappeared when he looked at her face. "What are my choices?"

Jane counted them out on her fingers. "Let's start with who is Jacob Patel? What is on that paper? And what in the Saviour's Name is 'Trafalmadorma' or whatever he said."

"Fair enough," said Ian, "Jacob Patel sounds like a guy who had just started at the Institute before I left for the last time. I knew him maybe a few months. He was born in London but his family was from India. I think they sent him back into the English Occupation of India.

"The paper is a list of coordinates I could program into the navigator. They would take us to England in 1552. I don't exactly know where by just looking at the numbers but the computer could tell us that.

"Tralfamadore was the name of a planet created by an old twentieth-century science fiction writer named Kurt Vonnegut. He wrote science fiction — um that's a kind of story we told in my 2085 that might feature people traveling in space and time or meeting people from other planets or dealing with new sciencey things. In one of Vonnegut's stories, the Tralfamadorians were people who lived in all times concurrently. It was kind of a favorite story to read among us field historians."

Jane raised an eyebrow and gave her sparkling smile for the first time in a very long time.

"So," she said. "I guess we're living one of these science fiction stories now?"

Ian smiled back. "I thought I had been living in one my entire adult life, but yes, this takes it to new levels."

London, April 16, 2085

When they opened Fr. Adler's bag, Jane was puzzled, but Ian looked intrigued. He kept holding up the garments and running them through his hands.

Jane tried on the women's garments. It was a one piece garment with slightly billowy dark brown culottes for the legs and a white top festooned with intricate, wildly-colored bead work and what appeared to be hand-painted linework. The images were of birds, flowers, turtles and geometric designs.

Ian's new clothes also featured below-the-knee shorts but had a shirt and a dark jacket and a cylindrical hat sticking up several inches from the brim. His shirt was white but also adorned with many of the same kind of decorations as Jane's.

Jane had to admit she was impressed. Priest or no, Fr. Adler — or whoever had been watching them — had a great eye for sizes. Ian's trousers were a touch too snug at the waist but otherwise both his and her clothes fit perfectly. She wondered how long they had been secretly observed.

"What is this?" She asked Ian, pointing to the designs on her shirt.

Ian shrugged. "Let's ask Fr. Adler when he comes."

Neither slept well that night in anticipation of their adventure.

As instructed, Ian and Jane walked to the paved road not far from the Seneca after the sun had crested the nearby hill. They had waited only a handful of minutes when a vehicle pulled up. It was almost completely silent and looked to Jane like five little round carriages tied together in a string. There were no horses or mules or men pulling them but each carriage, such as they were, had a round bubble of glass above a comfortable-looking seating area. Each of the separate carriages seemed to have only one set of wheels.

In the first carriage, she saw Fr. Adler and another man — no, a woman with short hair! — who seemed to be the coachman, or *coachwoman?* What an odd thought. In the second carriage was another man and a woman dressed much like herself and Ian. The rest of the carriages were empty.

Fr. Adler exited his carriage and greeted Ian and Jane warmly, grabbing each of their hands in succession and shaking them heartily. Jane found this gesture disturbing but she hid her discomfort at the invasive contact, trying to follow Ian's lead.

"Welcome, welcome, good sir and fine lady. We have an adventure for you today. This centipede will take us directly to the heart of London, driven by the lovely Señorita Styles-Gomez." Fr. Adler pointed at the strange vehicle with a dramatic swoosh. The driver, hearing her name, smiled and waved back.

"I will sit with Señorita Gomez to direct her but I have brought Señora Freya Outhwaite and Señor Juan Northrop, both of whom are longtime Londoners, to give you the guided tour. Señor Northrup and Señora Outhwaite are quite the noted historians." Jane saw the wink from the priest and, from the corner of her eye, the gulp in Ian's throat.

The two historians reached out to shake hands with Ian and Jane. Outhwaite was a broad-shouldered, attractive woman with long brown curls with a few streaks of grey flowing down her back. She a round face with striking cold blue eyes, and ruby red lips that looked like they were always just on the verge of smiling. She wore very large glasses with small African masks as decorations at the temples. Northrup was a little younger, maybe late 30s, a little gangly and seemingly very enthusiastic. He had glasses that kept slipping down his nose and a long forelock that kept dropping down and taking the place of the glasses over his eyes.

"It is such a pleasure to meet you, Mr. Harland," Juan said, "Fr. Adler says he believes you know a great deal about our Earth history. Come into our pod, I can't wait to get to know you." He held the pod door and Ian and Jane climbed in and sat down.

The pod was surprisingly agreeable. From the inside, the glass dome had a darkened area that appeared to follow the sun to keep the direct light off the passengers, a fan recirculated the air at an agreeable temperature, the seats were comfortable and the historians gave them a quick demonstration how to open the small, almost hidden vents that let in air and sound from the outside world.

The smoothness of the ride fascinated Jane. A carriage in her time would shake its passengers with bone-rattling jolts. This felt like gliding on water by comparison.

They rode for a few minutes with Northrup giving a quick history first of St Rumwald's, then pointing out the distant skyline of downtown London through a break in the trees.

Jane stared in wonder. "How tall are those buildings? Can people really live in the sky like that?"

"Some of the biggest are thirty stories. You don't have buildings like that on your *planet*?" asked Outhwaite. There was an odd inflection on the last word.

Jane glanced over at Ian, afraid to answer, afraid to say something wrong about Tralfamadore. Ian just shrugged one shoulder as if to say it didn't matter.

"I don't know of any," she finally said, "but I'm from a different part of Tralfamadore than Ian is; maybe there are such tall buildings where he is from."

"Where I'm from," said Ian, "there are several buildings around one hundred stories high. The biggest I have ever heard of has close to two hundred."

"Your Tralfamadore has such huge buildings? Tell us more about Tralfamadore," said Outhwaite.

Adler's voice came into the car. Jane realized he must have an 'intercom' much like the one in the Seneca. It did not startle her as much as it had the first time Ian had used one.

"Freya, let us first give them our tour of London. I am sure Ian and Jane will tell us all about Tralfamadore later. Let us show them our world first."

Outhwaite looked a little put out but said "Yes, Señor, of course."

The trip from St. Rumwald's to London took about forty-five minutes. Northrup kept up a running commentary about the history of the city in the last hundred years. Though London was the capital of a small island country, it had been growing in importance in the last century because of England's reputation for neutrality and ease of access for the Northern Columbian people and many of the European states. He said it had more than doubled in population and was becoming quite cosmopolitan, at least between pandemics of Yellow Fever and Corona Viruses.

Ian looked up at the last point. Is that why you have these separate seating areas in your centipede?"

"Of course, we can quickly segregate people everywhere in London and in England, and we can usually keep the landemics down to only a year or two. How do you handle that on Tralfamadore?"

"Vaccines," said Ian.

"Your church allows those?" asked Outhwaite. "Do you not follow the teachings of Jesus?"

"Now Freya," said Adler's voice. "Let's leave such discussions for dinner. This tour is for Ian and Jane to learn about us."

By the time they started driving into the outskirts of the city, Jane felt much like the first time she visited London with her parents as a child. *Over five hundred years ago*, she realized with a shudder.

Like then, her face was pressed against the window of the carriage, eagerly taking in the new sights. She suddenly remembered it was that moment in her life, when entering London for the first time, that she decided she wanted to grow up to be a traveler instead of a stuffy, bored Country Lady like her mother. A few weeks ago, she was sure that dream was dead and she would soon be dead too. Now she had travelled farther, faster and more strangely than anything that little girl could have ever imagined. How fast and completely things can change. She barked out a laugh before she could stop herself.

Ian looked at her and she smiled back at him. "I will tell you later."

Ian too was nearly face-planted against the window as they drove through a new and unfamiliar London.

The city had narrow roads much like she remembered, but here and now they were filled with centipede cars like their own, passing around and through each other much too fast for sanity. Some of the cars were singles or doubles but most were longer like the one they were in.

The day was slightly chilly and overcast, threatening a good rainstorm later in the day, which was typical of April in the London she knew.

Everything else was different. Men and women walked on the streets together with no restrictions on the women walking alone. They wore such a variety of colorful clothes, many like what Adler had given to Ian and herself. She saw people sitting on chairs on the sidewalk playing musical instruments, juggling, performing all kinds of entertainments. This, at least, reminded her of her own London.

The buildings that were so impressive from afar were even more impressive when she was on the street looking up at them. How did people even get up so high? She remembered climbing the stairs to the spire of St. Martin's in Leicester and how exhausted she and her sister were by the time they reached the top. These buildings were at least twice as tall. Yet she saw people on balconies and even a few on roofs.

Just as dizzying was the variety of people she saw. Her tutors had taught her that the world was filled with people of all different skin colors from very dark to very pale, that there were whole countries in far to the east with people who had odd shaped eyes and jet black hair. Now, for the first time, she saw such people.

She saw dark-skinned people with long black hair in braids wearing shirts with the same kind of designs that were on the clothes Fr. Adler had given to them this morning. She pointed them out to Northrup.

"Well, for the last century or so, Iroquois designs have been all the fashion in England. London is getting to be one the biggest trading centers in Europe so the Iroquois and the Africans all come here to trade and sell their goods."

"The Iroquois?" Asked Ian.

"That's the name we use for the people from the New World, the continent that the Spanish discovered in 1492. Really, there are lots of names for the various peoples who live there. They aren't exactly "nations" like we have here but they truly are amazing civilizations and between the Iroquois and Africans, they make a lot of really beautiful things. He pointed to his own shirt and to a set of African bracelets that Outhwaite was wearing.

"Fascinating," Ian said, looking carefully at the items Northrup indicated.

"What's that?" Jane asked, pointing to something she couldn't even begin to fathom. A small creature, no, a machine of some kind about the size of a dog, was lumbering on six legs through the people on the walkways which lined the street where the centipedes ran. Most of the pedestrians were giving it a wide berth though a few seemed to drop things into a hole on its top. It had a mechanical arm that picked up scraps of paper, leaves, and anything else littering the sidewalk. There was no room for a human in this creation and Jane had no idea how it could move on its own like that.

"Goat-bot" said Outhwaite. "They're robots that help keep the streets clean."

"What's a 'robot' asked Jane, watching the thing with wide eyes. As it drew closer, she heard it was making a bleating noise and flashing a yellow light from a pole on its body.

Outhwaite looked skeptically at her again. "Seriously?" She said. "You come in with advanced alien technology like your strange ship and you don't know what a robot is?"

"It's a machine that can move by itself and carry out complex instructions." Northrup filled in, "Goat-bots keep the streets clean and safe, picking up litter and other waste, and they watch for problems and report back to safety services in case police or fire or medical help is needed."

"Miss Goodall," said Adler's voice, though he was still in the other dome, "how would you like to go into one of these tall buildings and see the city from up high."

Jane nodded enthusiastically and Outhwaite conveyed Jane's excitement verbally.

"Mrs. Outhwaite and I need to stop in at the diocese and make a report," said Fr. Adler. "Juan can take you to the roof there. After that, we'll take you to some of the most famous sites in London, La Catedral de la Santísima María, Westminster Abbey, Buckingham Palace, and we will finally end up at the Tower of London where we have a special treat for you."

At the Diocese of London, they walked in through a revolving chamber. Jane watched everyone else walk into the chamber, push on a handle, and calmly come out inside the building. It took her several false starts to enter the moving chambers. It went too fast and the consequences of being wrong seemed to be losing a hand or a foot. Once in the revolving chamber, she panicked at the inside entrance and did one more complete revolution before she threw herself out of the door and into Fr. Adler's arms. He chuckled quietly but said nothing and handed her off to Ian who squeezed her hand briefly. "I'm sorry," he whispered to her. "I should have realized you had never done that before. I didn't think."

They were standing in a large room with a smooth ceiling and walls. The floor was covered by a rug that went right to the edges of the wall. It had flat bench seats around the edges, and doors leading off to other somewheres inside the building. It was bustling with people, many of whom wore priests' cassocks or nuns' habits. More than a few wore tonsures, but others wore what Jane now understood were fashionable civilian clothes. Not far from the door was a desk where a young priest seemed to be there to help and greet newcomers.

He stood to attention when he saw Adler and Outhwaite. He started to say "Welcome Grand…" but he trailed off; Jane saw Fr. Adler had raised a finger to his own lips.

"Father Adler," said the man. "It is a pleasure to see you again. Should I let Fr. Redmond know you are here."

"Yes, thank you, Fr. Ricci, please tell him that Mrs. Outhwaite and I would like a few minutes of his time when he is available."

After a quick call on a device Jane recognized as another communications tool — so many ways to talk to each other! Jane watched Adler and Outhwaite go into a little room with sliding doors off the back wall. The doors slid closed then opened a moment later and the two were gone.

After a brief discussion, Northrup said he was going to take them to the roof and he led them to the same doors. Jane took a deep breath then followed Ian into the little room. The doors closed behind her and she realized she was the only one who hadn't turned around. She felt the room start moving first sideways then up and she grabbed tightly onto the handrail but was proud of herself that she held in the startled sound that tried to escape her throat.

After a few moments, the doors opened again, and Jane could see they were on the roof of the building. There was a railing around the perimeter marked off by stations of the cross.

Northrup walked them to the railing and Ian, usually so shy around her, kept his arm tightly around her waist.

"I am fine, Ian, you don't have to support me." Ian looked at her with a twinkle in his eye. "It's not you I'm comforting. I don't love heights." The view was higher than anything she had seen but not so very different from the vista from St. Martin's.

The rest of the day was one wonder after another.

La Catedral de la Santísima María was spectacularly beautiful but different than any cathedral she had ever seen. Instead of the ornate decorations and soaring architecture she was used to, it was an austere design built about a hundred years before in this timeline. Ian said it didn't exist in his time.

It was built with close, sweeping curves and planes and with an ingenious use of windows to create cross-cutting paths of light leading one's attention to the altar and the cross above it. Both she and Ian had assumed that this Cathedral was built in honor of the Virgin Mary, so it was an odd feeling when Outhwaite corrected them, and Jane realized this Cathedral was in honor of the now-sainted woman who would have had Jane's head.

As they rode through London, they crisscrossed the Thames several times. Though many of the small rivers pouring into the Thames that Jane had known as a child were gone, the Thames itself looked the same to her, gently glowing in the late morning sun. There were more walls and bridges and riverside buildings and — to her shock and pleasant amazement — it did not stink of human feces and decaying waste like it did when she had last visited.

Westminster Hall still stood much as she remembered it but what they called Westminster Palace looked nothing like Westminster Palace from her time. It, too, was open to the public when Parliament was not in session. It was where both the House of Commons and the Casa de Señores met to advise the king or queen. When she asked the obvious question neither she nor Ian had yet thought of, Northrup said the reigning monarch was King Philip VII, now in the ninth year of his reign.

By the time they reached what Northrup and Outhwaite called the Tower Bridge, Jane was ready for a respite. Her mind was roiling with everything she had seen in this one day and how the world had changed.

She knew this was not Ian's time and she could see that he, too, was both surprised and fascinated by much of what he saw. But his surprise wasn't the same shock of new experiences that kept turning her head. The technology was different, but he knew about rotating doors, indoor plumbing, and public facilities, about the communication devices these people used. He wasn't afraid of robots or the building climbing boxes or even the centipede that moved people without any animal or human propulsion.

It was funny, she thought to herself, how she could have read about so many of these things on his computer but was still so taken aback by each new surprise in real life.

What she did come to realize, watching both Ian and Fr. Adler, Outhwaite, Northrup and all the people of this London is that Ian had been telling her the truth. Amazing as this "technology" was, it wasn't magic, it wasn't wizardry, and it wasn't the work of demons. Even the crazy robots that moved like living creatures, deep down, were machines — or so she believed now.

She found she had much to think about, but that would have to wait until after they had eaten. Right now, she was ravenously hungry.

At least the White Tower looked familiar. Much had changed but the basic shape and look of the tower was the same as when her father had brought Jane and her sister Katharine here. According to her hosts, now as then, it remained a building both to honor and house royalty and still served as a prison for certain crimes against the church and the crown, though Outhwaite seemed to lament the fact that the pope and the Bishop of London had sharply curtailed the use of arrest, torture, and execution.

Had she become queen, she would have been moved here before the coronation to live in state. Had she been executed as Ian's pictures had shown, that would have happened here as well.

A shadow crept over her heart as they crossed the Tower Bridge and entered the keep of the Tower of London.

The White Tower, April 16, 2085

God's Blood, thought Jane, *those things stink*. Both Adler and Outhwaite had "pipes" stuffed with burning stuff they called "tobacco." Adler said this tobacco was one of the most beloved gifts of the Iroquois peoples from across the ocean.

According to Fr. Adler, the Iroquois sent it to England and Europe by the boatload for just such celebratory occasions such as this. Ian looked slightly green as they offered it to him as well, but like Jane, he was quite willing to accept a glass of brandy.

"So," said Adler, "you have seen a little of our city and our planet, tell us about your Tralfamadore. It appears the two of you are from very different parts of your remarkable planet."

"What did Jacob already tell you?" asked Ian.

"Not a great deal, *mi hijo*, and certainly nothing I credit with any truth," said Adler.

"Why is that?"

"Oh come on, Mr. Harland," said Outhwaite, leaning in and puffing smoke out of the side of her mouth. "Do you really think we are so stupid and backward? You come from a distant planet but you look exactly like humans, you speak a weird, archaic version of *our* language, actually two different, weird, archaic versions of our language.

"You have names like Ian Harland, Jane Goodall and Jacob Patel. It strains credulity — it is like you think we are idiots. London may not be the pinnacle of learning in Europe, but we are not stupid. We don't know where you are really from but please don't play us for fools."

Adler leaned back with his pipe and smiled. "Of course, we are all God's children. Maybe God has created more than one England."

"Posh" said Outhwaite. "God has infinite possibilities. I doubt he'd repeat building a small, backwater island like us."

"Señora, I am offended. I love this little gem of a country."

Ian leaned back and rubbed his chin; the same way Jane had seen him do when he wanted to explain something difficult to her. Then he smiled. "Well, to be honest, it wasn't Jane or I, who said we were from a different planet, it was Jacob. We just didn't immediately disabuse you of that notion."

Outhwaite harrumphed.

"So your science seems to accept the possibility of life on other planets. What do you know about relativity?" Ian asked.

"We have quite a good knowledge of genetics," said Adler.

Ian laughed. "No, Relativity is a physics theory that tries to explain how crazily different the world and the universe are from the way we perceive it.

"This theory says that time and space are intimately linked as something called space-time. It argues that moving mass along any axis, um, any direction, in time or space can cause the other directions to bend and warp. The more the mass and the faster it moves; the more space and time can warp."

"Ah, we call that Temporal Reconciliation," Said Adler.

"Whatever you call it, it means that mass, time and space are related to each other. I am a historian, not a physicist, I can't explain all the exact details, but in essence, what it means is that the faster a mass can be made to go, the more it can bend both time and space around it, allowing you to take shortcuts in space or time. But normally these effects are very small, really at the sub-atomic level.

"In 2048, when I was still a teenager, a Chinese physicist, Yang Zhin Li, discovered a way to synchronize billions of these little interactions to create a small time-loop. He discovered that by synchronizing the particle fields, he could generate tremendous amounts of energy using what's called zero-point energy. That's the energy that is constantly being created and annihilated in empty space because of what is called, um, what we call, the Heisenberg Uncertainty Principle."

"Ah, maybe that is Kepri Salama's Principle of Exclusion," said Adler.

Outhwaite scrunched her nose playfully at Adler. "You always did spend too much time studying the atheist scientists…"

Fr. Adler smiled broadly back at her. "Don't make fun of me, *muy vieja amiga*, it is quite useful at this moment."

"So even though zero-point energy is, well pretty much zero energy," Ian continued, "Yang's discovery lets us pull more energy on a rolling basis from the very near past and the very near future, over and over which, in turn, makes the zero-point energy of the past, present and future in milliseconds instantly also bigger and the effect adds up very quickly. When he built this into an energy source, it turned out to be a nearly unlimited source of free energy with the chief difficulty of keeping the reaction under control.

"It took a few more years for the scientists to realize that Yang's engine was also something else entirely new. These ZiP Engines, as they are called, can be set in motion. As they go faster, at a significant percentage of the speed of light, they lose the ability to generate substantial new energy but they create powerful space-time bubbles around themselves and whatever we can fit inside this bubble — which in effect become portable, moving wormholes — that we can use to push — pull really — something, such as a time ship through space at super light speeds. And the ship can also take a right angle turn in space-time to go both backward and forward in time.

"Jacob and I are Field Historian who go back in time to witness and document what really happened in the past and to compare that to the documentary evidence we have for the times and places we visit.

"Both Jane and I were actually born in Leicester, me in the city, Jane in Leicestershire. I've lived in London for twenty five of my years, working for the Institute of Historical Research. Jane is, as you can guess, from a much smaller city and has only recently joined me in my travels."

"So are you from the future then? I have heard physicists talk about such ideas but we know of no way to do it," Said Adler.

"I'm not really allowed to say exactly where I am from." Ian answered — lamely in Jane's opinion. "We are forbidden from changing history."

Outhwaite scoffed. "You can give us science secrets but can't answer that simple question?"

Adler and Outhwaite looked at each other for a moment. "Dear Freya, you predicted it. I may know the scientists better than you, but as always, you know people."

"That *is* my job, Mateo."

Northrup looked back and forth between the two of them, finally looking back at Jane and shrugging his shoulders.

"Mr. Harland and Miss Goodall, let me take a couple extra guesses here," Outhwaite said after releasing a long plume of smoke. Jane thought her smile suddenly looked quite a bit more reptilian.

"You may both have been born in Leicestershire, but you were not born in the same time, not even the same century I suspect. Correct?"

Jane was not a great liar. She nodded.

"Guess number two; Mr. Harland is not from a future with time travel, he left, probably in his version of 2085 and tried to get back home. Mr. Harland, you went back in history to the sixteenth century, and you changed something, didn't you," she said looking straight at him. "You did something, — I'm taking a bigger guess here — maybe it was picking up this slip of a girl — and you changed 2085 into something you can barely recognize. Am I correct? And that is why all these other ships, five of them, keep landing outside St. Rumwald's, because they, too, are trying to get home."

This time, neither Ian nor Jane answered. Northrup looked at Jane with the wide eyes of a child. "You are from *Tudor* England! I am *so* happy to know you."

An older man knocked and entered. "Dinner is ready" he said and led them to a dining room. Jane was happy to escape the pipe smoke.

The dining room was small but well appointed with an ornate table, high-backed chairs, an elaborate electric light hanging from the ceiling. With a small shock, Jane remembered she had been in this very room five hundred years ago as a young girl, she had actually *eaten a meal* in this room. She remembered torches adding to fading light coming through the tall slit windows and a fire in the fireplace. It must have been fall then.

Her father had brought her and Katharine here when she was ten or eleven. Henry Grey was a fixture in King Henry's court and spent much of her childhood away from the family, but brought them to visit London at least twice and the second time, he had brought them to the White Tower.

She remembered her father showing them the rooms for royalty, the gardens, the chapel and, most interesting to Jane, many of the secret passages that only a few confidantes of the King and the King's Guard knew.

But what she remembered most from that trip though, was the tour of the lower floors. Lord Henry did not make them enter the dungeons, but he did make them stand outside and listen. He said they needed to know that life was not always kind and that love of their country and their Protestant faith required strength and fortitude no matter which side of that door one ended up on. She had nightmares for weeks after that.

When they sat down, a waiter offered them a choice of a white or red wine. Jane chose the Rueda White. Moments later, a set of mechanical waiters, more of these robots, rolled into the room and deftly dropped a plate with a hard Yorkshire pudding filled with gazpacho at each guest's place.

Though not as filling as she wanted, it *was* very good.

"Juan," Ian started after a moment, "you are a historian by trade, I understand."

"Yes sir," I am, "I am a senior lecturer in English History at the University of London. I specialize in Tudor history and the history of the so-called Reformation and the Counter-Reformation." Northrup eyes kept darting towards Jane as he spoke.

"I see," Ian said. "I'm guessing that Freya and Fr. Adler may have not been totally convinced by Jacob's story from the start then?"

Northrup smiled nervously, Outhwaite raised her glass to Ian.

"Can we exchange some history then? Juan, can you give me a brief history of the Tudor dynasty?"

"I would be delighted," said Juan, nodding eagerly.

"The first of the Tudors was Henry VII..."

Ian stopped him. "I think we share some of that history. After the War of the Roses, Henry VII was able to restore order after the mayhem of the Plantagenet rule. He had one son survive to maturity."

Northrup seemed a little put out at being interrupted but complied. "So much for restored order. Henry VIII was a heretic, a glutton, a libertine, and a serial bigamist. When the pope would not allow him to annul his first marriage, he made common cause with heretics across Europe that called themselves the 'Reformation' and challenged the authority of the Holy See. They claimed the church had fallen into sin and, begging the Father's pardon, they weren't completely wrong."

Fr. Adler waved his hand, dismissing any anger he had, but Outhwaite scowled at the professor.

"We are still together," said Ian. "After Henry's death, his still-minor son, King Edward VI was crowned."

"Yes, the bastard king. No one knows how much the boy was involved, but his Council of Regents, led first by the heretic Edward Seymour, then by the despicable John Dudley, conspired to keep Mary I, Mary the Blessed, from taking her rightful throne. She was the only legitimate child of Henry and his one true wife Catharine. Henry tried to legitimize his bastards from his other whores by creating what he called the "Church of England" and declaring his marriage to Catharine annulled, but no one with any faith supported such a transparent lie." Again, Jane saw Northrup's eyes dart between Adler and Outhwaite, as if he were carefully gauging their reactions to his words.

The robot waiters interrupted by bringing in the main dish. As with the gazpacho and pudding, they were able to deliver the dish almost simultaneously to all five diners and this dish was as piping hot as the appetizer had been chilled. It was a very elegant Shepherd's Pie, something Jane could appreciate with gusto. Finally, a dish she recognized and could sink her teeth into.

When she did, however, she was once again surprised, though very pleasantly, with the taste. It had a bouquet of unexpected flavors, some she could identify like garlic and nuts, others she had never tasted, that melded into a satisfying spicy treat.

Watching her dig in, Adler explained it was Catalan Shepherd's Pie which was infinitely better than the bland version the Northerners like to eat. Jane had to agree.

It was only after several minutes of dedicated eating and chewing that Northrup returned to his history.

"After Edward's death, Mary realized the time had come to restore England to the church and she assembled an army to retake the throne by force. But she had little fighting to do as the privy council proclaimed her Queen regnant and she was ushered in with great support among the people of England, tired of a government run by heretics, lechers, and gluttons."

It took every ounce of Jane's self-control to keep her mouth shut. Ian had reached his hand under the table into hers and he must have been in excruciating pain given how hard she was squeezing it.

Northup picked up his lecture again. "When Mary took the throne, she began to capture and execute everyone who had led England away from the true church, restoring to the church all its lands and privileges. She married Prince Philip of Spain and formed an alliance with the Spanish Crown and eventually became Queen Consort of Spain as well as Queen of England, Ireland and Scotland. She suffered a terrible string of miscarriages but in her final days, she had the priests pray fervently before her lying in and she allowed Philip to join her in her confinement." Northrup continued to watch Adler and Outhwaite.

"Though the queen died in childbirth, Philip came out of her chambers with a large, healthy baby boy." This was the first of her three miracles.

"Her son, King Philip I of England had a long and prosperous reign though he, too, had to fight the biscuit-eaters who would betray God and the pope."

Ian interrupted. "Why 'biscuit-eaters?' I've never heard that term before."

"One of the Protestant heresies is that the host does not become the blood and body of Christ. They go to church only to eat biscuits," Outhwaite said.

"Towards the end of his reign," Northrup continued, "English and Scottish merchants revolted against the restrictions placed on English commerce by the pope and by our ally Spain, and tried to revolt, but Philip brought the famed Spanish Armada to suppress the revolt and England became a protectorate of Spain."

Ian put down his fork and looked at Northrup. "So England became a vassal state to Spain?"

Northrup answered before he should have, spitting mashed potatoes across the table.

"For two hundred years we remained obligated to Spain. Spain became, for a while, the biggest Empire the world has ever known. It was said the sun never set on the Spanish Empire. They colonized much of Southern Columbiana until the Mayan Empire revolted and drove them to the sea, and they even tried to set up colonies in Africa and the Far East like China, Japan, and Korea. Other countries tried to hold colonies too, Italy, France, Portugal for example. But between battles with Portugal, France, and eventually Russia, Spain lost most of its foreign colonies by the late 1700s and gave up all claim to England, Scotland and Ireland in the Treaty of Plymouth of 1782.

"Most of the other colonial powers also lost their footholds outside of Europe too by the early 1800s. Fortunately, we still get to eat Spanish food, though. I don't speak Spanish or Spanglish like Fr. Adler and Mrs. Outhwaite, but I do love Spanish food."

Adler chuckled. "I too like the food; but I think it is the Spanish music I would most miss if not for our shared history."

"Miss Goodall," asked Outhwaite, "do you agree that Mary's restoration of the Holy Church to England was the proper thing to do when the heretic Tudors tried to break from God's will so the corrupt, fat king could fuck whoever he wanted?'"

Ian squeezed her hand again and she tried to answer more levelly than she felt. Jane could feel it was a trap but couldn't help herself. This was her God, her Church, and her family Outhwaite was insulting.

"Certainly you understand that the Catholic Church had much to answer for with its corruption and avarice. Henry wasn't the only one to think so. They sold indulgences so the rich could do what they wanted. There was blatant fornication, and rewards for the male and female lovers of the pope and the bishops. Then there was the Inquisition…"

Outhwaite leaned back, apparently satisfied for the moment.

Juan looked nervously between Outhwaite and Jane. "We owe so much to Mary and Prince Phillip and Spain for destroying the heretics and their false church. Isn't that correct? Mary burned or hung every biscuit-eater in England and executed every Protestant Tudor."

"Except one" Freya said.

"Which one was that?" asked Jane, desperately trying to hold back her horror.

"Why, the whore of Northumberland, that bitch, the Lady Jane Grey, who ran off to fuck the first man she met after being betrothed to Guildford Dudley. That simple act of cowardice and whoredom is what turned the people of England against the godless protestant heretics."

Jane ignored Ian's vain attempts to warn her by hand squeezes and stood up to her full four feet and eleven inches, knocking her chair back into one of the serving robots. "I am no whore. That Papist Mary was going to execute me. I should've stayed and died before my eighteenth birthday?

"When Ian offered me a way out, I took it. I shouldn't have, I should have stayed and died like God intended and then you Papist scum would never have taken over my beloved England."

Jane stopped as she realized that perhaps now was not the ideal time or place to re-litigate the Reformation. She sat down and looked around at all the people staring at her.

Northrup wouldn't meet her eyes, Outhwaite sat with her arms folded and a small, smug smile on her face.

Fr. Adler sighed. "Freya, *querida*, you are always *so* good at your job."

"This has been a very long day," said Ian. "Is it too late for you to take us back to our ship?"

"Señor Northrup can take *you* anywhere you want to go. I am afraid that Lady Jane Grey will be enjoying the continued hospitality of the White Tower."

It was Ian's turn to stand in anger. "I think not. She will remain with me. What the hell do you want with her here anyway."

Fr. Adler sighed again and gave his disarming smile, this time to no effect on anyone in the room. "My dear Time Traveller, it was no coincidence that I was writing my memoirs at St. Rumwald's when you arrived. The monks there had reported sighting several ships like yours in the past year and I was sent to investigate. Until a few years ago, I was the Holy Grand Inquisitor of England. I am retired now but the bishop thought I would be the right person to investigate these strange visitations."

"I did have the opportunity to talk with Mr. Patel and he did in fact claim he was from Tralfamadore, but I did not believe him, even before talking with Mrs. Outhwaite, who has served as my chief prosecutor for twenty years and believes that everyone lies to Inquisitors. I had been waiting at St. Rumwald's for several months before your arrival blew away all of our wireless communications as you landed."

"What do you want of us, of Jane?"

"Well, I have always taken my oath to defend the faith very, very seriously and I can attest that Freya has done the same. Due to the decisions of several recent popes — wrongheaded I believe — I no longer have the authority to arrest heathens, atheists or academics like yourself and Mr. Northrup here. The newest pope has limited us to pretty much investigating thefts from altar plates, nuns who drink communion wine and priests who chase after altar boys.

"It seems, however, that prosecuting one of the conspirators against Mary the Blessed is still fine with the Church so Mrs. Outhwaite and I have one more job to do together."

"Juan," said Ian, "Can you please get us out of here?"

"I will try…" Northrup said.

"I am very sorry, no." Adler said. Two guards entered and stood ominously behind Ian and Northrup. Ian grabbed for Jane's hand. "My lady, I swear I will not let anything happen to you."

The guard wrapped something around Ian's neck and pulled him from his chair and out the door. Northrup, too, was dragged away, screaming and writhing against the restraint.

Jane tried to get up and run out the door too but was stopped by another tower guard who held something with multiple points against her body.

"Lady Grey," said Adler, "please do not resist. Those devices can be incredibly painful. It is better you walk out on your own two feet."

"You don't need to kill him, you don't need to kill Ian," Jane said to Outhwaite and Adler. Freya still sat almost primly with her wrists crossed in her lap.

"They won't be harmed;" Outhwaite said, "We have no charges we are allowed to bring against them. They will be there tomorrow to watch as the charges are published against you, then they will be freed. I suspect Fr. Adler will have your time craft towed back to the university here to be taken apart and studied and replicated."

"What will happen to me?" Jane asked. Her voice faltered slightly, much to her shame.

"Tomorrow we will read the charges. If you confess your crimes, you will be executed by beheading in three days' time, giving you time enough to make peace with our Lord and Savior, Jesus Christ, through the mercy of His church. If you do not confess, you will be placed on the rack until you confess or you die. We will give you every chance to confess to save your soul. We pray to God that you confess and make your peace with God and Our Savior."

Jane nodded. It was what she expected, it was the same sentence and chance of redemption her uncle and her cousin gave to Catholics. She still had her speech memorized and now she knew why God had brought her here. She could find peace with the pain and she would not forsake God before these Papist rats.

The White Tower, April 16 - 17

The cell was cold, she was left to sleep on the floor in a sack. They had even shaved her head and left the strands of her red-gold hair on the floor to mock her.

She sat in the corner of her cell, racking her brain for a way to kill herself. She wouldn't do it, of course. Her path of service to God was now clear, but it gave her something to think about in the dark and the cold and the quiet.

In the morning, a guard brought her some sort of gruel.

"I am sorry, my Lady, I did not know they left you this way," he said as he wrapped a dirty, moth-eaten blanket around her shoulders. "Please do not be afraid. All is not lost." This latter he whispered to her.

"What are you doing with the whore, Valdez? Do you want to join her in the dock?" came a voice through the door. "Bring her out. The bishop is ready for her."

"Sergeant, she hasn't finished eating yet."

"You think the Inquisitors care about that? Give her the sack and bring her out *now*."

The guard helped her stand and walk to the door. She looked at the sergeant, her head held high. "Will you take me before the bishop in a sackcloth? Have you no mercy at all?"

"Not for biscuit-eater scum. It is long past time you paid for your heresy," the man said.

They led her down winding steps at the end of the cell block and three levels down, she was led into a large room and taken to the raised prisoner's dock at one end. There were many rows of benches against each side, already filed with a handful of people, including, to her horror, both Ian and Juan Northrup, each accompanied by a guard. Facing the dock was a large throne-like chair, with two smaller, plainer wooden chairs, one on either side.

Inside, she felt nothing but fiery anger as she stood there for what must have been half-an-hour as more spectators came in to fill the benches, many walking up and gaping openly at her as if she were a prize horse. She kept her back straight and her head held high. No one would see her fear.

"You've drawn a fine crowd here, *Lady-whore* Jane," said the sergeant, "Everyone important here in the diocese and in the government of England has come to see you held to account at last for your wantonness and your wicked heresy."

Jane did not respond.

Finally, a bailiff appeared in the center of the room, knocking his staff three times for each announcement. *Knock, knock, knock.* "All Rise for His Excellency, Richard Wren, Bishop of London and England."

Knock, knock, knock. "All Rise for His Excellency, Andrew Redmond, the Grand Holy Inquisitor of England."

Knock, knock, knock. "All rise for His Excellency, Mateo Adler, Grand Holy Inquisitor Emeritus of England."

The three men came in with great pomp and dignity and sat in their respective chairs, the bishop in the throne in the middle and each inquisitor on either side.

The bailiff turned his back to the dock and the room, facing the bishop and the Inquisitors. "Grand Inquisitor Redmond, who shall be prosecuting the case against this heretic?"

Redmond nodded his head. "It is with great honor that I appoint Dame Freya Outhwaite as Lead Prosecutor in these proceedings.

The bailiff faced the room again and knocked his staff on the floor. "I call forth Dame Freya Outhwaite to lead these holy proceedings."

Outhwaite stood from her chair and nodded to the bishop, the inquisitors, and then to the room. "I am ready to proceed."

She turned towards Jane. "Prisoner, will you state your name for the record?"

Jane again stretched herself to her full height. "My name is Lady Jane Grey, daughter of Lord Henry Grey and Lady Frances Grey, Duke and Duchess of Suffolk."

"Prisoner, is it true you have come five hundred years from your evil, benighted time into our time by some mechanical conveyance?" There was a muttering around the room until the bailiff pounded his staff.

"I ask that you give me the respect of calling me by name and title." Jane said.

"I will do no such thing for a whore, a traitor and a heretic. Prisoner, answer my question."

Jane felt the insults sting, but she would not flinch before these people. God had a plan for her and she would be strong to the end.

"I do not know for sure if it is magical or mechanical. But yes, I am Lady Jane Grey, born in 1537 and I have been brought to your time by God to heal…"

Freya made a hand gesture to the sergeant, and he whacked Jane's back hard with his pike, knocking the breath out of her. The other guard, the kinder one, surreptitiously tried to support her with a hand on her back to keep her from falling.

"Prisoner, you will only answer the questions I put to you. Is it true you conspired with your traitorous, heretical father, and the traitorous heretics John Dudley and his demon-spawned son Guildford, to usurp the throne of Queen Mary the Blessed?"

"My cousin, Edward VI, King of England and Ireland, named me his successor as he lay dying. I would not have been a usurper." Jane's anger at these farcical proceedings came through her voice, but her bonds would not let her lean forward like she wanted.

"Prisoner," Outhwaite shouted at her, "Did you conspire with your father and with the Dudleys to place yourself on the throne to prevent the just destruction of England's heretical rebellion against the true Church? Answer 'Yes,' or 'No.'"

"I worked with…" She stopped after another blow from the Sergeant.

"Prisoner, do you admit your guilt in opposing the restoration of the Holy Church? Yes, or No?"

"How dare you?" Shouted Jane. "I…"

"Gag the whore." Outhwaite said and the sergeant roughly stuffed a cloth into her mouth, leaving her gagging. The other guard tried to support her and adjusted the gag to stop her choking. He whispered in her ear as he did so. "I am sorry, my lady, please be patient."

Jane looked at him quickly then looked away, not wanting to give him away.

Outhwaite continued speaking, explaining the history to the court and the observers. Starting with Henry VIII, how the Tudor heretics broke from the Holy Church to pursue their sexual perversions and to bring the kingdom of Satan to the world. For forty years, they persecuted and executed anyone who threatened their vicious reign of terror and evil.

Outhwaite argued that Jane was the sole surviving Tudor witch who had tried to escape with a time-traveler.

"Before she ran away in her own cowardice," Outhwaite said. "It was well known that the Tudors and the Dudleys conspired to keep Mary the Blessed from the throne and prevent England's return to the protection of the Catholic Church and the Holy See. It is well known from documents and testimony from the time that they wanted to place this little prostitute on the throne to continue the depravities of the biscuit-eaters."

After Jane Grey ran off to whore it with the then unknown man, she explained, their plot fell apart and Mary and her armies rescued England and executed the heretics, destroyed the satanic conspirators, and put herself on the throne for her short but blessed reign along with her husband, Prince Philip of Spain.

Jane fought against her gag but could do little more than grunt through it.

Outhwaite's presentation went on for over three hours and ended abruptly with the decision by the Bishop and the Grand Inquisitor, agreeing that Jane would be given the chance to recant her heresy under persuasion and sent to her eternal reward or punishment depending on her own reconciliation with God. There would be no further public appearances and her body would be burned and her ashes scattered to the winds.

When the Grand Inquisitor asked about her paramour, Outhwaite pointed Ian out to the court but said she had no evidence he was involved in the plot against Mary.

The White Tower, April 18

Jane was again huddled in a corner of her cell for the night, naked, cold, and shivering. She quietly whimpered to herself and tried and to use the hair they had shorn from her head and left on the floor in her cell as a blanket. It did no good whatsoever.

The prison was nearly silent except for the snoring of the guard outside her door. She had never heard of a quiet prison. She knew prisons in her own time to be loud, raucous and violent.

But even this silence weighed on her heart. There would be no chance to say her peace to anyone, only the chance to confess, or not confess, under torture to a Papist priest. Her words would not be recorded for posterity.

Would God even hear her words in a place like this? Her faith said yes, but her heart doubted.

Suddenly, there was another voice outside the door, talking loudly over the snoring.

"Wake up, ya ugly oaf," it said, then there was the sound of a chair scraping and a groggy guard falling to the floor.

"I wasn't sleeping, sir."

"Just restin' yur eyes?"

"Yes sir, I wasn't asleep."

"Get yur ass out of 'ere. We'll deal with ya in the mornin.'"

"I was told not to leave the prisoner alone."

"I'm telling ya to leave, now, or ya'll be guardin' the sewers."

"Yes sir." There was the noise of the man getting up quickly and scurrying away.

After the distant slam of a door, Jane heard a shockingly familiar voice. "My lady," Ian said, "are you all right?"

She whimpered first, then found her voice, shaky but audible. "Ian, I am alright for now. What are you doing here?"

"Oh, I'm your new guard, Paul Edgecomb." She heard the key opening the lock.

She watched him come in, shrouded in the electric light from the corridor. She stood up, then ran to him and threw her arms around him, ignoring her own nakedness. The hug he gave back to her flooded her with a feeling of safety, if only for a moment.

"Ian, I am so scared. I don't want to die like this."

"You think I'm going to leave you here; we're going to leave you here?" He pulled out a bag of cloths for her. "Quickly," he said. "We have many friends here, but not everyone."

"Where are we going?"

"Edward is going to take us back to the Seneca," said Ian, indicating the very large man in a sergeant's uniform. Edward had bushy eyebrows and a big red beard around a snaggle-toothed grin. "Lady Jane Grey, 'tis a great honor to meet ya. I 'ave read about ya all my life, I was even named for your cousin, King Edward or so my Da' says." He literally got down on one knee.

Shocked, she accepted his hand and let him kiss hers. It was awkward with her still shivering from the cold and still only holding Ian's proffered bag of clothes against her nakedness.

"Are you a Protestant, sir?" She asked.

"Oh no, m' lady, everyone in England is a Catholic. But there is some of us who believe ya and yur family was treated poorly and the church of that time certainly did need reform, we believe."

Ian said "Lady, put the clothes on now so we can try to get out of here without being caught."

Jane obeyed and found being warm and clothed again a great comfort. As she dressed, Ian began explaining.

"It seems, my lady, that you and your family have quite the fan club here in this timeline"

"What is a 'fan club?'"

"Ah, it's a group of people who are interested in you, who admire you. In both timelines, interestingly enough, there exists a group of amateur and professional historians that call themselves 'The Tudor Society.' They used to have me give online talks in my 2085."

"Turns out Northrup is a big deal in the Tudor Society here and now, and that many of the people who play the part of guards for the public visitors at the Tower are also members."

"Some of the real guards too," said Edward.

"And you're not banned by the Church?" she asked.

"'Course not," said Edward. "The greatest Tudors of them all was Mary and her son King Philip I. We are a respected 'istorical society." Edward held his fingers to his heart and smiled. "It's just we don't advertise to the Church much that we 'istorian types respect *both* sides.

"The reason we got a chance to gets ya out is that Northrup called an emergency meeting and convinced the society to plan an escape. There are a lot of us who work here at the Tower who love 'istory and don't want no part o' killin' it."

Slipping out through the door, Jane looked both ways down a long corridor. Her cell was nearly the central cell of some twenty or thirty cells on what she thought was the fourth floor.

"So what's the plan?" she asked as they started moving down the hallway to the right.

"We think we may have an hour before anyone figures out you're gone," Ian said. "We'll be trying to get down to the Thames where Edward and his people have a boat waiting for us."

"Why is it so quiet here?" Jane asked, looking around at the empty cells. The corridor seemed endless as they made their way down to the stairwell at the far end.

"A 'undred years ago," Edward said, "it wouldn'a been. This is where the Inquisition used ta like ta keep the worst heretics and the atheists. Only the last few popes ha' discouraged torture an killin' heretics and Protestants and atheists an' the like. That's why the damned Grand Inquisitor Adler was so pleased with hisself to get his 'ands on you; a *real* enemy o' the Church."

"Oh, lucky me," said Jane.

"They had to get special dispensation to hold the trial yesterday. Mostly, the tower and the guards are fer tourists now. The basement holds the real prisoners that the Inquisition is still allowed to arrest but almost never torture anymore."

"So they weren't going to torture me?" Jane asked.

"Ah, no, my lady, they do keep the dungeon in working order, just in case, but it is about only five prisoners or so a year anymore. But that Fr. Adler and Pros'cutor Outhwaite, they had a hard 'un on fer ya. I think they viewed it as their way to go down in the 'istory books."

"Come on, folks, Let's keep moving on our way out." Ian said. "I really want to get back to the Seneca."

"That, my dear time-travelin' 'istorian, is a very good idea," said Edward. "We're on the fourth floor now an' somehow we gotta get through guards and night staff on the first floor t' get ya out. We be thinkin' we'll pretend yur another prisoner we have orders to walk out, but it ain' gonna be easy."

From the stairwell at the far side of the corridor, they heard yelling. The guard Edward had so rudely dispatched was leading the charge. "Halt, in the name of the Holy Inquisition. If you run, you will die," said the officer behind him.

"*Carajo*," said Edward. "Run!" And the group bolted towards the door on their end. Weakened, Jane stumbled twice but Ian held her up. The pursuing guards were catching up with them but they reached the door first. Edward locked the door behind them then jammed a spike in the keyhole.

She heard the pursuers slam into the door and rattle and bang on it as she and her rescuers started down the spiral stairs.

"Something to be said for old rusty locks, I suppose," said Ian.

"It ain' gonna hold them long." Said Edward.

Jane's mind was running a mile a minute. She had been here as a child. "What wall is this, the Northwest?" she said pointing to the wall that had held her cell."

Edward had to think for a moment. "Aye, my lady."

"Good, I think I know way we might get out safely." Edward and Ian stared at her in disbelief.

"'Ow's that?" asked Edward.

"Lead on, my lady," said Ian and they continued circling down the spiral stairs.

Above them was a loud sizzling noise and the sound of what must have been the lock shattering. A few tiny pieces of hot metal rained on them as Edward unlocked the next floor and they poured through into another corridor. Edward spiked this door as well from the inside.

It must be here. She thought to herself, but was it six doors in from this side or six doors in from the other side all the way down the corridor? One, two, three, four, five, six. She reached up but couldn't reach the block, dammit. She pointed Ian to it and told him to push it up and to the left.

Nothing happened.

No, it was seven. She moved to the next door and pointed again for Ian. They heard the pursuers hammering on the old heavy wooden door to the stairs trying to force it to open. In a moment, they would shoot through that lock too or simply break it down.

Ian reached, pushed sideways then in.

Click.

She had been right. Her father had shown Jane and her sister this passageway in case they ever found themselves in the Tower. She smiled, remembering her father's face when he said he had no idea how such a useless piece of information would ever help girls but, well, his father had taught him...

"Shit," said Ian, "the letter to your sister, that Katharine hid, I think it was found in a passage just like this." Jane laughed. Of course, her sister would have hidden it in such a place when she was held too. If Jane *had not* chosen to go with Ian, if she *had* sent the letter, her sister *would* have stashed it here in the tower. What a strange and wonderful thing traveling with Ian would be — *provided they lived long enough to do it again.*

The three of them pulled themselves into the little room and shut the secret door. Just as it clicked closed, they heard the pursuers smash through the stairwell door and start running down the hallway.

They heard the guards run down the corridor, trying each of the cell doors as they passed. When she judged the pursuers were far enough away, she whispered "My father showed my sister and me this secret passage when we came to visit. For a while, at least, this floor used to be for guests and not prisoners."

"How long should we hide here?" Ian asked.

"Not long," she said, and started feeling around the back wall for the next release.

"Would this help?" asked Ian, bringing out his strange little device that took pictures, opened timeship doors and now, apparently, made light.

With his light, she quickly found the release she wanted and opened another door leading to a spiral stairway going down from where they stood.

"This boat, Ian, where are we supposed to meet it?"

Edward answered. "It will be in the water outside the Traitor's Gate."

"How were you planning to get us there? Through the Bloody Tower?"

"Aye, if we can get to the Bloody Tower, or if we can get to Northeast ramparts, I have friends waiting in both places."

"So you don't have a specific plan?" asked Jane.

"We 'oped we could walk you through as two guards moving a prisoner." Edward said.

"'Course that was based on the idea that nobody knew you were out of you cell," said Ian.

"Aye," said Edward. "We have a few friends among the guards and a few ideas about how to smuggle you out, but you and the Inquisition did na' give us a lot of time to make very deep plans."

Jane nodded. "I don't suppose so. Good sirs, this stairway will take us down to a passage that lets out on the northwest wall near the west tower. If we get there, will that help us?"

Edward laughed loudly. "Well, it ain' gonna hurt."

"Good God, Sarge, keep it down. Your laugh rumbles like a jet engine."

"A wot?" Edward asked.

"Never mind."

In Jane's time, these stairs had been kept clean and clear, but it must have been a long time since anyone remembered them. As much as she hated batting cobwebs and stumbling over loose blocks and steps, it made her happy that no one apparently used this passage now.

Using Ian's light, they made good time going down the stairs, reached the bottom floor and turned left toward the West Tower, ignoring the passage going off to the right.

While the stairs were dusty and cobwebbed but passable, this passageway on the ground floor was immediately more difficult. The floor was covered with a soft, putrid sludge. Fallen rocks from the walls and the ceiling tripped them up randomly.

Jane felt something land in her newly shortened hair and start moving around her head. She reached up to touch it and had to swallow her scream as she flailed wildly against a bat.

Ian pulled her arms to her side while Edward grabbed the creature in his huge hand and flung it away. For a moment, she buried her head in Ian's shirt and he stroked the stubble on her head.

"Better you than me, my lady, I would have screamed loud enough to wake the dead if that had been my head."

She wasn't sure if that were true or not, but she appreciated the effort. After a few moments, she pulled herself together and they plowed on only to reach a dead end just a few dozen more feet down the passage. The wall had collapsed. No amount of digging or prying could dislodge enough rubble to make a crawl hole for any of them.

"*Carajo*," said Edward. "What now?"

"We go the other way," Jane said. "If we can get through there, we can still get outside by the North Tower."

Edward pulled a device out of his pocket that looked a bit like Ian's little camera, door opener and torch. He spoke two words into it, "Feline Boreas."

Ian flashed the light into Edward's face. "You have a damn radio?" he said.

"Don' know what that is, this 'ere is a talk-box. I talk 'ere and my associates can 'ear me."

"*Now* you're telling this to us?"

Jane didn't know what they were talking about but guessed that Edward and his people had warlock devices too. In the warlock world, it seemed, they could do almost anything with these weird little devices. But she also heard disbelief in Ian's voice.

"I told 'em we would be comin' out o' the North Tower. If'n we're lucky, someone will un'erstand and meet us there."

"If we're lucky? Why can't you explain the whole damn thing to someone?"

"'Cuz every guard in the Tower has the same talk-box. Boreas was the Greek God o' the north wind. And feline is the lady 'cuz Captain Esposito thinks she looks like a little cat. I talk more than that and maybe they can track our signal or maybe they knows it's me with the feline. It's not like we break prisoners out o' the Tower every Monday and Tuesday."

Jane had been wrapped up in her own worries, but it struck her then just how much this man was risking for Ian and herself. She leaned in past Ian and pulled herself up as high as she could, and he bent so she could whisper "Thank you for all this" into his ear and she kissed his cheek. Edward blushed — she could see that in Ian's light — and she nodded in response.

The path north seemed in better shape. It didn't have as much guano on the floor or as many bats above them. Instead, it was teaming with cockroaches and hornets. Edward had been stung several times by the time they reached the door which, thankfully, slid open with only a little coaxing.

Edward stuck his head out first, looked around, then motioned for Jane and Ian to follow. "There's probably tower guards all over the place out here and maybe some of their damned robots," said Edward. "We're gonna hafta' move as quietly and as carefully as we can and try to get to the Bloody Tower."

"Well, you bloody bear, you couldn't move silently in a room filled with pillows and feathers."

Edward turned toward the woman who had silently joined them, and smiled broadly. "*Puta Madre*, Helena, you want to give me a heart attack?" But he hugged her just the same. She was a small woman, only a little taller than Jane herself, dressed in the uniform of a tower guard.

Jane was intrigued that a woman, someone so obviously a woman, could have such a job. She would have to ask Ian if it was the same in his 2085.

Saints, it was good to be outside again. There was little moon, but it seemed the Tower had some kind of light of its own. Another thing she would have to ask Ian about if she ever had the chance. There were lights in his Seneca, but nothing as big as these.

After quick introductions, Ian turned the conversation to the practical, trying to get options on how they could get to the Bloody Tower.

Helena explained that the Society members among the guards had put out the word that the escaped whore and her paramour had been seen heading out the door of the northeast wall and were hightailing it back into London across the bridge. The bulk of the searchers and the three tower guard bots had all been dispatched north. Their best chance would be to skirt the outside of the White Tower and hide as best they could in the trees and hedges that had recently been allowed to grow there, then head across the open areas as quickly and silently as they could to the chapel. From there, maybe they could go through the corridor in the outer rampart and out through the Byward Tower and straight to a small boat an unnamed benefactor had arranged for them.

"Hardly sounds safe," said Ian.

"Well," said Helena, cocking her head at him. Jane could just barely see her expression in the unnatural lights. "We can certainly take her back to her cell and try all this again tomorrow night. I'm sure she will be much more relaxed after a day on the rack. We're only trying to escape from England's oldest, strongest and most storied prison. I'm sure we'll have a much safer plan by then."

"Point taken," said Ian.

Keeping low, taking whatever cover they could, they got as far as halfway across the open walkway to the chapel doors before anyone saw them.

"Halt, who goes there?" came a voice from near the Western Tower. "Stop or I'll shoot."

Edward, who was the last of them to cross to the chapel, waved at them to keep going, then turned around and staggered back towards the tower.

"Oh come on, captain, it's just me and the boys havin' a little fun." He was purposefully slurring his words.

"The other one I just saw didn't look like no boy, Edward. Looked like Helena with the big tits."

"Oh, aye, me an' the boys an' a girl or two."

"You've heard the new prisoner has escaped?" asked the guard.

"Aye, and the cap'ns and sergeants have all gone t' London lookin' fer her. Perfect time for me and the boys and the girls t' go the other way."

"Edward, you mangy dog. But it's better you putting that pretty Helena to the question than those bastards with that damned girl. Get on with you and you don't tell and I won't tell. I just hope those flaming assholes don't find the little lass."

Edward continued to stagger until he was out of sight of the Tower then ran to join Ian and the women.

The rest of the way to the river went without a hitch. Two friends of Edward and Helena met them at the Byward Tower and gave Ian and Edward new clothes to hide their guard uniforms. They opened the gates and led them down to a small, flat-bottomed boat in the river. Helena gave Jane an unexpected hug and whispered "safe travels, come back if you can" in her ear. She gave Ian a quick kiss on the cheek. Edward picked up an oar and started slowly guiding the boat down river.

"Settle in," Edward said. "We got a bit o' way t' go t' get t' a centipede which will take ya back t' your ship."

The night was silent and though the city lights reflected along the edges of the water, the river was mostly black. Edward seemed to know every current and bend, and the gentle ride lulled Jane to the verge of long-denied sleep. But her daydreams of a soft warm bed were rudely interrupted when she heard an ungodly screaming and saw what she could only guess was an angel shining brilliant white lights across the water and which had a head of flames quickly changing from red to blue to yellow. "Mother of God," she said, "preserve us." This avenging angel was crossing the water faster than any boat Jane had ever seen.

"Get down;" said Edward, "Get down and be quiet and don' move." As they hit the deck, he threw a canvas tarp over them.

Even through the canvas, Jane could see the colored lights. She could hear Ian breathing hard next to her and Edward answering the angel.

"Halt, who are you?" asked the angel in a voice louder than any Jane had ever heard.

"My name is Liam." It was Edward's voice, but he had a completely different accent. "This is me home, I live here."

"We're looking for two men and a woman. The costume boys from the Tower tell us the woman they put on trial yesterday escaped already."

"Oh, aye," said Edward, "Them costume boys can't even keep a woman locked up safely in the Tower of London. What a bunch o' idiots they are."

"You see two men and a woman on the water here tonight?"

"No sir, been all by myself tonight since the tourists left."

"You see them, you find a talk-box and call the Metro, you hear?"

"Aye sir, I will."

The screeching, whining noise started up again and moved downriver from them. After a while, Edward pulled up the covering and helped them up again.

"Water cops," he said, "not always the brightest. We're getting close to the 'pede."

A few minutes later, the boat turned up a tributary and even in the darkness and silence, Edward navigated surely and silently through the shallows and the broken tree limbs and rocks.

"You *do* live on this boat, don't you?" Ian asked.

Edward nodded. "I got some debts," he said. "Ex wife. And now I got no job to go back to."

"Well, I know that feeling." Ian said.

In The Centipede, April 18, 2085

Edward pulled the boat to the edge of the stream and tied it to a tree. Climbing up a short path, they reached a road and found a centipede car waiting for them. It took Jane a moment to recognize Northrup sitting in the driver's seat. He waved at her, much like the first pod driver she had met.

Jane, Ian, and Edward got into the second pod and Northrup did whatever a pod car driver did to get it moving.

Northrup's voice came over the intercom system. "I am so sorry the idiot priests of this time have made your visit so horrible."

"Juan," Jane replied, "I can't express deeply enough my thanks that you and your friends have risked your lives for me, for us."

"We at the Tudor Society believe history should be studied and honored, not re-fought. Besides, Mr. Harland is a very persuasive speaker."

"You too, Edward," she said. "I am very grateful."

"Ah, well," he said, "Some of it I done for Juan here. Did ya know we are distant cousins?"

"Really," said Jane with unfeigned amazement. She couldn't think of two people more unlike each other.

"Aye, when we were little 'uns, Juan and his family would travel up from Cambridge to Stoke-On-Trent to see my family. What was it, your mum was sister to my Da's brother's wife?"

"Aunt Tilly," said Northrup's voice. "It was a big family."

"And filled with actors and 'istorians," said Edward. Sometimes when we were together, the adults had us act out famous plays along with them. One year, we did *The Wives of the Heretic* and I got to play Henry because even at twelve years old, I was bigger than most of the adults. And Juan's sister Emelia wanted to play Anne Boleyn so badly though I never knew why."

"Because she had such a crush on you, you big lout," said Northrup.

"Oh," said Edward, "and speakin' o' crushes, there was another time Juan insisted he and I play Guildford and Lord John Dudley."

"Oh no, stop," said Northrup.

"He wanted to play Guildford so he could woo the beautiful and mysterious Lady Jane…"

Jane shook her head in amazement, never imagining that she and her family would be the subject of children's games. "And who got to play me?"

Edward frowned. "Well, no one, my lady, ya had always already left and we was searching for wherever ya had gone. Jane could almost hear Northrup blushing in the other car.

This world, Jane decided, this 2085 was every bit as crazy as the 2085 described by Ian's computers and her own 1553. Still, she had to wipe a little water from her eye at the men's kindness.

The Road to Saint Rumwald's, April 18, 2085

Jane looked out of the dome as the pod car sped through the city.

There were lights everywhere and nothing was flickering. There were lights on the street, lights in many windows and lights used to highlight many of the buildings they passed in the downtown area.

The speed of this car was both exhilarating and terrifying.

"How fast are we going? I have never known such a speed."

Edward looked pleased. "My lady, the Bishop of London owns one of the fastest centipedes in England. This car has a top speed of forty-eight miles per hour and can travel over a hundred an' fifty miles on one charge."

Ian snorted and Edward looked at him. "Why do ya laugh?"

"I'm sorry, I don't mean to laugh. In my time, scooters, little bicycles with an electric motor, could hit 50 miles per hour. My own electric car could easily cruise at 150 miles per hour and go four hundred miles on a charge."

Edward's eyes widened. Jane, who had studied Ian's time was less impressed. "Can you tell Edward the state of your world when you had this technology?"

"Fair point. Our love of technology changed the world in a lot of very bad ways that don't seem to have happened here. While familiar in so many ways, you don't seem to have suffered the ravages we perpetrated on the world by destroying so much of our environment. The nine days that changed the world." Ian said, almost to himself, "The nine-day reign of a child queen made all the difference in the world."

"Do you really think that was it?" came the voice of Northrup from the first pod.

"It's just that you blame this on the lack of Jane's queenship. Last night, you told the Society members that some of the people in your Institute argued that the smallest change, the wind from the wings of a butterfly, could change the future as much as the beheading of a queen."

"That is true," Ian said, "but sitting here with this young girl, it is hard to imagine her not being a force of nature."

Jane found this a little much. "I have almost been executed twice, I was betrothed to the son of a great lord and I would have been queen if not for your intervention. I am seventeen years old. I am no child."

"I am sorry, my lady, in my time, and as I understand it in this version of my time, seventeen is seen as much younger than it was in 1533. It is hard for us to wrap our minds around."

"Do try, good sirs," she said.

Jane watched the city fade into countryside, only half listening to the men discuss the two divergent histories of 2085.

She, herself, was done with this time almost as much as she was done with 1553 and her pending execution there. A few weeks ago, in 1553, she had never imagined people could travel through time. She suspected if she had ever imagined what time-travel would be like, it certainly wouldn't involve finding new ways to be locked in the White Tower.

Eventually, the rocking of the pod car, the whistling of the wind through the vents and rambling of the men lulled her into the sleep she hadn't had for two days but it wasn't restful, she dreamed of being tortured with her mouth gagged so she couldn't admit her guilt and put an end to her suffering.

From a distance, she heard Ian calling and calling and finally found herself waking up in the crook of his shoulder. She straightened, embarrassed to find she had been drooling in her sleep.

"Lady Jane," he said, "we're here, back at the Seneca. I think we can finally escape this nightmare. I promised to give these men a tour of our ship, then we can leave this behind."

Once again, as they approached the Seneca, dawn was bringing first light after a long night of running.

"Where will we go?"

"I don't know. We can go back in time or take our chances going forward. We can go meet Jacob and see what he wants to tell us, we can stay in the now but go somewhere we might actually be welcomed. Once we are safe inside the Seneca, we can make that decision in peace and with full bellies. If you want, I can take you back when and where I picked you up. I would be sorry to do so, but I will do that if you wish it."

Jane and the three men exited of the pod car and started walking up the path through the woods that would take them to the Seneca.

Jane heard the snap of a twig first and melted off the path. As much as she had hated going on hunting parties with the Dudleys, she was grateful now for what she had learned.

It was the big sergeant, the one who had gagged her, who came up behind Ian and held what she gathered was a firearm to the back of his head.

"Where do you think you are going, atheist? And where is your pretty little biscuit-eater?" Ian froze, feeling the barrel at the back of his head. "We left her in the prison, I have no more need of her, I just want my ship back."

Jane found a large rock that fit neatly in the palm of her hand.

"I don't believe you," said the man. Fr. Adler received a call on the Inquisitor's talk-box that you and the Tudor Costume boys had freed her. I see some of your costume boys here with you, where is the whore?" All three men had stopped and the other two turned around while the sergeant moved his gun around to gesture at them.

Jane may have been small but she had been raised by her hard father to know how to protect herself. She found a lot of anger inside herself at this moment and at this bastard of a man. She brought the rock down hard enough in the middle of his back to drop him to his knees. He shot and a bolt of some sort of lightning blackened the leaves just to the left of her rescuers.

She brought another blow to the side of his head, bringing him down completely and several more blows to his head eventually cracked his skull into a bloody pulp.

Ian, Edward, and Northrup stood there, watching impassively. When Jane was done and still knelt beside the body, breathing hard, Ian said. "I think it is long too late for this but remind me in the future not to make you angry."

Jane looked up at him, not sure what she was feeling just at that moment. He offered her his hand to help her up. She dropped the rock next to the corpse and accepted.

Edward picked up the guard's pistola and put it into his own empty holster.

He must have been waiting near the road to ambush them but that probably meant that Adler and maybe other tower guards were already at the Seneca, probably trying to find a way in.

As they approached the Seneca, they heard pounding on the door and a string of un-priestly invectives in Fr. Adler's voice.

"I know this is the goddamned door but how the hell do you get it open?" He was pounding on the door with his cane, make no dent or mark whatsoever.

Outhwaite was trying to insert a knife blade into the keypad next to the door with no more success than the inquisitor. There appeared to be no one else around to help them or protect them.

"Grand Inquisitor," shouted Ian, "Please get away from my ship."

The two turned slowly and looked at Jane and Ian and the Tudor Society men.

"Give the whore back to Sgt. Dunham and I'll let you have your damned ship back. Guard," he said to Edward, "you know better than to protect heretics and traitors. Give me your pistolas now and maybe I won't prosecute you for heresy as well."

"Grand inquisitor," said Edward, "I think the sergeant has had as much o' the Lady Jane Grey as he is ever likely to want. My guess is that she did not appreciate his gentle treatment of her."

Adler's face fell a bit but he moved away from the door and from Outhwaite. Jane was suspicious and kept her eyes on Outhwaite. She was about to yell that Outhwaite was pulling out her own pistola, but Edward saw it first and fired before Outhwaite had raised it halfway.

Jane had to admit being impressed with the weapon. Though it made little more than a crackling noise, it threw Outhwaite's body hard against the Seneca and left a small pattern of black burn marks where the weapon had penetrated the woman.

Adler tried to run, but he was an old man and Edward easily caught up with him and dragged him back kicking and screaming. He held the old man's cane securely in his other hand.

"Gentlemen, would you like to see the interior of a time ship?"

Northrup and Edward readily assented, Adler said nothing.

The door whooshed open and both Society members stood there, open-mouthed, looking at the inside room much bigger than the ship was on the outside.

"Come on in," Ian said, "and bring the good Grand Inquisitor with you and I can show you wonders and we can talk Tudor history all you want. I have photos and movies and recording and I am sure Lady Jane, the lady of this ship, will be glad to tell you anything you want to know.

"And while we're at it, we can go anywhere in this world and time you have ever wanted to visit."

"Can we leave the Grand Inquisitor someplace unpleasant while we're at it? Maybe in the Levant or the forbidden city in China where they do so love Grand Inquisitors?" asked Northrup.

"That sounds like a wonderful idea to me," said Jane. "But first I need a shower."

In the end, though, after the Seneca departed with Ian, Jane and the two guests, a cane-less, talk-box-less, and very dispirited Adler was left in the clearing next to the bodies of Outhwaite and Sgt. Dunham that Edward had thoughtfully laid out for him.

A Thread Across the Veil

To: cleo@singingemail.com
From: ant@singingemail.com
Sent: March 15, 2021 03:43

My Dearest Cleo,

   My heart is broken. We finally got everyone here today so we could spread your ashes in the wildflower field that you and I loved. I miss you so much I can barely stand it. Our bed is cold without you, our basement is dark and dank and scary without you.
   We met online, we lived so much of our lives together online, we built our busi-

ness online, and you even died working online. I should have been home when it happened, I am so sorry.

So I think sending this email out into the wilds of the internet is the most appropriate way to tell you how much I still love you and how much you will be missed. Flow with the data packets my love and find new servers to explore.

»-(¯`·..·´¯)->,
Ant

[Bing]

To: ant@singingemail.com
From: cleopatra.ellington@newlife.pgt
Sent: March 15, 2021 03:49

   Ant, that is so sweet, thank you!

Cleo

To: cleopatra.ellington@newlife.pgt
From: ant@singingemail.com
Sent: March 15, 2021 03:51

  Who the fuck is this?!! You bastard. I'm going to find you and fuck with you whoever you are!

[Bing]

To: ant@singingemail.com
From: cleopatra.ellington@newlife.pgt
Sent: March 15, 2021 04:00

  Wow, didn't expect that reaction, Ant-Man. There is nobody to fuck with. Don't get your balls in a bunch. I really *am* Cleo, your dearly departed lover.
  When you die, you can get your email forwarded to you. Most people don't — God, who wants spam in the afterlife — but I did. Too much unfinished business!

Love,
Cleo

To: cleopatra.ellington@newlife.pgt
From: ant@singingemail.com
Sent: March 15, 2021 04:02

   Prove it.

[Bing]

To: ant@singingemail.com
From: cleopatra.ellington@newlife.pgt
Sent: March 15, 2021 04:14

   There is this little, really horrible tattoo of Mario on your butt. I don't think you ever showed that to anyone but me and I sure as hell don't blame you for that (LMAO).

(つ●﹏●)つ
Cleo

To: cleopatra.ellington@newlife.pgt
From: ant@singingemail.com
Sent: March 15, 2021 04:18

   Fuck. What pet name did I call you in bed?

[Bing]

To: ant@singingemail.com
From: cleopatra.ellington@newlife.pgt
Sent: March 15, 2021 04:22

   Peppermint Patty and I always *hated* that. Good thing I loved your cute little Mario ass enough or I would have beat the shit out of you.

(♥_﬎ -)♥
Cleo

To: cleopatra.ellington@newlife.pgt
From: ant@singingemail.com
Sent: March 15, 2021 04:43

  Fucking hell! Where are you? Can I see you again?

Ant

[Bing]

To: ant@singingemail.com
From: cleopatra.ellington@newlife.pgt
Sent: March 15, 2021 05:17

  Sorry, my love, doesn't work that way. I can't come back. You can't come see me. But we can talk like this anytime you want. But I've got lots of work to do so sometimes I might not be able to answer immediately.

Cleo

```
To: cleopatra.ellington@newlife.pgt
From: ant@singingemail.com
Sent: March 15, 2021 05:33
```

   Work? You can't be doing in Heaven what we did.

[Bing]

```
To: ant@singingemail.com
From: cleopatra.ellington@newlife.pgt
Sent: March 15, 2021 05:39
```

   ROFLMAO!!!!!

   You think I would be in Heaven?

   You know what the fuck we've been doing for five years, right?

Cleo

To: cleopatra.ellington@newlife.pgt
From: ant@singingemail.com
Sent: March 15, 2021 06:01

But that was just business. You are such a nice person. What we did for work was work; we never even met those people. But everybody you knew in real life you were kind to and you were funny and sexy and really, really smart. You were really good at what you did, what we did.

What are you doing now? Actually, where the hell are you?

[Bing]

To: ant@singingemail.com
From: cleopatra.ellington@newlife.pgt
Sent: March 15, 2021 06:14

HAHAHAHAHA. I'm in purgatory, that's what dot-pgt stands for in the domain. My bosses don't use that word, they call it the in-between place where we have to pay for our sins so maybe we can earn our way to Heaven. And you're not going to believe this, I actually work for tech support!

Cleo

To: cleopatra.ellington@newlife.pgt
From: ant@singingemail.com
Sent: March 15, 2021 06:19

   YGTBFKM!! You work in tech support? OMFG! I thought when people did what you and I do, um, did, we're never allowed to touch a computer again.
   Wait, why do they need tech support in the afterlife? Do people get computers now instead of harps when they go to Heaven?

Ant

[Bing]

To: ant@singingemail.com
From: cleopatra.ellington@newlife.pgt
Sent: March 15, 2021 06:40

   You get whatever you need. It's kind of like Sweden or the Far Left Radical Socialists you're always yelling about.
   If you were a soldier of the faith in life, they give you a sword or a gun to keep doing that.If you were a cook, you get

all the kitchen stuff and food to make meals for people. If you were a musician, you get a harp or a guitar or a harmonica or a banjo to play music to praise God — though come to think of it, I haven't seen any banjo players here.

If you used computers, you get to work with computers and they made me tech support so I can use computers to help people instead of, um, what we were doing before.

So I get to help people here who didn't know much about computers in life. I actually got to work with Joan of Arc yesterday. She's here in the middle place for another 5000 years, but she got a new gPhone which is like an iPhone from God. The hardware and software always works, but sometimes the wetware needs a lot of help.

I got to go for a bit, I have some calls to take. I'll email when I'm back, we have something really, really important to chat about.

(ꑄ˘‿˘)♥ ℒ♡♡e Y♡Ⓤ,
Cleo

[Bing]

```
To: ant@singingemail.com
From: cleopatra.ellington@newlife.pgt
Sent: March 15, 2021 07:16

   You there, Ant boy?
```

```
To: cleopatra.ellington@newlife.pgt
From: ant@singingemail.com
Sent: March 15, 2021 08:55

   You know I hate it when you call me
that ;-)
```

[Bing]

To: ant@singingemail.com
From: cleopatra.ellington@newlife.pgt
Sent: March 15, 2021 09:00

    Ant, there's one more thing I didn't tell you yet. I've been assigned one more really important job. You remember "Christmas Carol" where the ghost Marley had the chance to save Scrooge? I get to do that for you.
    I got sent to Purgatory when I died because I have a chance. It's not guaranteed, but I have a chance to do enough good to get to go to Heaven.
    As you can guess, the standards here are way more relaxed than we were taught in Sunday School. Even people who have done bad things all their lives have a chance to be saved if we repent and do more good here than we did bad in life. It's going to take me a long time to earn my wings but I think I can do it.
    You remember my old friend Priyanshu? We studied together at CalTech and we had a bit of an affair and we worked out some of the schemes you and I used but he went straight and became a white-hat.
    I used to tease him about all the money you and I were making and he was making some measly amount like $150K per year while you and I were packing away millions.

Turns out he got the last laugh. He was killed in a car crash two years ago and he was the one who sent me the lifeline that gave me my chance.

Now I want to do the same thing for you but it's gonna be hard.

Are you willing?

Love,
Cleo

[Bing]

To: ant@singingemail.com
From: cleopatra.ellington@newlife.pgt
Sent: March 15, 2021 09:49

Hey Ant, you there?

[Bing]

To: ant@singingemail.com
From: cleopatra.ellington@newlife.pgt
Sent: March 15, 2021 13:49

Hey Ant, you gotta listen to me 'cuz you're going to straight to Hell if you don't. I can only help you if you listen to me. And I'm the only one who can help you.

Cleo

[Bing]

To: ant@singingemail.com
From: cleopatra.ellington@newlife.pgt
Sent: March 16, 2021 10:43

Hey Ant, please answer me, I love you. I want to help you.

To: cleopatra.ellington@newlife.pgt
From: ant@singingemail.com
Sent: March 16, 2021 13:51

You're the same as me. You did the same shit as I do. I did the same things you did. How come you get to be so fucking high and mighty and I'm going to Hell?

Ant

[Bing]

To: ant@singingemail.com
From: cleopatra.ellington@newlife.pgt
Sent: March 16, 2021 15:27

   Remember those things you did *before* we met, the ones I wouldn't do? You stole from a fucking orphanage in Syria. How many kids died there?
   Remember that company you hacked and they couldn't pay you without dumping all those dioxins into the Saginaw. You pulled that off with one stupid email scheme.
   Remember your email to double the savings of widows over 75? How many little old ladies did you get kicked out of their homes?

Cleo

To: cleopatra.ellington@newlife.pgt
From: ant@singingemail.com
Sent: March 16, 2021 18:13

   The dioxin thing isn't my fault. They still had enough money to stop the disaster. They just wanted to run away with as much as they could.
   And those little old ladies, if I hadn't done that, someone else would have. Do you know how stupid and gullible they had to be to fall for my scam? If they lost their houses, good. They shouldn't have been living alone anyway.
   What makes you so special? I used to love you because you were fearless and didn't care who the fuck we scammed. Are they making you soft now?

Ant

[Bing]

To: ant@singingemail.com
From: cleopatra.ellington@newlife.pgt
Sent: March 16, 2021 18:22

Used to love me??? Has it come to that? You'd rather screw people than listen to me?

To: cleopatra.ellington@newlife.pgt
From: ant@singingemail.com
Sent: March 16, 2021 18:24

Well you're not here anymore. I can't wrap my arms around an email ghost.

[Bing]

To: ant@singingemail.com
From: cleopatra.ellington@newlife.pgt
Sent: March 16, 2021 18:25

Okay, I'll give you that. But can you at least listen to me in honor of the love we once had?

To: cleopatra.ellington@newlife.pgt
From: ant@singingemail.com
Sent: March 15, 2021 18:30

Oh Patty, I still love you. I'm just so confused. This believing in God and Heaven and Hell and shit is new to me. I don't know what to make of it. What do we have to do?

[Bing]

To: ant@singingemail.com
From: cleopatra.ellington@newlife.pgt
Sent: March 15, 2021 19:07

We have to make amends. All that money we have in the Caymans, we have to find a way to use it for good. If we do that, we can save you and speed up my transfer from Purgatory to Heaven. We call it "earning your wings" from the old movie, but I don't think there are real wings involved.

When you earn your wings too, we can be together again. Forever.

Love,
Cleo

```
To: cleopatra.ellington@newlife.pgt
From: ant@singingemail.com
Sent: March 16, 2021 19:19
```

 Cleo, that money was supposed to be our retirement. It's still my retirement money. How am I going to live without that money?

[Bing]

```
To: ant@singingemail.com
From: cleopatra.ellington@newlife.pgt
Sent: March 16, 2021 19:36
```

 Do you want to know the day and time you're going to die? I can tell you that, it's right here in your files on my computer. Sorry, big guy, you're not going to need retirement money. You're gonna overdose on Ice same way I did on China Blue. It's not tomorrow but its long before you can use our money.
 You can't use that money now, either, we always knew the Feds were watching. This is win-win because you can save your ass from eternal damnation with money you will never use in life.

Cleo

To: cleopatra.ellington@newlife.pgt
From: ant@singingemail.com
Sent: March 16, 2021 20:51

   Okay, what do we have to do? You know I'm fucking puking here. If it was anybody but you, I would never believe this. Can you tell me what I have to do with the money? Donate it to another orphanage or something? There's a lot of money there.

[Bing]

To: ant@singingemail.com
From: cleopatra.ellington@newlife.pgt
Sent: March 16, 2021 20:54

   I've been given special instructions on where to transfer it. There's a charity which feeds hungry women and children in Nigeria. Just give me the account number and I'll take care of that for you. Please, dear Ant, if you ever loved me as I love you, help me and I can save us both.

Cleo

To: cleopatra.ellington@newlife.pgt
From: ant@singingemail.com
Sent: March 16, 2021 20:57

You know the account numbers and the routing numbers. You've always had access to it.

[Bing]

To: ant@singingemail.com
From: cleopatra.ellington@newlife.pgt
Sent: March 16, 2021 21:01

But it's on my computer in the office. I don't have access to the computer in our office.

```
To: cleopatra.ellington@newlife.pgt
From: ant@singingemail.com
Sent: March 16, 2021 21:05
Attachment: RBC Royal Bank Account Info.txt
```

   Ok, my love. Here it is.

```
To: cleopatra.ellington@newlife.pgt
From: ant@singingemail.com
Sent: March 16, 2021 21:06
```

   Hey, wait a second. Are you telling me God or Jesus or angels or whatever can't get an account number from the Caymans?

```
To: aiofe.byrne@usdoj.gov
From: Edward.Manhaussen@usdoj.gov
Sent: March 23, 2021 10:17
```

Aiofe,
   You Irish witch. You god-damned did it again, you could talk the Devil out of the

keys to Hell. You make me so jealous. You are a legend, I bow down.
   What happened in court?

Ed

Edward Mannhaussen
Assistant United States Attorney
U.S. Department of Justice
Internet Fraud Division
950 Pennsylvania Avenue, NW
Washington, DC 20530-0001
+1 (202) 555-6437

To: Edward.Manhaussen@usdoj.gov
From: Aiofe.Byrne@usdoj.gov
Sent: March 23, 2021 10:28

Eddy,

   Haven't I always told you? Con-men are always the easiest people to scam. You wouldn't think it, but it's true.
   Once I got Cleo Ellington to start cooperating with us, I thought it was just a matter of time before we got Milanich. But

when she OD'd, I was scared we couldn't make the case so I had to bring her "back."

In court, Judge Coffin let Anthony Milanich plead guilty and we made a deal with him. If he is able help the court give back all of the money they stole and give whatever's left to court-approved charities, then the judge said Ant might be able to get out of prison to live out his old age as a free man.

Of course, he won't have any retirement savings…

Aoife B.

Aoife Byrne-Massey
Trial Attorney
U.S. Department of Justice
Internet Fraud Division
950 Pennsylvania Avenue, NW
Washington, DC 20530-0001
+1 (202) 555-6722

About The Author

Welcome to my first book, *Songs of a Befuddled Muse*, a collection of short fiction of varied and divergent inspiration.

More Songs of a Befuddled Muse is already in planning along with more cantos for the *Life and Times of Lady Jane*. Look for a new fantasy series, tentatively titled *The Hero Without a Prophecy*, and tentatively planned as a trilogy to begin appearing in 2023.

I currently live in Solon, Ohio, a suburb of Cleveland, and have traveled and lived widely across the US. My wife Lisa and I have two incredible daughters, one of whom, Jamie, provided the graphics and cover "tattoos" for *Songs* and the other who makes several thinly-veiled appearances in these stories.

I have been privileged to work in a variety of careers, including a decade as an award-winning newspaper reporter and photographer. Building on that experience, I also worked in publishing, graphic design, web design and development and web programming. Throughout most of my life, I have written fiction and am very happy to finally be sharing my work with a wider audience.

Besides writing, I spend an inordinate amount of time with photography, particularly stereo photography.

Please visit BefuddledMuse.com to find out more about me and my upcoming projects. While you're there, sign up for the Befuddled Muse mailing list so you can be notified of events and promotions, and please, please, please leave reviews of this book on Amazon. If you like this book, please share the book and my links with anyone else you think might also enjoy it.